MW01264236

LOVE BEARS
ALL THINGS

Cameron Cole

ISBN: 1541377435
ISBN 13: 9781541377431

CHAPTER ONE

"Open the door!"

Isabelle trembled when she heard her husband, John, shouting and beating the other side of her bedroom door. Knowing John was drinking himself into a stupor, she had locked herself in her room hours before. She had listened to him curse, kick, and bang on the furniture downstairs. She had been quietly pacing the floor, praying that he would pass out before remembering to come upstairs and demand his rights as a husband. *Well, it seems my prayers won't be answered again tonight*, she had thought when she had heard his heavy footsteps move clumsily up the stairs.

"Open up, Isabelle! I know you're in there, and I know you hear me! This is your husband, John! I'm here to show you, my barren wife, how much I love you."

When he drank, he brooded over the fact that they had no children and she hadn't given him an heir to carry on his family name. Of course it was all her fault. It had never crossed his mind that the problem could possibly be with him.

"Oh, God, help me tonight! Please help me!"

She prayed harder as the bedroom door began to splinter as he pounded on it with his meaty fist. Her knees began to tremble, and she felt the room sway. When the hole in the door was big enough for John to put his hand through, he unlocked the door, opened it, and stomped into the room. Even though he was a short man, the flickering light from the kerosene lamp made John's shadow look long and distorted.

"Come to me, my darling," John said in a mocking tone of voice as he walked to her with outstretched arms.

Isabelle gasped, and her hands went to her throat. She slowly began backing away; he sprang toward her and grasped her shoulder. His thumbs pressed against her collarbone. Terrified, she dared not show any fear or pain.

"Why can't you give me a son? If you care anything about your miserable life, you will give me a son," he said.

She saw something in his eyes that she hadn't seen before. Was it desperation or insanity? Tonight she felt he would stop at nothing to cause her pain and punish her because she was barren, and she knew that he would enjoy every minute of it.

He placed his hand on her shoulder and began shaking her violently. She was more frightened now than she had ever been before. She took a deep breath, trying to hold back her tears; if she showed any fear, he would more than likely continue hurting her. She managed to place her hands on his chest; she felt that the only hope she had was to try and talk some sense into him.

When she spoke, her voice trembled. "You're right, John. I've failed you. Perhaps tonight…" She hesitated. "Will be the night I will conceive the heir we both so desperately want."

When she began to talk, he stopped shaking her and looked at her for a long moment, and then he drew back his hand and struck her with all the force of his anger. She felt her ear sting; she felt the throbbing pain begin. When he picked her up by the front of her gown, she heard it rip. When he loosened his grip, she fell back on the bed.

As her whole body went numb, she realized that all hope was gone. She couldn't escape this monster! Animal instinct took over when she saw him unbuckle his pants and watched as they fell to the floor around his ankles. She bent both knees then gave John a hard, swift kick in his stomach, knocking him off balance and causing him to fall to the floor. She sprang off the bed and darted to the door. Screaming and cursing her, he made an attempt to chase her. But his feet became entangled in his pants, and he fell back down on the floor. She ran down the stairs on to the front porch before he managed to get himself off the floor.

Wherever I go, I know he will find me, she thought as she turned her head from side to side, trying to decide which direction would be the safest way to run. *Perhaps it would be best if he finds me, kills me, and gets it over with.*

Hearing his footsteps coming down the stairs, she whispered, "Oh my God." Then she jumped off the porch, lost her balance, and slid on the dewy grass. When she regained her balance, she ran and hid underneath the low-growing limbs of a large crape-myrtle bush.

When John got to the edge of the porch, he paused and began calling her name. "Isabelle, where are you?" His voice was taunting. "Come here, darling. Come to Daddy."

She looked through the branches of the bush and saw him standing on the porch, leaning against one of the porch posts, holding his pants up with one hand, not having taken the time to put his belt back on. His other hand was balled up into a fist.

"If you come out now, I'll forget about all the bad things you've done to me, and we can start all over, just like you once said we should do. We'll just relax, and then everything will be fine."

When Isabelle didn't appear at his beckoning call, as he was accustomed, his tone changed. "You had better come here, woman. If you know what's good for you, you'll show yourself."

Isabelle's knees turned into jelly, and she sank to the ground. Her heart was pounding, beating so loudly in her own ears that she was sure that he could hear it and that the noise of her heartbeat would lead him straight to her. Her hands were clammy with sweat, and she could taste the metallic taste of her own blood where she had chewed on her lower lip. She heard their dog, General, begin to bark loudly.

Oh, God, help me. He'll lead John straight to me, she thought. Then she saw that the dog was barking and trying to lead John down the road away from her. She realized that General was trying to rescue her, because he knew the extent of John's cruelty, as he had been beaten and kicked by John as well.

John saw and heard the dog. He laughed and said, "Now I'll find you; you didn't think you could hide from me and old General, did you?" As he yelled into the night, his mad laughter pierced the night air. "I'm coming, and we'll find you!" He stumbled down the steps and followed the dog as it led him further down the road away from her.

She breathed a long sigh of relief. "I thank you, God, for General; tonight he seems to be my guardian angel."

She knew this was her chance to get from the front yard to the barn. She ran to a large oak tree draped with Spanish moss. Her fear was still so great that she was unaware of the sounds of the choir of crickets, katydids, and the deep-throat bullfrogs that were in the yard. Nor did she smell the fragrant smell of the honey suckle or her beloved rose bushes. She could still hear general barking in the distance farther away as she left the shelter of the tree and headed for the barn. After entering the barn, she softly closed the heavy door, leaned back against it, and pulled in great gulps of air. Her arms dropped to her side, allowing the torn gown to gape open and exposc the tops of her small breasts.

Even though Berry was in the back of the barn, he heard the creaking of the door as it opened and closed. He stopped rubbing and talking to the mare he had assisted as it gave birth to a colt. It had been a difficult birth. Berry had had to turn the colt and pull it out from the mother. But now it was over, and he had already gone outside and washed the blood and sweat from of his body. Leaving his dirty shirt outside, he was naked from his waist up. Berry straining his ears for any sound, trying to listen for any clue as to who had come into the barn.

Most likely it's Master John, he thought, because he had heard John calling and cursing his wife. If she escaped him, then he might very well take his anger out on Berry. Berry was more than willing to take John's abuse if it would spare Missus Isabelle. Sometimes it was almost more than he could bear, seeing the bruises on her arms, the haunted look in her eyes, and the defeated slump of her shoulders.

When Berry could no longer hear noise, he became afraid. Over the years, before his people had been freed from slavery, he had taken many a beating from John when he was drinking. He decided that if it was John, he would make himself noticed. Or was someone trying to sneak up on him? Maybe it was a thief, perhaps a gypsy, or an ex-slave trying to survive. Whoever it was, the person had the advantage over him, because he or she could see inside the barn by the light of the lantern but he couldn't see outside in the darkness of the night.

The mare became restless and began to neigh. He gave her a reassuring pat and then crouched down on his knees. Leaving the stall, he cautiously began to walk toward the front of the barn. When he neared the front, he gasped in surprise when he saw Isabelle leaning against the door. He noticed her torn gown and her long, brown hair in disarray. The combs had fallen out, and her hair tumbled across her face and down her shoulders. Tears were flowing down her cheeks, and her body was shaking. He could see that she was terrified. He wanted to go to her and comfort her, as he would his own wife or his children, but he was afraid that John would burst through the door at any moment. He just couldn't take the chance.

Berry was a tall and muscular man. His skin was lighter than most Negroes on the plantation because his grandmother was a Quad-roon. John's grandfather had purchased her in New Orleans for a house slave. Berry's real name was Washington. He had been nicknamed Berry because of the distinct birthmark on his right hip, which was the size and shape of a large strawberry. This birthmark had been on all the children born to his family for the past three generations.

In the ten years since the slaves had been freed, Berry and his wife, Sue Ellen, had chosen to stay on the plantation where they had been born and raised. Berry, his wife, and their three children still lived in the slave quarters and tended to Master John's farm. Master John had promised to give them a percentage of the profits that the land brought each and every year. Even though Berry had little education, he was intelligent enough to know when he was being cheated, but he was thankful that he had a roof over his head and plenty to eat, which was more than some of his friends and family who had left the plantation had now.

Berry watched Isabelle in silence for a few moments; he knew that he had to do something but was afraid to do anything. When he saw her body beginning to slump, he went to her. He was afraid that she was about to collapse.

"Missus Isabelle, Missus Isabelle, it's me, Berry." He spoke to her in a soft, soothing tone, a tone like the one he had just used to talk to the mare.

She gasped, her body stiffened, and her eyes widened with fear. When she realized who he was, she sighed with relief. "Berry, thank God it's you! Help me, Berry! Please, help me!"

Forgetting that her gown was torn, she held both arms out to him, and the gown opened to her waist.

CHAPTER TWO

As he looked at Isabelle standing in front of him, Berry was shocked. Her clothing was ripped, revealing her breasts. Her eyes were opened wide and filled with fear. Berry stared with his mouth agape. He could feel her fear and wanted to reach out to her, hold her, and comfort her, but he didn't dare. He had never held a white woman in his arms, and he never intended to. He hesitated for a long moment, and then in a comforting voice, he asked, "Missus Isabelle, what on earth has happened to yo?"

Fearing what might be behind her, Isabelle tried to talk, but her lower lip twitched uncontrollably. As Berry came closer, she could feel her body begin to relax.

"Talk to me, Missus Isabelle," Berry said. "Tell old Berry what's wrong."

Her mouth worked, but no sound came out. She tried again and heard her own voice, trembling, weak, and raspy with effort. "Oh, Berry, he hit me! And I think he's going to kill me. He's trying to find me now! I don't know what I'm going to do; I don't want to die!" She cupped her face with both hands as sobs shook her body.

Berry silently stood where he was and made no attempt to console her, even though he could see that she was working herself into a tizzy.

"He's walking up the road; he thinks I went up the road." She looked up at Berry as she spoke through hesitant sobs.

Berry became angry as he saw all the fear and distress Isabelle was suffering. He knew that John was responsible for all her pain. *He hit her! How low-down and dirty can a man get?* He wondered. He clenched his fists as he tried to control his anger. He knew what it was like to be beaten by John. He had been known to beat his slaves unmercifully when he had too much to drink. Berry had several scars from John's drunken rages.

Berry knew that he was in no position to stand up for this helpless woman standing before him, but he knew in his heart that if John came into the barn tonight to do her harm, he'd have to fight him. Berry knew that he was a better man than John. He felt that he could take him in a fistfight, but he also knew where he stood in society. He knew that any slave or free black man would be hanged without a second thought if he raised his hand to a white man. He knew that it would be in his best interest to hide Isabelle.

"He'll come back soon. He'll find me, Berry. I know he will," said Isabelle.

"He won't find yo," Berry said as he placed his index finger over his lips, "cause I'm gonna hide yo."

She nodded her in agreement. He walked in front of her and guided her to the back of the barn. As she followed, she realized that her breasts were exposed. She pulled her gown across her chest and then crossed her arms in front of her to keep the material intact.

Reaching for the lantern, Berry said, "Let me snuff out de light." He cupped his hand over the globe, took one puff, and blew out the light.

Berry's hiding place was a stall in the back of the barn. The stall was filled with hay. What no one knew, except Berry and his family, was that in the back of the haystack was a large hole. His children had hollowed it out for a playhouse. Inside the hole were a few old, ragged quilts and an old feather pillow leaking feathers through frayed edges. When they reached the stall, they heard the barn door open and John come inside, yelling her name and cursing. Both of them jumped. Isabelle began to shake and cry.

Berry placed his hand over her mouth and whispered, "Please, Missus Isabelle, be quiet. Yo must be quiet, or he'll find us. Now let's get into de hay." She nodded but didn't move.

When she didn't move, he got in front of her, took her hand, and led her as they crawled deep into the hay.

John began to stagger through the barn and stopped when he came to the stall where the lantern hung. He reached for it, touched the hot globe, and burned his hand. He cursed, drawing back his hand and swinging it to try to cool the pain.

"You're in here somewhere, aren't you, my lovely one?" he asked.

The horses became restless, kicking and moving around in their stalls. "Are you in the stall with the horses, my love?" he asked. "I'll find you. Just wait and see."

He retrieved the lantern and, after much fumbling, finally took a box of wooden matches out of his shirt pocket, struck one on the rough stall gate, and lit the lantern. He went into the stall and saw the newborn colt. "Well, my darling Isabelle! It looks like we have a new colt here. It seems like everything can reproduce around here except you." He laughed insanely. "When I find you, I'm going to give you one more chance."

He left the stall and began to walk toward the back of the barn, checking every stall as he passed by them. The swinging lantern cast eerie shadows. He stumbled around for a few minutes, but it seemed like hours for Isabelle and Berry. John was only a few feet away from them. When he couldn't find her, he became even angrier. He kicked everything around him and firmly said, "You're just not worth looking for." And left the barn.

Isabelle's body was trembling, and she was stifling a scream.

"It's all right now, Missus Isabelle. He done and gone to de house."

"Hold me, Berry." Her voice was filled with pleading and desperation. "I need someone to hold me before I fall all to pieces."

Isabelle put her face in the palms of her hands. She felt like a trapped animal with nowhere to run. She needed a kind word, some understanding and reassurance that everything was going to be all right.

Berry placed his arms around her and tilted her face toward him. He wiped the tears away from her cheeks with his hand and pushed a wisp of hair from her face. He wanted to bring her comfort and somehow ease her pain, like he would with any wounded being. She began to relax as Berry gently rubbed her back, but when he touched her shoulder, she flinched and pulled away. He heard her quick intake of breath. He knew this was where John had hit her. He began speaking comforting words, words from his heart.

She began to calm down, and her breathing becoming slower. Everything was quiet, except they could hear the soft neighing of the mare and the whimpering of the newly born colt. They could hear mice scurrying around as the moonlight spilled through the cracks in the barn wall. When Isabelle relaxed and lay back on the faded quilts, Berry knew he must get home to Sue Ellen and their children. Sue Ellen didn't like to be left alone after dark.

"Missus Isabelle, what yo aim to do? Go back to de house?" he asked.

"No!" she quickly answered. Her body once again stiffened with fear. "I wouldn't dare go back into that house, not tonight anyway."

"Don' yo think he'll be passing out soon?" Berry asked.

"I don't know; you can never tell about him," she said.

"How long has he been drinking?" Berry asked.

"He started this morning. And he's been acting crazy since noon. Soon after lunch, I heard him getting rough with the field hands. I went into my room and locked the door, trying to stay out his way."

"Oh, Lord, help dat man! He's gonna drink himself to his grave!" Berry was shaking his head as he talked. "I'll tell yo what. I'm gonna sneak in dat house and see what he's a doin'! Maybe he's passed out by now." Berry began to crawl to the opening of their little hideout.

"No! Don't go, Berry! Don't leave me," Isabelle pleaded as she grabbed his pants leg and tried to try pull him back toward her.

Berry pulled her hand off and proceeded to crawl toward the opening away from her. When she got hysterical, he stopped and backed up to her side. *How on earth am I gonna get myself out of dis?* He thought. *How am I gonna get home tonight?* Then a thought occurred to him. *I'll take Missus Isabelle home with me.*

"Missus Isabelle, now yo calm down. Don' get yer self in a tizzy. We will jus' sneak out of here. Den we goes to my house; yo will be safe dare. Den in da early morning, yo can sneak back to yer place. Master John is likely to sleep all day!" He said.

"No, Berry, I don't think I can ever go back into that house!"

"Well den, let's go to my house; my sweet Sue Ellen will make yo a hot cup of her herb tea. Yo will sleep like a baby. Den in da morning if yo don' want to go home, I'll see dat you gets to yer mother's. How does dat sound?"

"No, Berry. I'm afraid to move, because he's so sneaky. He could be hiding just outside the barn door watching the house and the barn, waiting for me. No, I'm not going to leave here tonight. I know he won't find me here!"

"We can' stay here tonight, Missus Isabelle," Berry replied. "It jus' ain't right. I'm gonna get home to my Sue Ellen. She'll be fit to be tied when she don' know where I is. Lord, help dis old black man."

Berry looked up to the ceiling and uttered a prayer. He thought, *I got to look out for her.*

"Berry, don't leave me. Please don't leave me here all alone." Isabelle reached out to Berry with trembling hands.

"Lord, help me out of dis mess. No black man should be where I is tonight," Berry mumbled as he moved closer to Isabelle. He put his arm around her shoulder. She began to relax against him. He finally soothed her, and she lay down on the ragged quilt. He lay beside her. She rested her head on his chest, and he began to talk to her in soothing tones. She soon turned over and fell asleep. His plans were to leave her when she fell asleep and go home and explain all of this to Sue Ellen, but he was very tired and fell asleep as well.

Sometime in the night, Berry's hands began to roam over Isabelle's body. And in his sleepy stage, he thought it was Sue Ellen that was sleeping beside him. In Isabelle's sleepy stage her body began to respond to Berry's gentle touch.

When it was over, they relaxed in each others arms. A rooster crowed in the barnyard, bringing them both to their senses. When they saw the slanted beams of light creeping through the cracks in the old barn replacing the moonlight, reality hit them. They bolted straight up. Isabelle pulled at the blanket and covered herself.

"Missus Isabelle, what have I done? Lord, I ought to be horse-whipped for dis!" Berry's voice was filled with fear, and his eyes were open so big that she expected them to jump out of his head. Isabelle realized it was her turn to comfort him.

"This never happened, Berry. Don't you worry about this, do you hear? No one will ever know. If you hadn't been here to take care of me, I surely would be dead by now."

"I know, Missus Isabelle, but I's liable to be dead befo' de sun goes down today." Berry was trembling. "If de Master finds out what I gone and done!"

After Berry calmed down some, the two began to plan how they could get Isabelle back into her house without being detected. Berry looked at Isabelle and shook his head.

"Lawdy lawd! Missus Isabelle, yo sho can' goes into de house looking like dat."

Her gown had ripped farther down in the front; even though she was tightly gripping it, Berry could still see some skin. Her hair was in disarray, and fear filled her eyes, as the fear of her husband overcame her.

Berry said, "I believe I has to go in de big house and fetch some clothes for yo."

"Yes, we must do something," Isabelle replied. Fear caused a chill to run up her spine, and her teeth began to chatter.

"I'll go right quiet like. I sho hope Master John done passed out cold," Berry said.

He began to make his was out of the hay. He knew that Sue Ellen would be in the kitchen preparing breakfast and worrying about him because he hadn't come home last night. When he got outside, he stayed close to the barn and looked all around. When he saw no one, he knew he had to make a quick dash to the house even though his knees threatened to buckle under him and his body shook with fear.

He ran to a side door where he knew there were stairs leading up to their bedrooms. Getting to the landing, he quietly tiptoed down the hall. To his right was John's bedroom, and across the hall was Isabelle's. Berry saw that the door to John's room was slightly ajar. He was afraid to open it, but with trembling hands, he quietly pushed the door open.

When the door creaked, Berry froze, thinking that he had awakened John and he would be dead at any given minute. But he looked inside and saw that John had passed out and was lying across the bed, fully clothed. With a sigh of relief, Berry went on across the hall to Isabelle's bedroom. He went inside and went straight to her trunk, opened the lid, and grabbed the first thing he saw. Berry knew that he had to work fast and get out of the house before anyone saw him. He paused for a moment, making sure there was no one in sight, and then he quickly made his way back to the barn.

After what happened when Berry and Isabelle were in the barn together all night, everything changed. Isabelle's self-esteem sank lower and lower. She wondered, *how in this world could I have done the things I did while I was in the barn with Berry? What kind of a woman have I became? Could it be that deep down in my soul, I've always been those dirty names John has called me all these years?*

But the one thing that changed for the better was that she was no longer afraid of John. Because now nothing seemed to matter. Because she was so burdened with guilt over what had happened with Berry. She couldn't stand the sight of her husband; she blamed him for her being in the barn that fateful night, and she especially hated the times when he came to her bed.

John had become kinder and gentler with her. He couldn't figure out what had happened to his meek, shy wife. She was standing up to him and would argue with him. He knew she didn't care for him, but maybe she never had. When he forced her to be near him, he could feel her cold distaste for him from across the table or across a room.

Berry also changed. He moved around the plantation like a ghost, never speaking unless spoken to, doing his chores as quietly as possible, with his head hung low and his shoulders slumped in defeat. He avoided Isabelle as much as possible

CHAPTER THREE

John was lying on the porch swing lightly snoring with his head propped up on a pillow, his feet hanging over the swing's armrest. A warm breeze and the gentle swaying of the swing had lulled him to sleep. Nearby Isabelle sat in a white-wicker rocker. She was gently rocking, holding a round embroidery hook with a pillowcase with a hand-drawn, rose pattern stretched tightly over it. She was embroidering colorful red roses and green leaves on the pillowcases. She was full of nervous energy and she tried not to think about the child she was carrying. Her skilled hands stretched and pulled the colorful thread through the material, making tiny, delicate flowers and leaves. They had come outside hoping to catch a breeze and were waiting for the house to cool off for the night.

Isabelle looked up from her work when she heard the rumble of wagons and the pounding of horses' hooves as they pulled the wagons up the road and toward the house. She laid her work down in a wicker chair next to the one she was sitting in. She stood up and walked to the edge of the porch and placed her hand over her eyes to keep the sun out of her face.

Then squinting her eyes, she looked down the road and saw a cloud of dust. She wondered who was approaching, because sometimes there were soldiers trying to find their way home, as well as stragglers, who would come down this busy dusty road, often stopping at their home asking for water and a short rest for themselves and their horses. Soon a caravan of gypsies came into view. Her heart skipped a beat when she realized that this was Mama Dora and Tomsk tribe. Her prayers were about to be answered.

Thank God! She thought as she closed her eyes. She felt that Mama Dora could mix up a medicine of some kind that would cause her to lose this unwanted child she was carrying.

If she had counted right, Isabelle was now four months pregnant. There was a possibility that the child was John's, but there was also the chance that the baby was Berry's. If it was Berry's, John would certainly kill her, the child, and Berry. It would be for the best if she saved all of them the disgrace and the pain. Well, hopefully Mama Dora could help her!

"John, John, someone is coming! John, the gypsies are back!" She was very excited.

"Oh, yeah." He sat up. "Well, I hope it's a decent tribe."

The gypsies came through this part of the country frequently, but they never stayed long, because their wandering spirits didn't allow them to stay in one place very long. They made their living tinkering and selling hand-mixed medicines they made out of bark, herbs, and plants that grew along the less traveled paths and the dirt roads they traveled. They were very skilled at fortune-telling, convincing their customers that they could see into the future.

"John, it's Mama Dora and Tomsk, the leader of this band of gypsies, once again! Look at their beautiful wagon; I simply love it!"

The wagon was ten feet long with porches on front and back. The body was made from beaded, tongue and groove match board painted bright colors and decorated with lion heads painted with gold leaf on the outside of the wagon.

Isabelle said, "I can't get over how beautifully their homes are made! It's such a joy to see this tribe of gypsies again."

Isabelle waved her hand in welcome. The drivers waved back. Then they left the road and turned into a field across the road from their house.

"Looks like that ragged, thieving tribe is back."

"Now, John, you know yourself that these gypsies don't steal. You know you like them. Why do you want to act like this?"

He smiled a lopsided grin and said, "Yeah, I guess you're right. They're very amusing, don't you think?" He got off the swing and sat down on the porch steps to watch the gypsies set up camp. John said, "Such beauty is not often seen in these parts."

He was looking at the two gypsy stallions, a type of breed from the British Isles. That were pulling Tomsk wagon. They were small, perhaps fourteen hands high, with thick-boned legs and feathering that started at the knee in the front and at the hock in the back covering the hock. They sported wide, thick tails that dragged the ground and wide, double manes.

"His horses are more beautiful than the horses hitched to the other wagons," John said. "I think it's because they're skewbald and I prefer piebald animals."

A piebald animal has huge, irregular patches of white on black; a skewbald animal has heavy patches of white on chestnut. The color of the animal is determined by the pigment underneath the coat. Piebald animals are pigmented under the dark patches and non-pigmented under the white patches, allowing for different color patterns.

The wagon train began to make a circle as they set up camp. There were at least fifteen covered wagons in this group of gypsies and several uncovered wagons as well. There were cages of cackling chickens and crowing roosters. Cattle dogs were herding the cattle and the sheep behind the wagons. Pots, pans, and numerous vessels were hanging on the outside of the wagons and noisily clicking against the side of the wagons as they moved along the uneven field. Musical instruments were securely tied to the back of the wagons.

She saw a tall harp tied to the top of a flat wagon. It never ceased to amaze Isabelle how these landless wanderers carried everything they needed to set up anywhere and called it home for the time being. Mama Dora and Tomsk were the leaders, and they had the most colorful wagon.

The gypsies' dogs were barking, the horses neighing, and the cows bellowing ready to be milked. Soon Isabelle and John saw the smoke from the campfires beginning to rise. Isabelle picked up her embroidery and sat back down in her chair, breathing a long sigh of relief.

The following morning Isabelle pulled the hand-crocheted shawl tightly around her shoulders to avoid the early morning chill that was sending goose bumps over her skin. She was out very early; the dew was still clinging to the bushes and trees. She knew she should have waited a few more hours before she visited the gypsy campground, but she felt she couldn't wait any longer to try and solve the dilemma she had got herself into.

She had been awake all night praying as she contemplated her next move. She felt she must act quickly before she talked herself out of aborting the unborn child. She already loved the child she was carrying. She couldn't help but wonder if it was a boy or a girl, and she felt it was a sin to take the child's life. She felt it was as great a sin as taking anyone's life, because this little, innocent unborn baby hadn't had a chance to see what he or she might have contributed to the world.

She had tried to abort her child once, using a long metal wire, but she had lost her nerve and stopped. She realized she couldn't do that to herself and the child. If Mama Dora would give her a potion causing her to lose the child, then she felt she would somehow be justified. She knew there would be a lot of pain; she also knew she could bleed to death, but she knew that she would surely die if she gave birth to a black child.

Nearing the campground, Isabelle could smell the smoke from the wood fires. She could smell the aroma of the brewing coffee, pipe and cigar smoke, and meat as it popped and sizzled over the open fire. When she neared Mama Dora's home on wheels, she recognized the teal-covered, bow-top wagon. She paused for a moment when she saw that Tomsk was outside skinning a rabbit; after he had skinned it, she watched as he split it down the middle and let its guts spill into an old, beat-up pan sitting at his feet.

Then he rinsed the blood off and stood up when he saw her. He held the rabbit in one hand and his knife in the other. The rabbit looked all pink and bare without skin.

"Welcome, Mrs. Isabelle," Tomsk said and smiled, showing his perfectly straight, white teeth. "I would shake your hand—that is, if I had a free hand." He laid the rabbit down and wiped the blood off his knife and hands and on to the grass.

"That's OK, Tomsk. I think I'll pass on the handshake," she laughed.

"Can't say as I blame you," he said.

A young gypsy woman who was camped next to him lifted a pot of coffee boiling on a bed of hot coals that had been banked up at the edge of the campfire. She politely asked Isabelle if she would like to have a cup. Isabelle declined. The gypsies were all friendly and welcomed her into the campground. Several invited her to join them for breakfast.

"Whose beautiful voice do I hear?" Mama Dora asked as she walked out on the porch, dressed in a long, flowing, red housecoat trimmed in gold braids. Her long, black hair, sprinkled with gray, hung loosely around her face. "I thought that was your voice!" She walked down the steps and put her arms around Isabelle. "It's so good to see you again."

Tomsk had placed the rabbit on a skewer and put it over the fire. He washed his hands and poured Mama Dora a cup of piping-hot coffee and handed her and Isabelle a cup. Then he pulled out a small, straight-backed chair for Isabelle to sit on.

"Oh, I'll not sit down now. I'll just drink my coffee, and then I'm going home. I'm so sorry I came so early! I should leave you now and allow you your privacy. I'll come back later in the day." Isabelle took a small sip of the coffee.

Mama Dora put her hand on Isabelle's arm. She could see that her guest was very troubled. "We are so glad to see you, my dear. Let's go inside the wagon, where we can talk. Tomsk, please keep our coffee cups full and call us when breakfast is done."

"Oh, no, I'll go on. I feel as if I'm hindering you," Isabelle said and began to pull away from her. She had become fearful and wanted to run away.

"Nonsense, you should know by now that you can't hinder a gypsy. Time means nothing to us. My people don't worry about what's going to happen tomorrow or what happened yesterday. Today is all we have, and it isn't guaranteed; that's why we live for the moment. The moment is all anyone can count on."

Mama Dora motioned for Isabelle to come in the wagon.

"Oh, how I wish I could have that outlook."

"You can't help it if you were raised to allow possessions and rules to stop you from living life to the fullest. That's just the nature of your race. Now on the other hand, my tribe was born to be free and to roam from place to place. We never worry about how or what we will eat or wear. We know that all things will come to us, as they always came to our ancestors."

Mama Dora went inside the wagon and held out her hand, bidding Isabelle to come inside. Isabelle paused, then climbed the three steps, and stepped inside the wagon. She paused and let her eyes adjust to the dim light.

Mama Dora propped open the makeshift door, allowing the sunshine to come inside, lighting up her beautiful home. Inside the wagon, Isabelle saw the ornate walls and ceiling, the small, cast-iron cook stove that rested in a wooden fireplace on the left of the wagon. Brackets for holding an oil lamp were mounted over a flat-top, wooden trunk that also doubled as a table; cupboards and closets were mounted to the wall to hold the contents securely as they traveled. A double bed was secured to the floor. On the bed, Isabelle saw a young, dark-haired boy who lay sleeping underneath colorful blankets.

Mama Dora went to the sleeping child and said, "Stephen, it's time to wake up and start a new day."

The boy rolled over on his back and put his arms over his head and stretched, but he didn't open his eyes.

"Wake up, sleepyhead; it's time to pay for your bed!" Mama Dora teased as she ruffled his hair. "Come on now. Get up. We have a guest, and I would like very much for you to meet her."

The young man sat up and pulled the covers close to his chest. He looked surprised when he saw Isabelle.

"Don't look so shocked, Stephen! We'll turn our heads while you make yourself presentable."

In a few moments, Stephen said, "Grandma, I will be honored to meet your guest." The two ladies turned and faced Stephen.

"Isabelle, I would like for you to meet my grandson, Stephen. He's our daughter Vaughn-Etta's son. Stephen, this is Mrs. Isabelle. She lives in the big house across the road. She and her husband, John, have always been friends with our people and have always been kind enough to allow us to camp on their land."

Stephen extended his right hand. As he shook Isabelle's hand, he smiled and showed his beautiful, white teeth. When Isabelle shook his hand, she thought, *did I feel the child inside me move, or is my troubled mind playing tricks on me?* Her hand went to her stomach. She was speechless for a moment, and then she said, "Stephen, it's nice to meet you."

"It's an honor to meet you, Miss Isabelle." He made a slight bow to her and his grandmother and quickly left the wagon.

"My, but he is a fine-looking boy," Isabelle said.

"Well, thank you. Now why don't you sit down, Isabelle?"

Mama Dora took two small, straight chairs that were hanging on hooks and were screwed into the framing of the wagon. Cushions were tied to their frames with colorful ribbons.

Isabelle took one of the chairs from her hostess. As she sat down, she asked, "How is Vaughn-Etta?"

A look of sadness came into Mama Dora's eyes, and a single tear fell down her lined cheek.

"Vaughn-Etta passed away two months ago." She wiped the tear away with the back of her hand. "She contracted consumption and died soon after."

"I'm so sorry! I shouldn't have asked." Isabelle placed her hands on Mama Dora's, and in a sad voice, she continued, "I had no way of knowing."

"Of course you had no way of knowing, sweetheart. We haven't been around for a while."

"I suppose you and Tomsk will raise Stephen." Isabelle knew it was the custom of gypsies that if the mother died, the children would be raised by the maternal grandparents. She was sure that this had been made clear to Vaughn-Etta's husband before Tomsk would consent to the marriage.

"No. Actually we want our grandson to see and live in both worlds. As you know, Vaughn-Etta married a man from your own race of people. They fell madly in love the first time they laid their eyes on each other. He's a good man and a hard worker. Vaughn-Etta would want her son to be with the man she loved so much. I feel he has much to offer Stephen. I feel very strongly that his destiny is not with the gypsies, although we would consider ourselves lucky to have him travel with us all the time. And if it's his decision to remain with his mother's people, then he will truly be welcome."

"You are such a strong, wise woman, Mama Dora." Isabelle sighed a deep sigh. "I wish I had only a fraction of your courage."

"You have more courage than you realize, young lady. But I can see that there's much troubling you."

"How can you know so much? Are you reading the tea leaves?" Isabelle had always been amazed at Mama Dora's knowledge.

"No. No, my child. I've given up on my people's religion. I worship the true and living God. Stephen's father taught Vaughn-Etta all about Jesus Christ and all about the hope he brought into this dark world. I'm raising Stephen in the faith as well."

"Then how can you know I am troubled?" Isabelle was puzzled.

Mama Dora threw her head back and laughed. "It doesn't take magic to see that you slept very little last night. Let's face the facts. It's just daybreak, and your shoes and stockings are wet with dew. If that isn't enough, you have put your dress on wrong side out!" Mama Dora laughed as she patted Isabelle on her leg.

Isabelle looked down at her dress; indeed, she had put it on wrong side out! She began laughing with Mama Dora.

After their laughter subsided, they both became serious. Mama Dora stood up and put her arm around Isabelle's shoulder. "Now tell me, child. How may I help you?"

Isabelle became uncomfortable. She began to unconsciously twist her hands in her lap. She dropped her eyes. She didn't feel that she could look Mama Dora in the eyes. "Yes, Mama Dora, I'm very troubled. I need your advice as well as your help."

She paused and then ran her fingers through her hair; still she couldn't look at Mama Dora. "I just don't know how to go about asking you for what I really need." Tears welled up in her eyes.

Mama Dora gave Isabelle a loving look and a gentle smile and said softly, "Child, why are you so afraid of this pregnancy?" She took her hand and lifted Isabelle's face up to look at her.

Isabelle's mouth flew open in surprise. Her body stiffened as she moved to the edge of the chair, causing the chair to creak. "How do you know I'm pregnant if you've stopped reading the tea leaves?" she asked loudly.

"One doesn't have to read the tea leaves to know when a woman is carrying a child. It shows first in a woman's face. But there's much fear and anxiety in your face and in your eyes as well."

"I'm terribly afraid to give birth to this child." Tears began to fall in earnest. She bit her lower lip to stop its trembling.

"Are you afraid for yourself or the child?" Mama Dora asked.

"Both of us," she answered, her voice trembling. "I'm afraid for both of us."

"Are you sure there's reason enough for all this fear?" Mama Dora took Isabelle's trembling hands into her own.

"Yes! Yes! Please believe me. I know what I'm talking about! Could you please, please, give me something safe to take so that I can lose this baby?" With pleading eyes, Isabelle looked into Mama Dora's kind eyes.

"Isabelle, I feel that every life that comes into this world is here for a purpose. Everyone has a job to do. Big jobs or small jobs, whichever that might be, God has an overall plan. And to deliberately take a life is wrong. We weren't given the power to decide who lives or who dies."

Isabelle's shoulders slumped in defeat. The two sat in a long silence.

Then Mama Dora said softly, "I feel that you are carrying a little girl, a beautiful little girl. I feel that if you will allow this child to live, you both will have long lives. Now there is obviously a dark cloud hanging over you, but that cloud will pass over. You will have much happiness in the future."

"Then it's safe for me to have this child?"

"Yes. You have your child. Everything will work out for you and the little one. I feel this child has a great talent. She will bring you much pride and peace," Mama Dora said.

"How do you know this if you've given up fortune-telling?" Isabelle questioned.

"Intuition, my child! My soul feels these things. We gypsies are not bogged down with pressures that most folks have. Our minds run as free as the wind. We learn to notice things in this world that others might miss. I feel as if I'm telling you the right things. No more black magic or trickery from the dark side." She squeezed Isabelle's hand tightly.

Isabelle knew what Mama Dora was talking about when she talked about trickery. Mama Dora had already told her some of the tricks that the gypsies did, like passing on signs to their kin who they knew would be traveling this way soon. Signs were left on rocks, trees, or fence posts. Most of the signs were circles, dots, or dashes. Perhaps in front of the house of someone whose fortune they had told, they would leave a sign meaning, "I have told them they will receive great riches."

Mama Dora got out of her chair and walked to a small trunk. She opened the trunk and looked at the labels on several of the bottles that were stored inside the trunk; she selected one particular bottle. She turned toward Isabelle and handed it to her. "Here, my child, take this medicine with you. It will help you with your morning sickness."

"Thank you for everything," Isabelle said as she stood up to leave. "I know that I can always count on you, Mama Dora."

Mama Dora smiled and nodded her head. "Take care now. Oh, by the way, please tell Berry to try and come over to our camp tonight. We are having a dance, and no one can sing and dance the way Berry can. Tell him to bring his Jew's harp."

CHAPTER FOUR

Isabelle's labor began just before daybreak on a clear spring morning. A sharp pain woke her from a restless sleep. She had gone to bed tired, because the last few days she had been working very hard and couldn't seem to sit still. In spite of her size, she had cleaned her room and the nursery, and she had also helped Sue Ellen in the kitchen. Sue Ellen had scolded her, telling her she needed to save her energy.

That same afternoon Sue Ellen had walked into the nursery and seen Isabelle dusting down the walls. She had said, "I can see dat my scolding ain't doing no good. Yer as restless as an old hen making her nest. De moon changes tonight. Mark my words, Missus Isabelle." She pointed her index finger at Isabelle and continued, "Yo birthing is near. Yo will drop dat baby soon. But if yo don' slow down, yo will be too tired to push dat baby out!" Placing both hands on her broad hips, Sue Ellen had turned and left the room.

Isabelle wanted her labor to start. She wanted to get this over with as soon as possible. Life or death, she had no way of knowing which one it would be until this child was born. She'd worried so much about the situation that she'd got herself into. She was tired of worrying and was ready to take whatever consequences came her way. She felt guilty every time she looked at her dear friend, Sue Ellen.

Sue Ellen was so proud for her and had been so kind to her since she had become pregnant. More times than Isabelle could count, she had heard Sue Ellen say, "De Master sho has changed since yo are in de family way. Life's got downright pleasant for all of us round here."

Sue Ellen made this remark to her in front of Berry several times, and he would drop his head and leave the room. They had never discussed what had happened in the barn that fateful night. Both were trying to pretend that it had never happened, both were hoping the child did, indeed, belong to John.

When a sharp pain shot through her back, it felt as if Isabelle were breaking in two. She couldn't move until she rode out the pain. She was breathing deeply and had broken out into a clammy sweat. *Oh God*, she thought, *it's here. My baby is almost here. This is the day that will seal my fate.*

As she lay there, all the horror stories about white women giving birth to black children came back to her. She knew that if the baby was black, then the doctor would kill it quickly, perhaps smother it with a pillow or cut the cord and not tie it off, allowing the child to bleed to death. The family would try to keep this disgrace secret, but truth always had a way of coming out. Isabelle knew that if the child was black, the doctor would first get John's permission and then simply snuff out the child's life. She knew that John wouldn't dare kill her then, but soon afterward he would do his evil deed and end her life, whenever he thought no one would know. If anyone did find out, she was sure no white man would blame him.

"Oh, let this child be John's baby! Please, God, I know I'm a sinner. Please forgive me! Have mercy on me!" She rolled her head from side to side as she fervently prayed.

Isabelle suffered alone. When the sun finally came up and was bathing her room with its bright light, the pains were coming closer together. She knew the time had come to wake up John. As her feet touched the floor, she slowly walked up the hall to her husband's bedroom, her hands holding her stomach. Not unlike someone walking to the gallows, there was a fear and dread in every step she took.

When John opened the door to Isabelle's weak knock, his sleepy eyes were soon replaced with excitement, and a smile crossed his face when he saw the pain in his wife's face. "It's time, isn't it?" With gentleness, he placed his arm around her shoulder to assist her to the big, four-poster bed in his room.

She pulled back. "No, John, take me back to my room."

As soon as she had entered the room, a chill had come over her body, as the horrible memories of John's cruel treatment of her in this room came back to her. Her eyes swept the high-ceiling room; the cream-trimmed, maroon color reflected John's masculine taste. The draperies on the window and the massive canopy bed were decorated in a cream color with an elaborate edging of maroon.

"Come on, Isabelle. This is the bed I was born in, and I want my son to be born in here as well. We've already discussed this." She was reluctant to move, but he picked her up and laid her on the bed. John fluffed a pillow, placed it under her head, and then went to the door and began yelling for Sue Ellen, "Sue Ellen! Come quickly! It's time; the baby is coming!"

Sue Ellen was in the kitchen making biscuits for breakfast. Hearing John's call, she quickly left the dough she was kneeling, reached for a potholder, and picked up the skillet of sausage she was frying and set it off the stove. Sue Ellen wiped her hands on her apron as she rushed up the stairs.

"Isabelle is in labor!" John yelled excitedly as Sue Ellen entered the room. "I'm going after Dr. Morris; take care of her while I'm gone," he ordered. He had already made arrangements with Dr.

Morris to be here when the baby arrived; he wanted the best for his child. He didn't trust the midwife.

"John, it's too soon to go after him. This could take all day." As Isabelle said these words, a contraction hit her, and her face wrinkled with pain.

"I want him here now. I've waited a long time for this day, and I don't want to take any chances." He bent over and gently kissed Isabelle's forehead and patted her stomach. "Son, please wait on Daddy to get back with the doctor before you make your appearance into this world."

After John left, Isabelle told Sue Ellen to go and tell Mama Dora to come because it was time for the baby. Isabelle had finally told Mama Dora about her fear and the chance that this child could be black. She had also told her that Berry could possibly be the father. The two had agreed that if the child was black, Mama Dora would somehow handle the situation. Perhaps she would tell John that the baby was so deformed that he shouldn't see it and then take it off to a safe place.

The doctor and John returned three hours later. Dr. Morris examined Isabelle and then went outside on the porch, where John was pacing back and forth nervously puffing on a cigar. John stopped short when he saw the doctor.

"Now, John, this is her first child, and this may take a while. You need to calm down." The doctor patted John on the shoulder.

"Is she doing all right? Is the baby OK?"

"Yes. Everything is going as expected. She probably won't give birth until later this afternoon." The doctor ran his fingers through his thinning hair. "I'm going to have to leave here for a while, John. I must go and see a very sick child over in the next parish. I promised the parents that I would return today. I'll be back as soon as I can."

John's eyes filled with fear. "No. You can't leave now." He reached into his pocket and pulled out a money clip. "Here's some extra money. Now stay," John ordered.

"That's a good offer, John." The doctor looked at the money John was offering him and shook his head. "However, I can't let the other family down," he said firmly and gave the money back to John. "Your wife will be safe. The gypsy lady is with her now, and they know how to deliver a baby."

John grabbed him by his coat collar. "You can't leave! I won't let you leave."

There was panic in John's voice. Dr. Morris could see that there was no reasoning with John, and he had heard that John had a terrible temper. With a sigh, he set his black bag down on the porch rail. Then the doctor began to reason with John, telling him how he would return before the baby's birth. John finally agreed to let the doctor leave.

After the final push that brought a new life into the world, Isabelle lay still and quiet and waited for some kind of reaction from Mama Dora. Isabelle heard no gasp of surprise as she lifted the baby and cut the cord. Then Mama Dora spanked the child, causing it to cry.

"It's a girl, Mrs. Isabelle," Mama Dora announced in a pleased voice and then added, "Everything is just fine."

Isabelle began to laugh and cry at the same time. "Thank you, God. Thank you for making everything all right."

Mama Dora hurriedly cleaned the newborn child and dressed her in a white gown Isabelle had made. When Dr. Morris walked into the room, she wrapped the baby in a blanket and handed the crying child to him.

Dr. Morris beamed with pride as he laid the baby beside Isabelle. "There's nothing like the miracle of birth. When the child is as lovely and perfect as she is, then it is a double blessing. Like I've already told you, she is definitely a beauty. I can't wait any longer for you to see her and for her to see you."

As Isabelle unwrapped the baby from the blanket, he continued to talk. "I told you there was no need to do all the worrying you did while you were carrying her. I'm so sorry I wasn't present when she was born. Now I think I had better go tell John what's going on and ease his troubled mind." The doctor chuckled. "I'll bring him in when you get her all cleaned up," he said to Mama Dora as he turned to leave the room.

"I'm going to the kitchen to fetch more water," Mama Dora said.

After they left the room, Isabelle looked down at the child who lay by her side. She saw the thick head of hair, the small nose and lips, and the light-olive skin. Isabelle smiled and looked toward the ceiling and whispered another prayer of thanksgiving. Everything had actually worked out well today. God certainly was with her. Then like all new mothers, she undressed her child and counted her fingers and toes. Then she pulled up the little gown and explored her baby's body.

Isabelle rolled her over and gasped when she noticed the small birthmark that was shaped like a strawberry. The mark was so small that she realized few people would notice it until the child grew more. But the one person who would know was Sue Ellen, because she had seen this very birthmark on every child she had given birth to. Isabelle realized that she would have to keep the child as far away as possible from Sue Ellen and John. She quickly rolled the child over and wrapped her securely in the blanket.

She managed a smile when John entered the room. She could see he was trying to hold back his disappointment that she hadn't given him the son he wanted so badly; she could read the hurt in his eyes as he walked up to the bed and looked down at the child.

"Here, hold her," Isabelle insisted.

"No, she's too small." John shook his head.

When Mama Dora walked into the room, she put a pan of water down on the dresser and walked to the bed. She picked up the child and handed her to John.

When John took the child, his hands were shaking. He looked down into her tiny face, and a huge smile came crossed his face. His eyes gleamed with pride. "You are so beautiful, and I would never think of trading you for a son. Your little brother will be born next, right, Mom?" He laughed and looked at Isabelle.

Dr. Morris walked up beside John and put his hand on John's shoulder. "I think she needs rest before you start planning another child," he teased. "It looks like you could use a little break yourself." He took the child from John's arms and laid her beside Isabelle.

"Yes, I'm sure she needs a rest. So thoughtless of me, darling. You've worked today. One of the neighbors, I don't know which one, brought over some chicken and dumplings this morning. Would you like to try some of them?" She nodded her head. "Then I'll go and get you something to eat." He turned and left the room.

Soon John was back upstairs with a steaming bowl of chicken and dumplings. He pulled a chair to the side of the bed. Then he sat down and began to spoon the food into her mouth.

As she ate the food, Isabelle could see a smile on his face. As Isabelle looked at her husband, she thought, *He's almost handsome with all the hard, angry lines gone from his face. I almost wish this moment would last forever.* But she trembled with fear when she remembered the birthmark. *If John ever sees the birthmark, then he will know the truth, because he's seen that birthmark all of his life.* She became so frightened that her teeth began to chatter and her body started to tremble.

"What's wrong, sweetheart?" John stood up in alarm.

"I'm sorry. It's just that I'm not very hungry. I'm so tired. Would you mind if I took a nap?"

"Of course you're tired. You've had a rough day. I'll take our daughter into the nursery and let you sleep." He reached out for the small bundle that lay by her side.

"No, John, leave her with me."

"Why? You can't rest if she wakes up. You should have let me get a wet nurse to feed our baby. Taking care of her will simply wear you out! I think it would be best if I take her into the nursery," he insisted.

"No, John," she said firmly. "Remember, I've worked all day bringing her into this world, and I want her to be close to me now. Please don't talk anymore about getting a wet nurse. I simply don't want to hear about it anymore," Isabelle said firmly.

"Well, I'm certainly not going to argue with you now, and I'm sure she wants to be close to you, too." John left the room, pausing at the door for one more look at his wife and child. Moments after he closed the door, he opened it again and stuck his head inside and said, "What are we going to name her?"

"I would like to name her Jane Ellen, after my great-grandmother and your aunt."

John smiled and closed the door.

Six months later Isabelle was taking a nap while the baby slept. Jane was starting to cut her teeth and had been crying a lot. Isabelle and John hadn't been getting much sleep. When Jane woke up and began to cry, Sue Ellen came quickly into the room.

She picked her up and began talking to her. "Listen, young lady, don' yo wake yer po tired mother. What are yo crying bout now? I knows yo can' be hungry, cause yer mama jus' fed yo." Then Sue Ellen felt her bottom. "Lowdy lawd! child, yo are soppin' wet."

At the sound of Sue Ellen's voice, Jane began to coo and spread her mouth into a smile.

"Yo pretty little thang." Sue Ellen held Jane close and kissed her underneath her fat, little chin. "Yer Sue Ellen's girl, ain't yo, honey? Well, Sue Ellen's gonna change you. Yer even wet on yer little gown!"

Sue Ellen talked as she held Jane in one arm and opened the chest of drawers with her other one and took out a diaper and a clean gown. Then she sat down in the rocking chair and removed the wet diaper. When she saw the birthmark on Jane's hip, Sue Ellen's hand stopped in midair, and she gasped as her stomach clinched into a painful knot.

Sue Ellen's gasp caused Isabelle to wake up. She sat up in bed and saw her child in Sue Ellen's arms and Sue Ellen's plump face filled with pain.

The two women eyes met for what seemed like a long time. Sue Ellen was the first to speak. "Now I knows why yo never let me give Jane her bath or change her clothes," she stated coldly, her tone clearly conveying her contempt for Isabelle. She stood up and handed the baby to Isabelle. "Here's yer chile."

"I'm sorry, Sue Ellen." Isabelle's voice broke. She realized that she had broken the heart of a dear friend, a friend who had always been there for her. Would she ever stop paying for her sins? One of John's beatings wouldn't hurt as much as the pain-filled look in her best friend's eyes. *Oh dear God, I wish that Berry and Sue Ellen would move off the plantation. I can't face Sue Ellen every day.*

Isabelle dropped her head and asked Sue Ellen, "Would you hand me a washcloth, please?"

When Sue said stiffly, "Yes, ma'am," with piercing contempt in her voice, Isabelle knew it would be useless to try and tell her what had happened that night in the barn. She knew Sue Ellen would never understand or be able to forgive her.

After she handed Isabelle the washcloth, she asked coldly, "May I be 'scused, Missus Isabelle?"

"Yes, you may."

With the swish of her long skirt, Sue Ellen left the room.

Sue Ellen walked to the barn, where she knew Berry would be doing the evening chores. She was so full of anger that she could hardly control herself. Berry had betrayed their love and their marriage vows. He had sworn, not long ago, that he had never been with anyone else. She walked rapidly, her feet stomping the ground. She had always trusted Berry, but the mark on the child's butt was enough proof not to trust him anymore. She knew for sure that baby was Berry's child. She had heard the story from Berry too often: how all the children in the past three generations of his family bore the light-colored mark in the shape of a straw berry on their right hip.

Sue Ellen began to mumble, "Dat black dog, he been sleeping wit' Missus Isabelle, and she done bore his chile. And he ain't told me nothing bout' dat."

She paused and raised the tail of her apron to wipe the tears from her eyes. In an angry voice, she continued to talk to herself, "I'm gonna scratch his eyes outa his black ugly face when I get a hold of him. They ain't no scuse for messing round wit' Misses Isabelle." She shook her head. "No, there ain't no 'scuse. I had him enough babies. I been good to him, and I ain't never refused him. He never needed to visit no whorehouse. John thinks dat baby's his. Well, there are two fools here: me and Master John!"

"Berry, where are yo?" Sue Ellen asked in a demanding voice as she entered the barn. When she opened the door to the barn inside, she paused and let her eyes adjust after leaving the sunlight of the day and entering the darkness. She placed her hands on her hip and looked around. "Berry! Where are yo? I'm gonna slap yer black face. I know what yo been keeping from me! I know why yo keep a going to dem gypsies. Yo been laying wit' Missus Isabelle! Master John's gonna have yer hide when he finds out, and I'm bout tell on yo myself!"

When Sue Ellen entered the barn, Berry was in the first stall. When he heard her accusations, he began to tremble. He had hoped this day would never come. After Jane's birth, he had felt safe because the child had blue eyes and olive skin and her hair wasn't kinky like his other chillun. He had been sure that she belonged to Master John. Berry walked out of the stall with his shoulders slumped and head bowed low.

"Berry." Sue Ellen let out a long sigh and shook her fist at him. "Yo done gone and done me wrong. Dat chile of Missus Isabelle's is yer chile; now don' yo try to lie out of dis one, Berry. I saw de birthmark, de same birthmark dat all my chillun wear." In a choked voice, she finished her sentence, "Berry, yo done went and broke my heart," and Sue Ellen began to cry.

"Sugar-ins," Berry said as he put his arm around her shoulder and led her to an old bench that sat in front of the stall. "Sit down, and let me tell yo what happened. Let me 'splain. Yo know how Master John was always drinking and cursing at Missus Isabelle. Yo told me to take care of her."

Sue Ellen nodded her head. Berry paused, scratched his head, and then continued, "Well, yo member last year when Master John got so drunk he was hitting; on Missus Isabelle? She hid from him and spent de night in de barn. Yo member, don' yo?" He nudged Sue Ellen with his elbow. "Yo member yo said yo met her coming outs of de barn de next morning when yo went to work at de big house? When yo got to de big house, yo said Master John had broken down her door and broke up a lot of things in de house. Yo said it took you two days to clean it all up."

Sue Ellen remembered and slowly nodded her head. She did remember that day and several days after that, because Isabelle had been agitated and worried. She'd had bruises all over her face and arms. Sue Ellen also remembered all the questions Isabelle had later asked her about babies and getting rid of unwanted one.

Dreading to tell Sue Ellen about what had happened, Berry cleared his throat and looked off into the distance. "I was in de barn dat night helping a mare wit' her first foal. Master John was a stomping and hollering for hours. Den all at once, he stopped. Dat skerd me, cause I feared he had done gone and killed Missus Isabelle.

"'Bout twenty minutes later, Missus Isabelle comes sneaking in de barn wit' her clothes half-tore off. She was squalling her eyes out. She never did notice her gown was tore and her bosom was showing. She was turning blue where Master John had been a hitting on her. I can' hardly stand to see no woman squall like she was a doing. I jus' meant to soothe her because Master John had been beating on her. Sue Ellen, I didn't mean for anything else to happen."

Berry looked at Sue Ellen with pleading eyes and continued, "Den Master John come into de barn jus' kicking everything and a cussing. Missus Isabelle was about to faint on me. I sho didn't want Master John to find her, so we crawled in de hay our chillun play in.

"Den she wouldn't let me leave her. I was so wore out, and when I got her settled down, we both went off to sleep. I had been working wit' dat mare for more dan two hours, and I had my shirt off. I could feel her tits rubbing up against me.

"Sugar-ins, I thought it was yo I had hold of. Yo know I didn't mean no harm. I sho didn't mean to hurt yo. I only care for yo. I love Misses Isabelle, but not like dat. I never had Missus Isabelle but dat one time. I ain't never went after no white woman, and Master John ain't never went after no black woman. We been lucky to be on Master John's plantation. I sho was hoping dat chile would be Master John's."

Berry shook his head. Berry wished Isabelle had told him this was his child but maybe she didn't know herself.

Sue Ellen looked at her husband with the beginning of compassion and heard the truth in his voice. She stood up and said, "Now what are we gonna do? Master John don' know yet, but Missus Isabelle does. Maybe we'll be safe here for a while. Dat baby looks more like a gypsy dan she does a darkie. Her skin is light. Dat is, if it don' turn. She ain't' got no thick lips or wide nose like de rest of us; dat may save your black hide."

"Po Missus Isabelle. If Master John finds out, he will kill her and dat baby. He'll sho kill me." Berry shivered.

"Missus Isabelle sho does love dat child, and Master John struts like a rooster. It would be good enough if he did know after the way he's done treated everybody. What are we gonna do, Berry? I'm afraid to stay here too long!" Sue Ellen sobbed and shook her head.

Berry took Sue Ellen into his arms and gently began to stroke her hair. "Sue Ellen, I sho am a lucky man to have yo. I love yo, Sugar-in. Yo gave me some mighty-fine chillun, and yo are de best wife a man could have. I sho' hope yo don' decide to leave me."

"I'm hurt, Berry. I don' know if I can forgive yo jus' yet." Sue Ellen pulled herself away from Berry and began pacing the barn floor. "Berry, we gonna get away from here. Now fore some big-mouth sees de birthmark. I hear tell some darkies are heading up north, but I don' think I could stand all dat snow and cold weather. dey say dey don' treat darkies no better there than dey do here. We gonna lose our little, ole house and garden plot. We ain't got no money. What are we gonna do, Berry?"

"What about New Orleans? I hear a darkie can make a living shining shoes there. Tell yo what, I'll go see de gypsies and ask Tomsk what it's like in New Orleans. There's a place called the quarters; dey say there are a lot of people doing all sorts of things for a few pennies. I'm a hard worker. Maybe I could drive a delivery wagon or even get a job wit' a band in one of dem clubs Tomsk talks about. I can sing and play my Jew's harp. I'll talk to Tomsk tonight."

Berry knew that he had to leave soon. If Sue Ellen saw the birth-mark, then it was only a matter of time until John would notice it.

Berry walked toward the flickering lights of the gypsy campfires. The laughter and music the gypsies were making seemed to beckon him as the notes reached him in the cool night air. The air also carried smells of cedar wood burning and food cooking. As he reached the camp, five children dressed in brightly colored clothes and shaking tambourines and two barking dogs ran out to greet him. Berry began to relax and for a moment forgot about his troubles. He envied the gypsies and their freedom. They didn't need wealth to make them happy. Of course Berry had never had much money, either. He hadn't saved any to care for Sue Ellen and his children. He was a freed slave, but being a black man in itself was still a kind of slavery.

He knew the gypsies gave no thought of tomorrow and what tomorrow would bring. They only lived for the day. They had no calendars and didn't seem to care what year or month it was. The gypsies never owned land or paid property taxes. They valued their freedom above all else. They traveled in their little caravans from one place to the next. Berry's people couldn't live like the gypsies. The war had been over for four years, but it seemed they would always have to answer to the white man's laws. Berry hoped he could find some answers. Maybe Mama Dora could tell him what to do; she was a very wise lady.

"Welcome, Berry!" With a motion of his hand to sit, Tomsk said, "Come join us for supper. Mama Dora can make some of the best rabbit stew you've ever eaten. Viva, get Berry some stew." Viva was a young gypsy girl.

"Don' mind if I do, Tomsk. Dat stew sho does smell mighty good."

Even though Berry had just eaten, the aroma of the stew was more than he could resist. Berry sat down flat on the ground. He had never learned to sit very long in gypsy fashion, sitting on their feet with knees bent. When Viva handed him a bowl of stew, the gold bracelets on her arms made tinkling sounds. Berry savored the stew and said, "Tomsk, yo sho are dressed mighty sharp tonight. What's going on?"

Tomsk wore a bright-yellow, full-sleeved shirt. His black trousers were tucked into black, shiny boots. Berry noted all the gold around Tomsk neck and on his hands. His sash was yellow and black.

"Well, Berry, Tinker and I are going into town tonight to try and make some money."

"How yo gonna to do dat?" Berry asked as he took another bite of the stew.

"Tinker has some new wares. He also has a new medicine that cures just about anything. Don't you, Tinker?" He asked the man sitting beside a square wooden box that held his new medicine.

"Yeah, well, dat's jus' dandy, but I need to buy my Sue Ellen something," Berry smiled at Tinker. "Yo got any red ribbons?" Berry knew he couldn't afford to buy her much because they would need all he had saved when they moved, but he sure was sorry for what had happened between him and Missus Isabelle. Maybe ribbons would take some of the hurt out of Sue Ellen's eyes.

"Yes, Berry. I sure do. I'll get you some. How many do you need?" Tinker stood up and walked to his elaborately and colorfully painted brush wagon with a half door and glazed shutters. Located at the back of the wagon was a set of steps. The outside was equipped with racks and cases fitted on the outside frame of the wagon, allowing Tinker to carry his trade items.

"Bout this much." Berry measured by putting his left arm out and his right fist near his nose. "Sho wish I could make money like yo gypsies do."

"Maybe you could, Berry." Mama Dora laughed as she walked up behind him. "You needing some extra money?"

"Yes, ma'am. I'm needing money to get off de plantation. I been thinking on Orleans. Do yo reckon an old black man could make a go out there?"

"I'm sure you could." Mama Dora sat down in the circle of the campfire. "You can play that Jew's harp and dance. I know you could make a living."

"Are yo folks headed for Orleans?" Berry questioned nervously.

"Yes. We will be heading for New Orleans pretty soon."

"Could me and my family travel wit' you" Berry's voice was pleading. "I sho do need to get away from Master John." He slowly shook his head. "I sho do."

"Yes, Berry, if you're in trouble, you can go with us. What are friends for?" she said. Mama Dora knew that John was capable of being very cruel and mean. *Could it be that John has discovered Berry and Isabelle's secret?*

Tomsk quickly stood up, dropping his bowl. The dogs were quick to lap the spilled stew off the ground. "No! I don't think he should ride with us. We have enough trouble with our own tribe. We sure don't need a black man's family riding with us; you know the white folks don't trust us anyway. It might be a bad idea and bad luck traveling with a black man."

Berry buried his face in his massive, calloused hands, and his shoulders began to shake. "If you can' take us dat will be all right. I understand." Berry's voice choked up.

Mama Dora could hear the desperation in his voice. She knew he was a man laden with a heavy burden. She wanted to help him. "Tomsk! Sit down, and behave yourself. That's no way to treat a friend," she scolded. Then in a kind voice, she said, "Berry, let's go inside the wagon." She stood up and offered Berry her hand. Mama Dora knew about Berry's problem, although she didn't know that Sue Ellen had confronted him.

Isabelle had finally confided in her and told her the dark secret about Jane's birth father. Yes, Mama Dora would do all she could possibly do to help her friends. Two people who had been caught up in an evil man's wrath. She was being given the opportunity to help Berry leave the plantation. And she had prayed every day that God would give Isabelle a path of escape.

Mama Dora led Berry to her brightly painted, barrel-roofed wagon. When they entered the wagon, her grandson was in there. "Out with you, boy. Get out there, and eat your supper before it gets cold!" Her command got the boy to scampering.

Mama Dora pulled up two cane-bottomed chairs and placed them opposite each other. The two sat down in the chairs, facing each other. She took both of Berry's hands into hers, looked him in the eyes, and said, "Berry, you and your family must go to New Orleans. I feel that is where your destiny lies. You and your family will find happiness in New Orleans. Don't be afraid to take this chance; do not be afraid of your future."

CHAPTER FIVE

Earlier in the day, Tomsk and his tribe had set up camp. They were camping just outside the city of New Orleans. Just after lunch, Tomsk asked Berry to ride into the city with him. He wanted to look things over to decide where the best place was to set up their food booth, and he would need Berry's help setting it up. They also needed a place for the tinker to sell his wares.

"What do you think about New Orleans, Berry?" Tomsk asked as the two men rode into town.

"Sho is a mighty fine town, Tomsk; it sho is." Like a small child, Berry's eyes were filled with wonder.

"Let's drive to Jackson Square. I think that will be our best place to set up. We've done well there in the past. Lots of gold and silver coins come our way there, Berry." Tomsk gave Berry a sly grin as he lifted the heavy, gold chain that hung around his neck. He kissed the chain. With a satisfied sigh, he said, "Yeah, lots of gold for the tribe! People will even pay to watch us dance. Especially our beautiful ladies!"

"Why don' yer moving bones stay in Orleans if dare's dat much gold here?" Berry questioned.

"There's not enough gold in this world to buy a gypsy's freedom. Now I'll be the first one to admit that the town and all of its buildings are grand. But all of this is not to be compared to one night of sleeping under a blanket of stars with the earth as a mattress."

"Well, dis ole darkie don' like to sleep under de stars. I wants a roof over my head."

"Yes, of course you do, Berry. I don't expect you to understand how we live or what lies in a gypsy's heart. I'm sure we can find you some work here."

"I'll do any kind of work I can find. What kind of work is dare round here?" Berry asked.

"Well, for beginners, there are lots of services you can do. For instance, you could set up a booth her in Jackson Square. You could sharpen scissors, offer to clean chimneys like you did on the plantation, or even shine shoes," Tomsk explained.

The two men rode into Jackson Square. Berry was admiring the statue of Andrew Jackson and the St. Louis Cathedral when he saw a group of white men who had blacked their faces in attempt to impersonate Negroes. They were singing and dancing on Market Square.

"What on earth is dat?" Berry asked.

"That's a negro minstrel show, Berry," Tomsk said.

"Dem folk's ain't Negroes!" Berry's eyes were filled with disbelief.

"No, they're not, Berry. They're certainly not Negroes!" Tomsk shook his head.

"Don' seem fair, Tomsk. De one thing ole Berry can do well is play music. Now white folks done gone and blackened their faces and done took my job away from me!" Berry's voice quivered.

"Now, Berry, just calm down. There's a place in this town for you and your Jew's harp. As a matter of fact, sometimes these people will hire black folks as talented as you are to teach the white folks to sing and dance like you do. There are a lot of bands in New Orleans, and most of them are Negro bands," Tomsk reassured him.

"Dat be fine. Ole Berry don' mind playing his Jew's harp for da white man. Jus' long as I feeds my family. Yes, sir, long as Berry feeds his family!" Berry took his harmonica out of his pocket and began to softly play a tune.

Tomsk pulled on the reins that he held in his hands. "Whoa!" he said while stopping the buggy.

"What yo doing?" Berry asked after removing the harmonica from his mouth and gently tapping it on his pants leg to remove any spit that he might have left in it.

"A thought just came to my mind, Berry. I'm half-minded to look up Captain Reeves. He's Stephen's pa, you know." Tomsk put the brake on the surrey and leaned back in his seat.

"Why yo want to look him up?" Berry asked.

"Because he's a very rich and influential man. Since my daughter died, we've been raising his son, and he's been mighty kind to our tribe. The last I heard, in addition to owning a shipping line, he had also bought into a theater here in New Orleans. I hear they have the top singers in the world performing in this grand theater."

"And what's dat got to do wit' me?" Berry wondered.

"I thought perhaps he would give you and Sue Ellen a job of some kind. Probably not your music, but maybe cleaning or gardening. I'm sure with my recommendation, he will help you all he can."

"So where does we find dis man?" Berry asked anxiously.

A wide grin crossed Tomsk face. "Probably down on Basin Street. He had a place there, and he has a quad-roon down there."

"What's dat?"

"Berry, a quad-roon is a woman of mixed blood!"

"Oh. Yes, I know all bout dat!"

CHAPTER SIX

At lunchtime John came out of the sugar-cane field and went to the plantation house to get some lunch. He was in a hurry, because he needed to go to the barn and sharpen the crescent-shaped blades called sickles. The sickles were used to cut the sugar cane. He liked to keep the blades as sharp as possible to get the maximum work from his hired hands.

John sharpened his sickles, knives, and hoes on a large grinding stone. He wanted to get the blades sharpened and back into the field during the worker's lunch hour. When John finished the blades, he walked to his plantation house called Willow Grove. It was a superb, brick and stucco plantation house built several years before he was born. It stood in the center of a rolling hill, overlooking a willow-lined stream. The stream flowed into a bayou, which emptied into the Mississippi River a few miles from John's house.

As he neared the yard where huge, live oaks and willows stood, light-green Spanish moss was intertwined with them and was swaying with the wind. From this distance, with the noonday sun washing across the trees and yard, the old house looked much like the mansion John remembered as a child, when it had stood in its full grandeur. Since the war, John hadn't had the extra money or the man power to keep the house and grounds as he wished he could keep them. However, since Jane's birth, he had taken more pride in his house and grounds, doing what repairs he could.

John paused to think about the yesterdays of his life. John Sims Bradford hadn't always been the cruel, unfeeling man who often drank himself into a stupor rather than face the situations that needing a level head to solve. By most standards, John Bradford was not a handsome man, mainly because of his short neck. His head seemed to rest directly on his shoulders. He stood just five feet eight inches tall. His best feature was his beautiful eyes, which were framed with unusually long, dark eyelashes. On the occasion when he did smile, you could see the smile in his eyes. He had an aristocratic face and thick, curling, blond hair, like all the Bradford men.

As he slowly walked toward the side porch, John remembered when there had been slaves and a happy family living, all of them working together in harmony. When the war had come to this part of Louisiana, John's father had freed all his slaves. Several had chosen to stay loyal to the family and work for the small houses and plots Joseph Bradford had offered them. The beautiful old house hadn't been damaged when the Yankees moved through their parish.

Memories of the past brought John's mind to thoughts about Berry, the best field hand he'd ever had, and John wondered where Berry was and why he had left the plantation so suddenly. *At least Berry could have told me where he was going.* John remembered the look in Berry's eyes when in one of his drunken rages, he had whipped him. *Could be that I whipped him just a little too hard. Oh, the sorrow I have caused so many people.* John shook his head. Berry and John were the same age, thirty-four. They had played and worked together as they had grown to manhood. John realized how much he missed Berry.

When old man Bradford had died, he had left everything to his only living son. John's two older brothers had been killed in battle. A younger sister had died in infancy. John hadn't gone into battle because he had bouts with malaria and sometimes was in bed for days.

"I don't understand," John said aloud, "why has my life always been such a miserable mess."

He was nineteen when his father had died. John had continued to work the land with the same success his father had. Now he continued his sad reverie, thinking about the past. A strong wave of melancholy overwhelmed him. The brothers he had lost during war had hastened his mother and father's deaths as well. All the deaths, grieving, and sudden change of lifestyle had caused so much misery, more than John could handle.

All the upheaval and uncertainty the war had brought him. It had also brought him shame. John breathed a deep breath and let out a deep sigh, as he once again relived in his mind being with the only girl he had ever loved. Her name was Magnolia Du-Bois'. Her family owned a large plantation a few miles from his plantation called Willow Grove. Growing up, John had attended school and church with her. The two families had visited each other occasionally. John had always thought she was beautiful and wanted to become her beau.

Magnolia had begun having a suitor at an early age; his name was Thomas Milford. His father owned a stagecoach station and a hotel. The two had met at a shindig. It was two years before Magnolia father would let Thomas call upon his daughter. Shortly after she became of age to see Thomas, they became engaged.

Soon after their engagement, the war had started, and Thomas had joined the solders. Reassuring Magnolia that the war wouldn't last very long, he then explained to her that she wouldn't want to marry a coward. He had said that if every able-bodied man would join the cause, then they would probably all be back home in a month, six months at the longest.

She had anxiously waited a year before she received word of his death in battle. How her world had shattered. It was almost more than she could bear. John began to visit her occasionally. She turned to John for comfort, and as time went by, she began to lean on him more and more. He began to see her more often and fell in love with her. He was blind to everything she said about Thomas, refusing to see how much she still loved him. Her dark, curly hair, blue eyes, and petite figure drove John wild with desire to please her. Being a short man, her petite figure made him feel secure—she fitted against his shoulder.

The two were together every chance they could for a year and a half. John asked her to marry him, and she accepted his proposal. They received her father's blessing. The wedding had been planned; the invitations had been sent.

Then Thomas had come back home. When Magnolia saw him, it was the happiest day of her life when she held this starved and crippled man in her arms once again. Magnolia was tearful when she had to tell John their wedding was off, but she knew she must follow her heart in spite of the hurt she knew it would bring him. "I just feel I must. You see, he's had a hard life since he joined the army. He's been kept as a prisoner of war for a long time."

"So you're telling me you are calling off our wedding because you feel sorry for Thomas? That doesn't make any sense," John had said in a loud voice. Magnolia had paused and looked at John. Her heart went out to him, but she realized he must let her go.

She had said, "Yes, John, I do feel sorry for him, and I'm sorry for what I am doing to you, to us." She had looked off into the distance, and then in a firm voice, she had said, "But he's the man I love the most."

John often replayed this conversation in his mind. Since then, John had never been the same.

He had later married Miss Isabelle Blount, a close neighbor. They had been friends for years. Since they were close neighbors, her father had been able to help him with the problems he had with running Willow Grove. After Magnolia had left him, John drank too much trying to forget her. He was not able to hold his liquor, and when he drank too much, he became a violent man.

He felt that gentle Isabelle could help him with his drinking problems, and he knew that she could help him with running the plantation. However, Isabelle lacked the fire in her character that he had so much admired in Magnolia. It may have been this passive quality in Isabelle that later led to their marital problems. However, today John felt like his life was going to be better. He knew that his new daughter had given him the incentive to do better and not to drink so much. Maybe Isabelle could give him a son next time.

As John reached the edge of the side yard, he saw George, the coachman, and Isabelle drive off in the old surrey. He wondered what had happened in the parish. He knew that since Jane had been born, Isabelle did not like to leave her with anyone; therefore, he felt the need to check on her. *It won't take but a minute to check on Jane, and then I'll go back to work,* he thought.

Just a few moments alone with little Jane would make his day. She had become the apple of his eye. The heir he had waited for would have to come later. He now had his beautiful daughter. Sure, he had been disappointed when the doctor had stepped on the porch and announced the child was a girl. He had prayed for a son to carry on the Bradford name and inherit this huge, old plantation. However, once he saw Jane and held her small body in his arms, all thoughts of a son left him.

He loved Jane immediately. He was glad they had chosen Jane Ellen for her name. He could barely remember his younger sister, but now she would have a namesake. He had been surprised that his daughter's skin was a dark-olive color and that her hair was very black, so different from his and Isabelle's blond hair and light complexions. He figured that she had inherited the dark complexion from his grandmother's Indian heritage.

These characteristics brought back more memories of Magnolia. A thought crossed his mind. *If I had had a child with Magnolia, she would probably look a lot like Jane.* Yes, Jane had caused him to change. This change had made his life with Isabelle better. Isabelle even seemed prettier to John since she had given birth to Jane. John had not been able to understand Isabelle's dark moods and seemingly unhappy attitude since Jane's birth. He had even talked to the doctor. The doctor explained that sometimes new mothers began to be maudlin after childbirth, feeling tearful and emotional.

Today John slipped into the house and into the nursery to hold his eighteen-month-old child, He picked up the child from her bed, where she was quietly sitting, kicking, and cooing. Then sat down in the old rocker and bounced the child on his knee. He played peekaboo and patty-cake and beamed with pride as she laughed. He loved to hear the sound of her laughter.

"Your daddy loves you, angel child," he said lovingly as he tossed her into the air and caught her. Jane's laughter filled the room as they played. John did not realize that Ripley, the new woman that had taken Sue Ellen's place, had just fed Jane her lunch just before he came into the nursery. She threw up her recently eaten dinner. The mess went all over the clean, neatly pressed dress that Jane was wearing and on the floor.

"Oops, Daddy done gone and made his little princess sick. I am so sorry. I didn't realize you had just eaten. We'd better get you all washed up before Ripley sees what a mess we've made."

He really didn't care if Ripley became angry with him; cleaning up the child he loved so dearly just gave him that much more time with her. He unbuttoned her dress and pulled it over her head, and then holding her in the curve of his left arm, he poured water out of the pink, flowered pitcher into the bowl that sat underneath it. The pitcher and bowl sat on a washstand near Jane's bed. He noticed the neatly folded towels and washcloths that Ripley had left stacked beside the pitcher and bowl. Apparently she hadn't taken the time to put them away properly.

He pulled out a towel and washcloth. He put the washcloth into the bowl of water and wrung it out. Then he laid Jane on her back on the bed. She giggled as he washed her face and under her chin. After he'd washed her fat, little tummy, he powdered her with the sweet-smelling powder Isabelle had always put on her. Then he rolled her over on her stomach to powder her back. When he removed her diaper, he saw the birthmark. His mouth flew open in shock.

John was brought back to his senses when Jane rolled over and began to say, "Dada!" His anger exploded as he put things together. *So this is why Berry left the plantation. He knew the truth would eventually come out, and he knew I would kill him for what he and Isabelle had done. This also explains why she has been so cold all these years. Isabelle and Berry were lovers!*

Running his fingers through his hair, he paced the floor. He stopped his pacing when another thought crossed his mind. *The old saying that the husband is always the last to know. Did everyone else know about my wife's infidelity? Were they all laughing at me behind my back? Now I understand why she refuses to leave Jane with anyone else and why she's been so protective with her. There was the lie about having the baby blues. Ha! The joke is on me.*

Jane cried softly, trying to get her father's attention. John automatically went to the bed and picked her up. But unable to dismiss those thoughts, he laid her back down again. The child whom he had held so dear only a few moments ago had now become tainted, dirty, someone who brought shame to him.

A deep sadness overcame him as he realized that he had once again lost someone he loved so dearly. There would always be a void in his heart that Magnolia and Jane had filled so completely. Tears fell down his cheeks. He wasn't quite sure he could hold up under all this pain, hurt, and anger that he was feeling. He needed a drink, and he needed one now. His thoughts went to the liquor cabinet located downstairs in the dining room.

John was so engrossed in his pain that he had forgotten that Jane was lying on the bed. He heard a thump and then a loud cry when Jane fell off the bed and onto the floor. He picked her up automatically and said a few soothing words to her. When he heard Ripley footsteps on the stairway, he quickly put a clean dress and diaper on Jane's trembling body. He then began to walk the floor, carrying her. *I must act like I know nothing*, he thought, *until I figure out what must be done.*

"What's de matter wit' my baby?" Ripley asked as she opened the door and stepped into the nursery. She smiled when she saw John holding the baby and said, "I didn't know yo were here."

"Yeah, I had to come back to the barn to sharpen the sickles. I thought I would check on Jane while I was here. I'm afraid I let her fall off the bed. She threw up on her dress, and when I washed her up and turned around to get her another one, she rolled off the bed. Oh, it looks like I forgot to clean up the floor. Take care of that, will you, Ripley?"

Jane was still crying and trying to get over her fall. John said, "Here. Take her. I need to get back to the field." John held the child toward Ripley. She took her and gently soothed the child with gentle words.

"Where's Isabelle?" John asked as he opened the door.

"Oh, she went to Master Cannon's plantation. Yo know his pappy died last night, didn't yo?"

"No, I didn't know he died. I knew he had been very sick, but I thought he was getting better."

"Dey said he got better for a few days. Yeah, dey said he actually sat up and talked and laughed wit' his wife and children. I guess dat was jus' his way of saying good-bye to dis world. I fried some chicken and made a cake. Missus Isabelle had George run her over there. I'm glad she's finally getting out of de house. I guess she thought Jane would sleep while she was gone," Ripley explained as she smiled and looked at Jane. Jane had put her tiny fist in her mouth and was chewing on it, making a sucking noise, as she looked at her father with accusing eyes.

"Well, I'll see you at suppertime. I need to get those blades to the field."

As John walked down the stairs, he breathed a sigh of relief. He hoped Ripley hadn't noticed how nervous he was. He hurried down the stairway and into the dining room. His hand shook as he opened the liquor cabinet and grabbed the first bottle within his reach, opened it, and drank it down. He devoured the fiery liquid as if it were water. When the Scotch hit his stomach, it burned for a time, and then he became numb. A sweet relief from his shock and pain. When he heard the back door close, John placed the cork in the bottle and quickly replaced it in the cabinet. *I can't be caught drinking. I've got to plan.*

"That bitch, that low-down bitch," he mumbled.

Tears began to flow down his cheeks, and his shoulders began to shake as he thought, *I've lost again. First Magnolia, and now my precious little Jane. Yes, and my wife, not that I have ever loved her much, but she is mine and has brought great shame to me. Who would have thought that quiet Miss Prim and Proper Isabelle would have the audacity to have a black lover? That just proves that you just never know what's going on around you.*

Well, she sure picked the wrong man this time to make a fool of! She is going to pay, and pay she will. So will Berry when I find him! Jane's not my child, and there's no doubt she belongs to Berry. I've seen that birthmark all my life. I know all about where it came from. They can't fool me! Oh, Jane, I'm going to miss you.

What am I going to do? I can't let her know I'm wise to her secret until I decide what to do. I can't let her find out I'm drinking again. I gave up my drinking for a child who's not mine. I'll play her little game until I find a way to get even with her. It's a shame. Here I am, the only living Bradford, and I have no heir. This is ironic. A Bradford slave's seed is reigning heiress to all this land.

Everything will go on as usual. I'll be the same devoted father I've always been. Jane deserves to die, and die she will. I must do it quickly, without raising any suspicion. I won't let anyone think anything has changed at my place, because I don't need any more scandal than there probably already is. I wonder if Ripley knows. Probably not, because Berry had already left the plantation before she came.

John brushed the tears from his eyes.

Sue Ellen! Sue Ellen knows. I'm positive of that; she would have spotted the birthmark quickly, because all of her children had been born with the same mark. Well, Jane must go! I can't allow her to live in my home much longer. The proof of my wife's infidelity must go, and so must Isabelle. How and when, I don't know just yet.

He took the liquor bottle back out of the cabinet and sat it on the table. He heard footsteps coming down the hall.

"Is dat yo, Master John?" the cook, a small black woman, asked as she stuck her head in the door.

John quickly stepped in front of the table to hide the open bottle of Scotch. "Yes. It's me, Abigail. I'm taking a short break from the fields."

"Yeah, yo need one. It sho is hot out dare, ain't it?"

"Yes, it is mighty hot. Do I smell something burning?"

"Lawdy lawd! I sho hope not!" She quickly turned and walked down the hall.

John picked up the bottle and went outside. He stood on the porch and breathed deeply, hoping the air would help clear his head. He felt disoriented, angry, and very lonely. With his shoulders slumped, he walked to the barn where he had left the mule. He untied the mule, got up on the saddle, and kicked the mule hard in his side. The mule raised his head and looked at John with a startled look in his eyes. John pulled out and used the whip on the mule's rear, and the mule ran faster than he had in years. Dust rose from the dry roadway as John made his way back to the field.

"Come here, Sam!" John called out as he as he rode to the edge of the cane field. Just then he remembered that he had forgotten to bring back the sickles he had sharpened.

"Yeah, boss?" The skinny black man answered as he neared John and the mule.

"I left the sickles back at the barn. Send one of the young boys back to get them. I want this field finished today! Do you understand?"

He gave Sam a vicious look.

CHAPTER SEVEN

"Pat a cake; pat a cake; make a little man. Roll him over; roll him over; throw him in a pan!" Isabelle's mother, Mrs. Gate, was sitting in a rocking chair in the parlor, holding Jane in her lap, and playing games with her. Jane was clapping her hands and laughing with glee. Mrs. Gate's was a tall, thin woman with graying hair. There were lots of worry lines in her face.

Isabelle sat on the sofa across from her mother. She was enjoying the scene before her. "Mother, isn't Jane beautiful?" she asked.

"Yes. She's so beautiful. She brings hope and innocence to our war-torn lives. It's so good to see new life after the cruel war years, when we saw so much suffering and dying. We are truly blessed that our homes were also spared the destruction that so many of our friends and family had to suffer. How sad our world has become."

"Let's not talk about the war, Mother." Isabelle stood up and walked to the window. She glanced outside, and then she turned around, crossed her arms, and leaned against the wall. "Jane is growing so fast, Mother. I'm simply going to have to make her some new clothes."

"I think this little princess deserves a ready-made dress! Why don't we go to New Orleans and do some shopping? I would like to buy my favorite granddaughter a new dress. In fact I have to be in New Orleans on business next week. Why don't you have Ripley go with us to take care of Jane while we shop?" Mrs. Gates suggested as she ran her fingers through Jane's hair.

"I don't think Ripley would want to leave the plantation right now." Isabelle shook her head. "Her husband is down. You know he has a broken leg, don't you?" Isabelle asked as she ran her fingers across the top of the dresser. "This needs dusting." She shook her head.

"Well, no, I didn't realize there was anything wrong with him. How did he break his leg?" Mrs. Gates talked while trying to hold Jane, who was squirming to get out of her lap.

"He fell through the barn loft. It seems that he was in the loft throwing down hay with a pitchfork when the floor fell through with him. He crawled on his belly and finally made it out of the barn, but it was several hours before anyone found him. His leg was very swollen when he was found. John went and got Dr. Morris. The doctor told him to stay off his leg for several weeks."

"Well, then taking Ripley is out of the question. We could take someone from my plantation, but Jane wouldn't know her. I think it would be best if we just leave her with Ripley and her daddy," Mrs. Gates said.

"Mother! I've never been away from Jane overnight! I don't know if I can just leave her!" Isabelle's body stiffened.

"Now, Isabelle, you know John worships her, and Ripley will guard her with her life." Mrs. Gates's voice was soothing.

"Did I hear my name called?" John opened the door and walked into the room.

"Yes, you sure did. I was just telling Isabelle that I have some business in New Orleans to attend to, and I think she needs a holiday. I told her I want to go shopping and buy some new clothes for Jane. After all, it will soon be Easter." Mrs. Gates smiled at her son-in-law.

"Well, I certainly agree with you, Mother Gates. I will take care of Jane while you're gone." He took Jane from Mrs. Gates's arms and held her close. She began to squirm to get down. "Now, baby, let your daddy hold you. Don't you ever get too big for your daddy," he said.

It was getting harder and harder for John to play the part of the perfect husband and father. When no one was around, he would ignore Jane, but when Isabelle was around, he acted like the perfect father. He had decided this was the best way to handle the situation until he could decide what to do about her. Maybe if Isabelle left for a night or two, he could find a way to solve his problem. But Jane could sense the change in her father; she began to cry and reach for her mother.

"Now, little Miss Jane, if you'll be kind to your daddy, I'll find you a surprise," Mrs. Gates said as she got out of her chair.

"A gift! You have a gift for our baby Jane! Did you hear that, Jane? Grandmother has a gift for you," John said. He held Jane tightly, squeezing her far too hard, deliberately trying to cause her pain.

"Let me see now. Where did I put my purse?" Mrs. Gates asked.

"It's over there on the piano, Mother," Isabelle said as she walked across the room and brought the purse to her mother.

Mrs. Gates took a small, pink-velvet box from her purse. She opened the box and took a small ring out of it. The velvet box caught Jane's attention, and she began to reach for it. Mrs. Gates caught her hand and placed the tiny ring on her finger. "Do you remember this ring, Isabelle?" she asked.

"Yes, Mother," Isabelle whispered. Her hands went to her heart. "But I must admit that I had almost forgotten about it."

"Oh, you must never forget about this ring, my dear. You wore it when you were a baby. Now let me tell you the story about this ring one more time. Someday you will tell this story to Jane, and then Jane can tell it to her daughter." She gave Jane a kiss on her chubby, little arm and removed the ring from her finger. Then she handed the ring to Isabelle. "Do you see the little flower on the inside band of the ring?"

"Yes, Mother," Isabelle answered as she looked closely to see the tiny symbol the goldsmith had placed there when he had made it. The symbol was a Lilly which was a trademark for this particular goldsmith so that people could identify the authenticity of his work.

"Isabelle, my father had this ring made for me when I was born. He was so happy to have a daughter after having five sons. His specific request was that the ring be given to the first daughter in our family line. I wore the ring. Then you wore it, and now it's time for Jane to wear it."

Mrs. Gates placed the ring back on Jane's finger, and then she slipped a narrow pink ribbon under it and securely tied the ribbon around Jane's wrist. Jane began to try to pull it off.

"Now, little lady, you have two fine pieces of jewelry. You must become accustomed to being a grand lady," Isabelle said with pride.

"Two?" Mrs. Gates asked.

"Yes, she also has a locket that came from the Bradford side of the family. It is so beautiful. The front of the heart-shaped locket has small rosebuds and leaves engraved on it, which made it the heirloom of the Bradford family. The delicate heart has a picture of John's mother inside. On the back, it has the letter *B* engraved by the jeweler in old English lettering. John gave it to Jane shortly after she was born. I can't believe you've never seen it. I'll get it and put it on her!"

CHAPTER EIGHT

John left the parlor. He went to his study and closed the door. He shook his head as if to clear his mind. Then he sat down in a chair behind the massive desk, opened a desk drawer, and took out a bottle of bourbon. He removed the cork and took a large swallow. Having to play the part of a loving father to Jane was almost more than he could bear, but seeing the locket that belonged to his dear, departed mother was simply asking too much. He couldn't remain in the same room with them and watch Isabelle place his mother's locket around Jane's neck.

The child had no right to impersonate a true Bradford. The very thought of that turned his stomach. Isabelle had played him for a fool. He was sure of that. He felt that everyone knew that Jane was not his child. He couldn't stand to think that society saw him as a foolish man. *Yes, the time has come when I must get rid of the evidence of Isabelle's sin out of our lives. I must kill the child!* This thought made John shudder. *I should kill Isabelle, but if Jane disappears, I can watch her slowly die or lose her mind.* The thought of sweet revenge took all his doubts away. He smiled an insane smile.

⇒‖⇐

Two hours later Isabelle knocked on his door. "John, may I come in?" she asked.

John quickly hid the bottle, lit a cigar, and puffed on it hard, making himself light-headed, he was trying to fill the room with smoke, hoping to cover up the smell of liquor. A few moments later, he answered, "Yes, you may, my dear!"

Isabelle entered the room, smoothing the front of her dress and tucking in an unruly lock of hair that had fallen out of the comb she was wearing to keep it up. She said, "John, I've decided to go to New Orleans with Mother tomorrow. We'll probably be gone overnight. Will you see that Ripley takes proper care of Jane?"

She began to cough. She fanned her hand in front of her face to steer away the heavy cigar smoke.

"Well, yes, of course I will, darling. I'll also enjoy the time I will get to spend with her. This will be a good opportunity for the two of us to be together. Without you, here I can spoil her silly!" John said in a gentle tone.

He stood up from his chair and started walking toward Isabelle. Then he remembered that he'd been drinking and didn't want her to smell the liquor. He knew that she wouldn't leave Jane with him if she thought for a moment that he had started drinking again.

He sat back down in his chair and said, "Isabelle, don't you worry about us. We'll do fine. It's about time you got out of the house for a while. You've been through so much since Jane's birth. Your baby blues do seem to have greatly improved, but there are times when I've seen you looking off into the distance like you have lost your best friend. You must go and enjoy yourself! I'll even write you a check so that you can buy yourself a few nice things."

"Thank you so much, John. You are such a generous man."

CHAPTER NINE

I sabelle and her mother left for New Orleans early the following morning. John spent most of the day in the cane fields overseeing the harvesting of the fields. Lately he had paid very little attention to what was going on around him, because his mind had been on how he could successfully remove Jane from his life. But he realized that just his presence in the fields would keep the field hands working.

Around two o'clock he noticed that the wind was blowing and the sky was getting dark. He had to put his hand on his hat to keep the wind from blowing it off his head. The wind blew harder and began to blow up dust and small seeds from fields. *This is going to be a bad storm* he thought. Then he yelled at the man closest to him. "Let's go to the house before we're all blown away!" But his voice couldn't be heard because of the wind.

"What yo say, boss?" The man cupped his hand over his ear to hear.

John walked closer to the man and said, "Go tell everybody it's time to go home."

"Yes, sir," the black man said.

John and the tired crew began to hurry to their shelters. As they neared the plantation, John noticed that a band of gypsies was hurriedly setting up camp across the road from his house. He could tell from the leader's wagon that this wasn't Tomsk and Mama Dora's tribe. There was no way of knowing where this tribe was going or where they had been. *They are probably stopping off here to wait out the storm*, he thought.

He smiled a satisfied smile, and an evil glint came into his eyes when he realized that the perfect plan had been laid at feet. *This is my way out of this shame. I will kill Jane and tell Isabelle that the gypsies took her!*

They had never had any trouble with any of the gypsy bands who had drifted in here, but it was commonly known that some gypsies would steal and had been known to kidnap children. With the way the storm was coming in, he knew that it would be several days before Isabelle could make it home. Hopefully the gypsies would be gone by then. If not, John knew that it would be their word against his.

When John walked into the backyard and saw Ripley frantically trying to take the clothes off the clothes line, he rushed over to help her. "You sure are scurrying around. I've never seen you move this fast before," John said and laughed.

"Oh, Master John! I've got to get dese clothes off de line befo' dat *bad* storm gets here. It's getting closer. I can smell de rain in de air." She looked up at the sky. The sky was becoming darker as the storm moved in. She placed an armload of clothes into a wicker basket sitting on the ground.

"Yes, I agree with you, Ripley. I feel like we are in for a bad storm as well. Grab the rest of those clothes. I'll carry the basket in the house for you." After she jerked the clothes off the line, John picked up the overflowing basket and carried it inside the house.

"I'm afraid Misses Isabelle and her mother will be gone for several days. I'll bet de creek will rise and dey won' be able to get back home as soon as they wuz planning to," Ripley said as she took the clothes basket from him and put them on a bench in the long hall that divided the house.

"Yes, I'm worried about that, too." John leaned against the stairwell.

"Don' you worry none, master. I can take care of dat beautiful child of yers." With both hands, she began to smooth her clothes and her windblown hair.'

"I know how well you can take care of Jane, and don't you think we don't appreciate you. But you know, lately you've been looking very tired and run-down. I guess between taking care of Jane and Wash, you're working too hard."

"Yes, sir. I do get tired, Master John. But don' yo worry none. I be fine."

"How long has it been since Wash broke his leg?" John asked.

"'Bout three weeks, I guess." She frowned.

"Well, I'll tell you what. As soon as you get those clothes put up, you can go home before the storm hits full force."

"What?" Her eyes opened wide.

"You can go on home, I said. You have a houseful of young children and a helpless man. I know your children are all afraid of storms, so go on home and take care of them." John spoke in a soft tone of voice.

"Thank yo, Master John. Thank yo. I'll fix yo and Jane some supper 'fore I leave."

"No. You must go before the storm hits. Just finish putting up those clothes, and then go home to your family. I'm perfectly capable of feeding Jane and myself. I want you to get some rest," John insisted.

"Yo are a good daddy, Master John. Yo sho are!"

She looked at John with respect in her eyes.

CHAPTER TEN

John watched until Ripley left the yard and walked in the direction of her cabin. Then he turned and walked up the long staircase and into the nursery. He stood over Jane's bed and looked down on the small child who was sleeping so peacefully. He wondered how such a beautiful, innocent child could cause so much heartache. *Yes, you are beautiful,* and for a moment, the love he once had for her flooded his heart and brought tears to his eyes.

Jane stirred in her sleep, stretched her small arms above her head, and smiled an angelic smile. He recalled his mother saying, "When children smile in their sleep, they're talking to angels." He stood looking down on Jane and began to have doubts about his ability to carry out his plans. He didn't know if he could actually kill the child he had loved so much before he had found out the awful truth. One moment he wanted to pick her up, hold her close, and protect her, and then the next moment, he became very angry and wanted nothing less than to destroy her. But most of all, he wanted to hurt and destroy Isabelle. With all the conflicting emotions, he left her room and went downstairs to the liquor cabinet.

The storm moved in with a fury. Lightning danced around and lit up the room John was in as he walked the floor and drank. The fury in his heart was as wild and out of control as the storm outside seemed to be. The darkness of the night had fallen several hours past. John decided the time was right. It was time to take Jane out and dispose of her; it was time to get her out of their lives forever. Once again he cursed Isabelle.

"Why didn't she let the doctor know that Jane was of mixed blood? It would have been so much easier on all concerned if her life had been snuffed out when she was born!" he mumbled to himself. He picked up a candle holder and the flickering candle from his desk and slowly walked up the stairs and to Jane's room. She was fast asleep, rolled over on her side, sucking her thumb.

"No matter what comes or goes, Miss Jane, one thing won't change. You are a very pretty little thing," he said as he held the candle over her crib and looked at her for a long moment. The candlelight shining into her eyes awakened her. She opened her eyes and reached both arms out toward him.

"Dada," she said.

He picked her up and held her tightly in his arms.

"It's just too bad you have to die, little Jane, but I'm not going to have a black child carrying my name."

John didn't notice that Jane was dressed in a new calico dress or that she was still wearing the ring his mother-in-law had given her. Nor did he see that the Bradford locket was still hanging around her neck. He wrapped Jane in a pink afghan that Isabelle had crocheted for her while she was waiting for Jane to be born. In his drunken state, he didn't think about any of these things. He was in a big hurry to get to the bayou. He needed to get the evil deed done before he lost his courage.

He paused for a moment and held her close to his body before he stepped off the porch and into the darkness. The huge storm clouds had darkened any light coming from the moon or the stars.

The cold wind hit his face. His feet slid on the wet grass. After he caught his balance and walked a few feet, he went into a chuckhole and twisted his ankle. This made him even angrier. Jane began to cry as the cold rain hit her.

"Stop that crying right now, or I'll go ahead and kill you with my bare hands!" he threatened and began to walk faster. As he neared the bayou, the lightning flashed and the thunder rumbled, seeming to shake the ground. The live oaks all covered with moss and willows swayed in the wind as the rain came down harder. In his hurry to carry out his plan, John had forgotten to get his coat and rain hat. Because tonight his heart was filled with hatred and murder, he was getting soaked and uncomfortable.

When he arrived at the bayou, the waters were raging. The currents were strong, and the riverbanks were swollen. John paused to look at the child once more. Even though the light was subdued, he could still make out her features. He felt that this was the last time he would see her olive skin and beautiful eyes, her black, curly hair, not kinky curly like the black children he had known. *How had she escaped the kinky hair?*

Jane began to squirm, trying to get down out of his arms. She cried, calling out "Dada" again.

"Don't you cry; this will all be over soon," he said in a soothing tone.

He hated himself because she could still get to him when she called him Dada. Soon she was crying loudly, and her small body was stiff with fear. John continued on toward the water. He could hear the rushing sound the water made as it splashed against the limbs and trees on the way to the main river channel.

"Come on now; don't cry so hard. You're going to be all right," he said to the child as he stood on the bank. "You're old Berry's child. What a shame." A deep sigh escaped his lips, and salty tears mingled with the raindrops that ran down his face.

John continued to mumble to himself, "Here I've wanted a child all these years, and when I finally get one, you turn out to be Berry's!" The more he thought about his wife's unfaithfulness, the stronger his anger became.

He swung the child back to throw her out into the deeper part of the waters. But as he brought her forward, he couldn't let go. He stopped, swore, and let the child fall on the banks of the bayou. He looked at the rapidly rising swirling waters and said, "I'll just leave you here. The water is rising so fast, it won't be long until you are swept away. That way you will be washed out my life forever, and I won't actually be the one to do it."

He stood there and looked down at the child. For some reason, he felt better since he had decided not to actually drown the child himself. In his drunken state, John felt that when she did drown, somehow it wouldn't be his fault. Of course it wasn't his fault. The blame lay with Berry and his floozy wife, Isabelle. After all, he had been forced to deal with this situation that was beyond his control. He knew that this last act of mercy would cleanse his conscience.

He looked down one last time and saw that her blanket was caught on some branches. She was crying loudly. He hoped the gypsies wouldn't hear her cries and come looking for her. They were not too far away. The thunder had lessened in the past few minutes, but it was still raining heavily. John knew he needed to leave this place before someone heard or saw him. He turned to go back to the house. He knew it would not be long before the child died. He didn't want to witness that. He ran toward the house, dragging his wounded leg, slipping and sliding on the wet grass.

John thought he heard a man's voice, but he didn't stop. He had to hurry. Stumbling from drunkenness, he rushed to the lane that took him to his house. The lightning continued to light the way for him. The cries of the child gradually slipped away from his hearing.

CHAPTER ELEVEN

"Whoa, whoa! Now take it easy. Now just calm down; it's going to be all right," Brother Malcolm Hatfield said in a soothing tone to the horse pulling the surrey his family was riding in. He was trying to get the horse under control. The horse was spooked by the terrible storm. The lightning flashed illuminating the sky and ground all around them.

The thunder that followed the lightning was loud, seeming to shake the earth. The rain was coming down hard and fast. A few miles behind them, lightning had hit a huge oak tree standing close to the road. When the bolt of lightning hit the tree, there had been a terrible noise when the tree had split in two. Then the loud thunder had followed as one-half of the tree hit the ground.

Malcolm, his wife, Sarah, and their children, Seth and Lydia, had barely escaped being hit by the fallen tree. Had they been a few minutes later, the tree would have landed on top of the surrey.

Malcolm had said aloud, "Thank you, Lord!" He realized that his horse was spooked with fear and was about to endanger them all. He had to try to control his own fears in order protect his family. He had to put his trust God to deliver him from this terrible storm.

Malcolm was a large man and stood six feet, two inches tall. He wasn't fat, but he had a large, muscular frame. He was simply a huge man with dark skin and shoulder-length, black hair. His top lip was lined with a heavy mustache. But he couldn't really be called handsome due to his huge ears and large nose. Everyone who met him soon realized that he had a heart made of gold. He had been called into the ministry when he was twenty-two years old. Sarah had been by his side for fifteen years. They had buried three of their five children in tiny graves in the family cemetery.

"It's such a dangerous night to be out. No wonder our horse is spooked. Besides the storm, I didn't like the looks of the gypsy camp we just passed." Sarah's voice quivered with fear.

"Daddy, Daddy," little Lydia called from the back of the surrey, "are we going to die? I don't want to die." Her voice choked up, and she began to cry.

"No, baby girl. We are not going to die, at least not tonight anyway. We must pray and then let our faith lead us through this perilous time. Remember the story of how God delivered the children of Israel, leading them through the Red Sea. Now if he led them through a big, big, old sea, then you know he can get us through a storm!"

Malcolm talked as he wrestled with the reins. There was another bolt of lightning and a loud clap of thunder. The horse reared its front feet high in the air. The horse's neighs were loud, and its behavior became more and more frantic. Malcolm wasn't sure how much longer he could hold on to the reins. He feared that the horse would bolt and run. He tightened the reins in an attempt to force the horse back to the ground. His front feet came back down on the road, but the horse had a mind of his own. No matter which way Malcolm pulled on the reins, the horse headed to the side of the road. Soon Malcolm could feel the surrey's wheels sinking into the soft earth; they were stuck. The horse paused for a moment and began panting for breath.

"Now Bob has really got us into some trouble!" Malcolm said to Sarah as he dropped the reins in disgust. "I don't know what to do." He breathed a long, heavy, disgusted sigh. The rain was blowing into the surrey, drenching their already wet and cold bodies. Malcolm knew that he must cover Bob's eyes so that he couldn't see the lightning.

Turning to Sarah, he said, "I'm going let Bob catch his breath, and then I will need your help. Can you hold the reins and help us get Bob out of the ditch? I'm going to have to put something over his eyes." He looked around but didn't see anything big enough to go over the horse's head. "Sarah, I'm afraid I'll have to use your wrap."

He looked down at the quilted wrap that lay across Sarah's lap. Although the wrap was soaking wet, it was still very beautiful. It was made out of white squares of material. Each square had a different color of butterfly embroidered on it. The wrap was quilted in tiny, neat stitches. Her mother had made it for her, so Sarah had taken extra good care of it.

Seeing his wife's reluctance and the frown that had come across her face, he knew how much the wrap meant to her. "I'll try not to ruin it, but our very lives may depend on your quilt," Malcolm explained.

"I understand," Sarah said as a tear fell down her cheek.

"Seth, get out of the buggy. After I put this over his head, I'll need you to talk to him and try to get him to calm down."

After Sarah took the reins, Malcolm and twelve year old Seth got out of the surrey and walked toward the spooked horse, talking calmly as they moved to his head. Seth ran his fingers through the horse's mane, but as they were about ready to put the wrap over Bob's head, another bolt of lightning illuminated the sky, causing the horse to panic even more. It took the two of them several minutes to place the wrap over Bob's head. It was taking all of Sarah's strength to hold on to the reins. As she stood up in the surrey and pulled with all her strength, her hair was a matted mess from the severity of the wind and cold rain.

Finally after they blindfolded Bob, they were able to calm him down by rubbing and talking to him. As the storm began to subside, the wind died down, and the thunder and lightning slowed to an occasional streak and rumble.

"Good job, Sarah. Now we are going to try to get out of this mud." Malcolm was sweating and out of breath. "Hold on tight to the reins. Seth, go to the back of the surrey and push. I'll guide the horse." As soon as Seth reached the other end of the surrey, Malcolm said, "On three, let's go."

As the horse pulled and Seth pushed, slowly the surrey began to inch its way out of the mud and back on the road. The two mud-coated men got back inside the surrey. They traveled only a short way before Sarah said, "Malcolm, stop!"

Malcolm stopped and looked at his wife as if she were insane. "Why do you want to stop? We just got started." Malcolm's patience was wearing thin.

"Hush." She placed her index finger over her lips. "Be quiet, and listen. I think I heard a child crying," she whispered.

After listening a few moments, Malcolm also heard the cry. "I hear something, too, but it could be an animal," he remarked.

"Or it could be a ghost!" Lydia cried, petrified with fear.

"Stop that sniffling, and try to help us listen. Perhaps one of us will hear what we heard a minute ago. Someone must be in danger; we can't leave here without trying to help!" Sarah sternly commanded her daughter.

When everyone became silent, they all heard the cry coming from the bayou. "What on earth? There must be a family stranded out in this terrible storm." Malcolm looked at the swollen bayou. "I'll go and see what's happening down there."

"I'll go with you, Dad," Seth said.

"No, Son, you stay and protect your mother and sister and try to keep Bob calm."

As Malcolm walked toward the raging waters of the bayou, the crying became louder. When he reached the riverbank, he saw a pink bundle caught in the branches of a tree, and he knew that the crying was coming from this bundle. He realized that the cry was getting weaker. There was very little movement from the blanket. He could hardly believe his eyes and ears. He cautiously went to the banks of the bayou, being very careful on the soft earth. He didn't want to lose his footing and fall into the angry waters.

When he got as close to the child as he dared, he leaned over, stretched out his body and his arms, and rescued the child. As he straightened himself up, he thought he heard someone running away. At least it sounded like long, lumbering steps. When he looked to his right, he saw a man running away from the bayou. Malcolm called out to the man, but he was too far away to hear.

Looking down at the tiny bundle he held in his arms, Malcolm eyes filled with tears. He was holding a child someone hadn't wanted. The child was wrapped tightly in a pink, afghan. The afghan had kept the child from slipping into the bayou. Malcolm unwrapped the afghan and saw that the child was a girl. Her arms began to reach out to him. Her color was blue, and her body trembled from the cold.

"Poor baby, poor little child," Malcolm crooned to the child as he held her close to his heart. While trying to warm her shivering body, he couldn't stop the tears that flowed freely down his cheeks as his heart went out to the child. He looked around to see if the baby's mother was nearby, but Malcolm saw no one. He stood quietly and looked toward the heavens. "Now I understand why you had me out in this raging storm tonight. Blessed be the name of the Lord."

Malcolm and Sarah were returning from a revival in Des Allemands, a parish twenty miles from their home congregation. Brother Rules was the preacher who had been hired to hold the revival, but on the day before it was to begin, his mother had died. He had sent a message to Malcolm asking him to please come and conduct the meeting in his place. Malcolm had almost refused to come because of the short notice.

And the fact that he was trying to decide if he should take another church that had been offered to him. There were things in his own congregation that needed his attention before he could move to another church in another parish, where the salary is more, but he wasn't fully decided if this move would be in the best interests of him or his family. He had prayed about the matter and decided that he truly should hold this revival, because he knew that people had already begun to travel to the church. He had decided his family should go with him and told Sarah to pack enough clothes for a week.

Overwhelmed with emotion, Malcolm could hardly speak. He returned to the surrey and handed the baby to Sarah.

"Malcolm, what on earth?" she questioned as she took the soggy shawl.

Malcolm swallowed hard. "It's a child, Sarah, a small girl. She—she was almost in the bayou. It looks like all that saved her life was the afghan that she's wearing catching on a limb. She's almost chilled to death; take her clothes off, and put on dry ones. What a night! What a strange night this has turned out to be."

"I agree," Sarah said as she began to take the wet clothes off of the child. "Lydia, open the trunk and try to find something dry to put on this child." She turned her head toward Lydia, who sat in the back of the surrey. Her eyes were wide open in disbelief.

"What do you want me to get?" Lydia asked.

"It doesn't matter. Anything you can find that's dry," Sarah said.

"Well she's not getting any of my clothes to wear!" four-year-old Lydia said.

Sarah saw the pouting lips of her daughter and realized that she was already envious of the child. "All right then. Lydia, get me something dry out of the trunk. Don't be so slow. This child is freezing."

"Mama, what are you going to do with this baby?" Lydia asked in a hateful voice as she opened the trunk and removed one of Sarah's dresses.

As Sarah undressed the child, she noticed the gold locket that was around the child's neck. Then she noticed the tiny ring on her finger. The ring was secured with a pink ribbon tied around her wrist. "Malcolm, look! This child has on gold jewelry! I wonder where she came from and why she was in the bayou. Do you think she's a gypsy? Or was she kidnapped by the gypsies?"

"I don't know, Sarah. I simply do not know all the answers," Malcolm said.

"What are we going to do with her?" Lydia asked again.

"I suppose we'll keep her! I'm certainly not going to leave her out here," Malcolm said in an irritated voice as he climbed back into the surrey. "The attitude you have, Miss Lydia, is anything but Christian. We just rescued her, and already you're wondering what we're going to do with her!"

"No one wants to leave her here, Malcolm." Sarah placed her hand on Malcolm's knee and gently patted it. "There's no need to yell," she said softly.

"Please forgive me for yelling. I'm sorry I yelled. It's been a very stressful and frightening night. But it's not been as frightening to us as it was to this small child. I've never felt the forces of evil as strongly as I felt them tonight. Satan was surely on a rampage. I firmly believe that God is in control and that he sent us here at this specific time to rescue this child from death. He must have a powerful plan for her. May we be worthy of this task that God has set before us."

His hands trembled as he pulled on the reins to get the horse moving. They rode silently for a while. Then the child began to cough.

"Malcolm," Sarah said, "why don't we stop for the night? I'm afraid we'll all catch our death of pneumonia if we don't get out of these wet clothes."

"I think that's a good idea, Sarah. I've had about all the excitement I can take tonight."

Soon they arrived at an inn. Malcolm carried their trunks upstairs to their room. After changing into drier clothes, they went downstairs for a meal. The cook served them hot mush floating in cream and cold corn bread. They also got some warm milk for the baby. Then they went back upstairs to their room. There were two double iron beds in their room. After much discussion, the small group decided that Seth and Lydia would sleep in one bed. Malcolm and Sarah would sleep in the other bed. They made a temporary bed for the baby in a large dresser drawer.

There was one ladder-back rocking chair in the room. Sarah sat down in the rocker and began to rock the baby. The group began to softly sing, "Rock-a-bye baby in a tree top, when the wind blows, the cradle will rock." They sang, Sarah hummed, and soon the child was asleep. When Sarah moved to get out of the chair and laid the baby down, Jane's body jerked, and her face wrinkled as if she were going to cry. Sarah settled back down into the chair and once again rocked and hummed.

"I wonder who could be so cruel as to abandon this child," Sarah whispered as she looked down at the sleeping baby. "I wonder how old she is."

"That's just one of the many things we don't know about her." Malcolm shook his head. Malcolm could hear the stress in his wife's voice when she talked about the child. For a moment, he could feel her pain. He realized just how much she missed the three babies they had lost.

"What's her name?" Seth asked.

"We don't know, Seth. But everyone must have a name. Let's pick one for her. Seth, you can go first," Sarah said.

"What would be a pretty name for my new sister?" Seth was proud because his mother asked him to pick a name for the baby.

"Mama, you know Seth can't pick a girl's name. He hates girls!" Lydia smirked.

"Yes, I can! Let's name her Abigail," Seth said.

"I don't like Abigail. It sounds too old-fashioned," Lydia scoffed at Seth.

"Why don't we name her after my mother? She had a pretty name; her name was Callie. Do you children remember her?" Malcolm asked.

"Yes, Daddy, we remember her," Lydia said.

"She was nice," Seth added.

"That's a good idea. We'll call her Callie Ann. After all, she does have on a calico dress. And her cries are now almost as loud as the calliope we heard that time we watched a steamboat going up the Mississippi." Sarah said,

"Children, it's been a long, hard day. I think it's time to blow out the lamp and try to get some sleep." Malcolm stood beside the bed and stretched his arms high above his head. "Children, kick your shoes off and get into bed. I'll cover you up, and we'll say a prayer together tonight."

Sarah finally made Callie comfortable in her makeshift bed. After the lamp had been blown out and they could hear the deep breathing of Seth and Lydia, Sarah and Malcolm began to discuss the child they had found. They were both very concerned about the new baby who had come into their lives. Malcolm felt that she was truly a gift from God. In fact he felt this so strongly that he hadn't mentioned finding her parents or even asking the innkeeper if anyone was looking for a missing child. Sarah's heart had gone out to the child the minute she had seen her, but she had some misgivings about keeping her.

As they lay side by side that evening, Sarah quietly asked, "Malcolm, what are we going to do about this baby?"

Malcolm lay quietly for a few minutes before he answered. "Sarah, I want to keep the child. I don't know why, but I feel like God has given her to us for a reason. And I feel we must trust him. Can you accept the responsibility of another child?"

"Of course I can, Malcolm. You know I can accept this baby. But because I have lost babies myself, I know that some mother's heart must be breaking over the loss of this darling little girl. She must belong to someone with money and position. Her clothes and jewelry seem to belong to a wealthy family. What if the gypsies stole her and then decided they didn't want her? Or maybe they became frightened for some reason, so they just left her to die on the bayou."

"That doesn't make sense. I think they would have removed her jewelry, don't you?

"Probably, but I think we need to report this to the authorities and see if there are any reports of a missing child."

"You know, Sarah. I feel that she was deliberately thrown into the bayou. I told you I heard someone running away, didn't I? I'm afraid that if I report this, I'll only be putting her in harm's way. It's just a gut feeling I've got. However, I will go to the Post Office soon. Mrs. Allen hears all the news. She will know if anyone reported a missing child. We will just be quiet and listen. When we are sure she's safe, then we will tell the story of how we found her."

Silently they lay in the dark, listening to the sounds of the night. Sarah broke the silence when she said in a low voice, "Malcolm, what if she's a gypsy?"

"What do you mean, Sarah?" He rose up on his elbow.

"Well, you've said many times that most gypsies will steal and that they seem to have a pact with the devil himself. They can predict the future, tell fortunes, and they move around like a leaf in the wind."

"If she's a gypsy, then we will raise her differently; we will teach her God's ways, and everything will turn out all right. You'll see, Sarah; you'll see."

"Everything seems to be happening so fast. So many new things," said Sarah.

"What are you talking about?" Malcolm asked.

"Well, this child, the new church. Do you think we are doing what's best, moving to the new church?"

Malcolm lay down and put one arm under his head and the other arm around Sarah. "I'm going to take the church," he said.

"You told the congregation we have two children. How are you going to get around that one?"

"I'll simply tell them God has blessed us with another child to raise. I feel that we must take this wonderful opportunity. The church is well established with almost thirty members, and you have always dreamed about living closer to a town. There's a good school for the children. The house they offered us is better than anything we have ever lived in. They also promised to pay me ten dollars more a month. Just think of all we could buy with the money. I think we should take the new church and trust in the Lord, as we always have."

Malcolm leaned over and kissed Sarah on the cheek. Soon they were both asleep. Malcolm trusted in the Lord's will, and Sarah trusted in Malcolm and his faith to make the right decisions.

In the bed across the room, Lydia was wide awake and fuming.

CHAPTER TWELVE

"Isabelle, doesn't the world look clean, washed, and all brand new?" Mrs. Gates said as she took a deep breath of the fresh morning air. Then she placed her hand over Isabelle's hand.

The buggy they were riding in was slowly making its way home. They had already got stuck three times traveling through the soggy earth. The wagon wheels were making deep cuts in the road. The wheels and sides of the buggy were splattered with mud. The driver and the two ladies had mud splattered all over their clothes.

"Isabelle, I've enjoyed our shopping trip and being with you so much! Getting out once again makes me feel like there is much hope in our lives. I feel that there is a new horizon, and I know we must put all the anger and fear behind us. We must put that terrible war behind us, although we'll never get over losing and missing all those fine young men!"

Mrs. Gates touched her brow with her gloved hand. Isabelle's father and brother had both been killed during the Civil War, leaving her one brother, Robert, and Mrs. Gates to run the plantation. Their home had been heavily damaged, and a lot of work had needed doing. Most of the freed slaves had agreed to stay on and help with the rebuilding. They also helped with the production of the tobacco and sugar-cane crops, which luckily had brought high profits the last few years.

Isabelle's mother had been so busy with refurnishing and re-modeling that she had not visited Isabelle in a while. Besides she didn't like John very much. She didn't realize the extent of John's cruelty to Isabelle, because Isabelle did a good job of hiding it. Her son, Robert, had had to help John and Isabelle out financially several times with the Willow Grove plantation.

"Isabelle! Isabelle!" Mrs. Gates said as she took a closer look at her daughter.

"What?" Isabelle looked at her mother with surprise, because her mind was wandering elsewhere.

"Why, Isabelle, you haven't even heard a word I have said!"

"I'm sorry, Mother. What did you say?"

"I said doesn't the world look clean today. It looks and feels like spring," Mrs. Gates repeated herself.

"Yes, Mother, it is a beautiful time of the year." Isabelle spoke with a trembling voice.

Mrs. Gates looked closer at her daughter. She saw dark circles under her eyes and a worried expression on her face. "Isabelle! What's wrong with you? You look terrible today! You need to pinch your cheeks and at least bring a little color into your face!"

"Oh, Mother, don't worry. I just didn't sleep well last night."

"It is difficult to sleep in a strange bed, isn't it? Mine was comfortable, and I slept quite well."

"It wasn't the bed, Mother. It's just that I miss Jane so much." She sighed deeply and tears came into her eyes, and then she said, "I'm also so worried about her."

"She's fine. There's no need to worry. It's just that this is the first time you've ever been away from her all night. Your feelings are the feelings every mother has the first time she leaves her baby. It's foolish for you to worry about her, because anyone can plainly see that John worships her. You know that she's well taken care of. You are such a worrywart, honey." Mrs. Gates didn't know anything about her daughter's dark secret.

"You're probably right, Mother."

Isabelle had had a bad feeling deep down in her soul ever since she'd left home. It was a feeling of dread. A feeling of things about to change and change for the worse. The stronger the storm had got the night before, the stronger her feelings of disaster had become. Because she had slept very little, her nerves were on edge.

Even though she realized the driver was doing his best, tapping the horses on their rumps with his buggy whip, urging them to work harder at pulling the buggy through the soft earth, it seemed to her as if the buggy was crawling at a snail's pace. The driver knew the danger of the horses getting stuck and perhaps breaking a leg trying to get out of the mud. All the reasoning didn't calm her nerves or calm the deep fear in her heart, a fear that couldn't be explained. Perhaps these feelings she was having were what the gypsies called second sight.

"We'll be home before dark, and all your fears will be over, you'll see. I'll leave you alone to gather your thoughts," Mrs. Gates reassured her daughter.

The two rode in silence for a while. Then Mrs. Gates pointed toward the swollen bayou to the left and said, "Oh, look, how sad!"

Isabelle looked in the direction her mother was pointing. She saw a small, swollen baby calf floating down the stream. "What a storm. I've never seen anything like it." Isabelle said and shook her head.

When they finally arrived home, the carriage had barely come to a rolling stop when Isabelle stood up. She picked up her long skirt tail and began to step out of the buggy without even giving the driver a chance to assist her.

"Watch your step, Isabelle! Those steps are muddy and slick!" Mrs. Gates cautioned her daughter.

"Yes, ma'am, I'll be careful," Isabelle said as she ran up the porch steps and to the front door.

Ripley opened the front door and held out both hands to Isabelle. Isabelle saw the pain in her eyes. "Oh, Missus Isabelle, I's afraid yo wont get back home for a while." Ripley voice broke as she talked, and tears filled her eyes.

Isabelle felt the icy fingers of fear griping her heart. Something was terribly wrong! "What's wrong, Ripley? Is John all right?" she asked.

Ripley nodded her head.

"Then what's wrong? Is Jane all right?" Isabelle's voice rose. "I need to see Jane." She walked past Ripley and started up the stairs.

"Jane's ain't here, Missus Isabelle!" Ripley said with reluctance, and she wrung her hands.

Isabelle turned toward her. She held on to the stair rail for support, because it seemed to her that all of her strength was leaving her body "What do you mean by 'she's ain't here'?" Isabelle asked in a low, impatient voice.

Ripley was speechless and unable to move for a moment. Isabelle began to climb the stairs and was soon in Jane's room. When she looked around the empty room, she began to panic. She began to breathe heavily, her chest heaving and gasping for breath. She felt as if she were going to pass out.

Ripley was soon at her mistress's side. "Lawdy Lawd! Missus Isabelle, sit down befo' yo fall down," Ripley said as she led Isabelle to the rocking chair in the nursery.

Isabelle tried to pull away from her but became more light-headed and had to sit back down.

"Sit here, Missus Isabelle. I's get a wet rag for yer head."

Isabelle nodded her head as Mrs. Gates entered the room. When she saw Isabelle's white, distraught face, she asked, "What's wrong? Is something wrong with Jane?"

"She's gone! Missus Gates, she gone!" Ripley voice was frantic.

"What do you mean she's gone?"

"Master John thinks de gypsies slipped in de house late in de night and stole her!" Huge tears rolled down her cheeks.

"You don't mean to tell me that Jane has actually disappeared, do you?" Mrs. Gates couldn't believe what she was hearing.

"Yes, ma'am, we can' find her nowhere!"

Isabelle pushed Ripley hand aside and reached for a blanket that lay in Jane's crib. She clutched it close to her body and stared off into space.

"Where were you and John? Didn't you hear whoever came into the house?" Mrs. Gates asked.

"Missus Gates, I was not at de house. After yo all lef', Master John told me to go home and he would take care of little Jane."

"You don't mean to tell me that you left her by herself with John, do you?" Isabelle asked. She tried to stand up, but her knees felt very wobbly. She sat down quickly, dropping the blanket to the floor.

Her actions frightened Ripley while she told them exactly what happened. "When Master John told me to go home, I asked him if he knew how to change her diaper an' give her a sugar-tit. He laughed and said he did. He said he wanted to spend some time wid her, and he told me to come back de next day."

At this point, Ripley put her face in the palm of her hands and began to talk through muffled sobs. "It ain't my fault, Missus Isabelle! What else could I do? He's de Master."

When Mrs. Gates looked at the two women, she realized that she had to calm them down to make sense of what was being said. She didn't feel that any real harm had come to her granddaughter. She placed her arm around Ripley shoulder and said, "We're not blaming you for anything that has happened. It's not your fault; please try to calm down."

Meanwhile Isabelle had got out of the rocking chair and picked the blanket up off the floor. Holding it close to her heart, occasionally she would put the blanket to her nose and smell it. Mrs. Gates realized that Jane's sweet smell was still on the blanket and that it was bringing her daughter a small measure of comfort. She went to her daughter, took her hand, and led her back to the rocking chair. As obedient as a child, Isabelle allowed her mother to lead her. She sat down in the chair.

"Now, Isabelle, honey, before you allow yourself to become more upset, let's try and think this through. I think we need to talk to John before we jump to any conclusions. After all, we both know he loves her dearly! If she's gone, I'm sure he has found her by now. You know he will look everywhere." Mrs. Gates was kneeling beside her daughter as she talked.

"Yes, Mother, I'll try to calm down and wait for John." Isabelle knew in her heart that there was no need to wait on John. She felt that somehow John had discovered that Jane wasn't his. *He's seen the birthmark! When he changed her diaper, he saw it. Dear God in heaven, in his anger, John has done away with my baby.* Isabelle's thoughts were so strong that she rose halfway out of the chair.

"What are you doing, Isabelle?" Mrs. Gates asked.

I can't let Mother know my thoughts or my guilt, Isabelle thought quickly and said, "Mother, I want to see if any of Jane's things are gone." When she stood up, Isabelle became very light-headed and had to quickly sit down once again.

"That's a good idea, Isabelle. Ripley and I will go through her things. You just sit there and watch me and tell us if anything is missing." Ripley went to the dresser, opened the drawers, and started holding up Jane's clothes one at a time.

"Thar's nothing missing except her calico dress," Isabelle said.

"Where is the afghan I gave her?" Mrs. Gates asked.

"It's gone, Missus Gates; we always kept it in de top drawer," Ripley said. "And de last time I saw Jane—" She paused and wiped tears from her eyes. "She was wearing all dat jewelry yo gave her."

Several hours later the sun had begun to set, and a mist began to rise over the land. The three ladies were frantic with worry. They were in the front parlor, looking out the window and waiting for John to arrive. The sound of brakes being applied to the surrey and John's cursing the horse signaled to the ladies that their wait was over. They ran out on the porch to meet him.

"Where's Jane?" Mrs. Gates asked.

"Why didn't you bring Jane home, John?" Isabelle demanded. She didn't even notice he was walking with a limp.

John paused on the porch steps. He looked at the three women looking down at him. "I don't know how to tell you all this, but Jane's gone. I've been looking for her ever since I discovered she was missing." John spoke in a tired voice.

"What happened, John? Why weren't you watching her? Why didn't you let Ripley stay and help with her?"

As Isabelle talked, she walked down the steps and stood eye to eye with her husband. As she waited for him to answer, she saw that he looked very tired. He looked as if he hadn't slept in a few nights. His eyes were red, swollen, and bloodshot. His shoulders were slumped in defeat; as she stood there, she could smell the strong smell of whiskey coming from his body.

Well, I can understand why he would take a drink. Perhaps he is also grieving the loss of Jane. Oh my, how could I even think that thought? Of course she isn't lost! This is only a dream, and I will soon wake up.

"Let me sit down, and I'll tell you all I know," John said. He went to one of the wicker chairs on the porch, sat down, pulled off his hat, and laid it beside him. He began, "In answer to your questions, Isabelle, I let Ripley go home because I wanted to spend time with my little girl. Yes." He nodded his head. "Just me and Jane. I love her so much."

His voice broke. He leaned forward in his chair and continued, "Now Ripley didn't want to go home, but I told her in no uncertain terms that I was capable of taking care of my child. I know how to change her diaper and make her bottle if she wants one. After I fed her supper, she went to sleep in my arms. I laid her down in her bed and then slipped downstairs. I hadn't been downstairs long when I heard a knock at the back door. I went to the door. There stood two gypsy men."

He glanced at the women. Then shame overcame him, and he looked down at the floor.

"What were their names?" Isabelle asked. Isabelle and Mrs. Gates had pulled up a chair and were sitting close to John. Ripley was standing behind Isabelle, leaning on the back of her chair.

"Rogue and Pierre. They're from that mean, thieving band of gypsies who came through here three years ago. They said they were looking for a mule to buy because one of their mules had died on their journey, and they needed to replace it soon so they could get on the road as soon as the storm broke. They offered me a good price, and since I hadn't used the mule for a while and he was getting old, I agreed to sell it to them. We went to the barn, but when we got there and they saw the mule, they backed out of the deal. They said they didn't need a mule after all. Now here's what I think happened. I think while we were in the barn, another gypsy slipped into the house and kidnapped our baby Jane."

"Did you look in on her that night, John?" Isabelle asked.

"No. I'm sorry to say I didn't. It was the next morning before I discovered she was missing." John looked up at them but dropped his head, unable to look them in the eye. He looked past them and off into the distance.

"Did you go to the gypsy camp and look for her?" Mrs. Gates asked.

"Yes, ma'am. I did. But the gypsies had already left."

"John, when you were talking to Rogue and Pierre, did they say where they were headed?" Mrs. Gates asked.

"When did you start looking for her? Where did you go to look? Have you talked to the sheriff?" Isabelle fired these questions at John.

"Wait a minute!" John held both hands out in front of him. "I can't answer but one question at a time! Mother Gates, I'll try and answer your question first. I assume the gypsies were headed to New Orleans, but you know how they are. They are subject to go any way the wind blows.

"Isabelle," he said and looked at his wife, "I began hunting for Jane early this morning, just as soon as I discovered she was missing. First I went to the gypsy camp. They had already left, but there were wagon tracks that crossed the tracks that the gypsies had made. But looked like they could have been made the night before, could have been made by someone who came to run the gypsies off. Maybe that's why they left in such a hurry."

"Have you been to the sheriff?" Isabelle asked.

"Yes, I went to the sheriff's office and told him what had happened. He was very upset. He said he would start looking for her."

"John, you say that the gypsies left that night. How could they travel in the storm, as bad as it was?" Isabelle spoke in a low, accusing voice.

"What are you saying, Isabelle? What are you implying?" John began to fake a cry, but for a fleeting moment in time, Isabelle saw the madness, laughter, and cruelty in his eyes. She knew in her heart that John had something to do with Jane's disappearance.

Mrs. Gates said, "Now the last thing you two need to do is to go at each other. You both love Jane. Now is the time to cling to each other and support each other. We'll find Jane. I know we will."

Isabelle hung her head in sorrow.

CHAPTER THIRTEEN

Callie sat quietly in the small, primitive church. The church had been built by slave labor many years ago. It had been built for the Protestants to worship God and also served as a gathering place for the local people to get together for parties, funerals, and weddings.

Callie's first memories were of sitting in small country churches along the bayous of the Mississippi. This particular Sunday morning she was daydreaming, gazing out the church window. Even at the age of sixteen, she was taken with the beauty of the bayou. There had been an early morning rain; but now the sky was clear and a brilliant blue. There were no dark clouds, only a few great, big, fluffy, white ones. The sun was seemingly kissing the cypress trees that were laden with Spanish moss. The moisture and the moss still clung to the trees and sparkled like tiny crystals, and sun-rays danced among the trees. Callie jumped when she felt Lydia's elbow punch her rib-cage.

"You'd better start paying attention, Callie!" Lydia whispered. "You know what Pa told us, don't you?"

Callie nodded her head, and her eyes went back to her pa, who was standing in the pulpit. This big, raw-boned man whom one couldn't call handsome was good-looking in Callie's eyes. His voice was gentle and soothing as he preached. He had never been a preacher who screamed to get his message across to the people in his audience.

Callie heard him say, "Even in these perilous times, you must love your neighbor as yourself." Callie loved her father and was happiest when she was with him. Being an ordained minister of the gospel, he sometimes traveled from town to town, parish to parish, leaving his family behind much of the time. When he returned home, the wagon would be laden with food, cotton, material, or whatever the people could afford to give him. He would accept these gifts in exchange for his preaching and teaching of the gospel; therefore, there was never much money in the household. At this age, this did not bother Callie.

Lydia punched Callie again. "It is almost time to sing."

Lydia squeezed her eyes into tiny slits, the way she always did when she wanted to boss Callie. Lydia had always been bossy, always giving Callie and her brother orders. She loved to follow them around. If they made a mistake, she would run to tattle on them. Sarah was constantly saying, "Lydia, you shouldn't tell on your siblings so much." This made Lydia unhappy.

"Lydia, would you and Callie come up and sing?"

Malcolm looked at his daughters with love. He felt that their singing was one of the rewards he received for serving God. Life as a preacher was hard, and there were times when Malcolm would have to take other jobs in order to make ends meet. But it was times like these, when the girls would raise their voices in praise to the heavens, Malcolm knew he was truly serving God. He loved to hear them sing. Lydia had a good voice, but it was Callie's voice that caused the congregation to really sit up and listen. Malcolm thought that he was listening to the voices of the angels each time he heard them sing.

Lydia was nineteen now. Most young girls Lydia's age were already married. It looked to Callie as if her sister might be an old maid. She had grown up to be very tall and thin. Her nose was much too big for her face, and she had inherited her father's big ears. But she did have some good features: her hair was brown, long, and silky, and she had a smooth and unblemished complexion. If she smiled more and was a nicer person, maybe more young men would noticed her.

Lydia and Callie stood before the congregation singing a beautiful, old hymn. Callie's voice rang out loud and clear. Floating through the rafters of the old church, her voice took prominence over her sister's. Callie had grown up into a real beauty: her olive complexion was flawless; her blue eyes with the long, dark lashes were filled with innocence; and her figure had matured early.

Lydia had always hated Callie from the night she had been rescued from the bayou. Her father thought the young child was an angel sent to him from on high. Lydia felt that her father didn't love her as much as he did Callie. When Callie became old enough to sing, she joined Seth and Lydia as they sang at church services. Callie had such a sweet voice that took the limelight away from Lydia. Callie was a beautiful young lady, and her sweet, clear voice worshiped the Lord with an innocence that the people in the congregation responded to. This just added flame to Lydia's envy. Today Lydia stood stiffly beside Callie, and Lydia's eyes were cold when she looked at her sister.

When the church services were over, the congregation told the girls how beautifully they sang. But their admiring eyes lingered longer on Callie, and they said to her, "You are a born singer."

Lydia's eyes traveled to her father. She felt that he loved Callie much more than he loved his own flesh and blood. Lydia felt the fury rise in her stomach. Her eyes became glazed and fixed with hatred as she glared at Callie. Callie felt Lydia's cold stare fairly boring into her body. She turned toward her sister and placed her hand on her arm.

"You sang so well today Lydia," Callie said and smiled. "I wish I could take my voice as high and clear as you can. Could you teach me how, Lydia?"

Lydia's face softened slightly. "Callie, I sing from way down in my stomach. You must learn to breathe deeply and sing from down in your stomach as well."

"Thank you, Lydia."

Callie was so relieved to see that Lydia was not really mad at her. She couldn't stand for anyone to be angry with her, and Lydia could be so cruel when she became angry. She would tell her mother lies and get Callie into trouble. She had actually caused Callie to get several whippings. Callie didn't understand why Lydia disliked her so much and why her mother always believed Lydia.

"Callie, Callie." Her father was trying to get her attention.

"Yes," said Callie, turning toward her father. She immediately saw the short, stocky, white-haired man standing beside him.

"Callie, this is Mr. Lester Moore. He is a professor of music, and he teaches at the state university in Baton Rouge. He is Carl Moore's brother. Their father died last week. I preached his funeral. You and Lydia sang some songs before the service, remember?

"Yes, Daddy, I remember. It's nice to meet you, Mr. Moore. I'm sorry about the loss of your father." Callie extended her gloved hand. He had a firm handshake, and he held her hand a little too long for her comfort.

"It is nice to meet you, Callie, and thank you for singing at my father's funeral. Even though my heart was heavy with the loss of my father, I must admit that I enjoyed your singing. It touched my soul and brought me comfort. I realized as I listened to you sing that you have a gift, a beautiful gift." His hand went to his face and played with his handlebar mustache.

"Oh, by the way," he said, dropping his hand and smiling "as your father said, I am a music teacher, and I have a proposal for you. I would like to give you music lessons and help you develop your voice. With your beauty and a trained voice, you could have a lot of success singing onstage or other musical events. There are many people, especially in big cities, who enjoy hearing and seeing music performed. You could be another Jenny Lind. People are starving for culture and refinement."

Jenny Lind was a Swedish opera singer, often known as the Swedish Nightingale.

Callie's mouth dropped open in surprise. "My goodness! I would love to make people happy with my singing, and I would just love to improve my voice. I know I need some training in my breathing."

Callie could hardly control herself. She seemed to be rattling on about singing. She felt like dancing, shouting for joy. She had never had anyone tell her that she might become successful as a singer. However, her mood quickly changed when she turned to Lydia. When Callie's eyes met her sister's, she saw the cold, evil hatred in Lydia's expression. Her facial structure was fixed with a scowl, and her lips were white and drawn into a thin line.

Callie turned back to Mr. Moore and said, "My sister has a good voice also. Actually she's really more talented than I am. Can she come with me?"

"Yes, your sister does have a great voice," Mr. Moore said without enthusiasm. "Perhaps she might like to have some lessons as well. If your parents can make do without both of you girls, then I would be happy to work something out."

Callie could feel the hesitation in his voice. She knew that he didn't really want to take Lydia. Callie looked at Lydia and said, "Oh, Lydia, this all sounds so wonderful. Do you think Pa will let us go that far away at the same time?"

Lydia's eyes remained cold as she looked with hatred at the man who was causing her pain. She turned and abruptly walked away without saying anything.

Callie sighed, and her shoulders slumped in hurt and disappointment as she watched her sister walk away. She lifted her head when she felt her father's hand on her arm.

"Don't worry, honey; she'll get over it." Her father's voice was soothing. "Why don't you go and catch up with her? You two will have to walk home. I must stay over for a meeting with the elders, and your mother will also stay, because the ladies are planning to have dinner on the ground soon."

Malcolm smiled with pleasure when he mentioned the coming dinner, when the ladies would bring their special, home-cooked recipes and then serve them from the makeshift tables. The men would set up sawhorses covered with wide planks, and the ladies would cover the tables with tablecloths they had brought from their homes. He would eat lots of good food, and more people than usual would attend the service. And he would preach to more people; he enjoyed reaching out to a large crowd.

"All right, Pa," Callie said quietly. "I'll see you soon."

After Callie told Mr. Moore good-bye, she slowly left the church building. She dreaded the walk home with Lydia. Callie didn't like to be with her sister when she was in one of her hateful moods. Lydia was sitting very still in the surrey and didn't see Callie as she approached. She was staring off into the distance, her body stiff and rigid. Her eyes looked like cool, blue stones when she finally looked at Callie. Mr. Moore's praise of Callie was almost more than Lydia could bear. Lydia knew that she had a good voice; in fact, it was a beautiful voice. But she knew that she would never be a beauty like Callie. She was just a big, overgrown girl who would never be pretty.

It seemed that beauty such as Callie's was all that mattered to the men of this world. Just look at her father. Since they fished

Callie out of that river, her father had fawned over the little, dark-haired girl who was likely to be a gypsy!

These thoughts made Lydia even angrier. Her temper boiled when she thought about Sean Roberts, a young man who had attended a nearby revival where her father was preaching. Sean had come to the revival every night and would sit with the two sisters, praising their singing. He would talk to Lydia as if he were interested in her. She had fancied herself in love with him. Then she had noticed that his eyes kept lingering on Callie when he was talking to her. She had realized he was just using her to be with Callie, because her father thought that Callie was too young to be alone with a young man.

What would all these people who were fawning over Callie think if they knew that she was just another one of those dirty gypsies? Up to this point, Lydia had not considered telling Callie what she knew about that fateful night she had been fished out of the river, because her father had warned the whole family about telling anyone. He felt that Callie was a gift from God and that God's wrath would be against anyone who betrayed this precious gift.

"Pa says we have to walk home. He has to stay over and meet with the elders." Callie's voice brought Lydia back to the present.

"I am not walking with you!" Lydia's voice was, of course, hate filled. "Just go on! I won't be far behind." Lydia crossed her arms in a matter-of-fact way. Then she glanced at the church-house door and saw her father standing in the doorway watching the two girls. Immediately Lydia got down from the surrey and began to walk by Callie's side.

As the two girls walked along, Callie noticed all the beauty around them. The noontime sun was hot, and a thin line of perspiration formed above her upper lip. The sun seemed to be dancing in their path, peeping in and out through the trees and casting playful shadows on the ground. They had walked about a mile down the road when Lydia's voice became gentle. "Let's take the shortcut home. We'll cut across the field and cross the creek; going that way will get us home sooner."

Callie agreed, because these were the first words Lydia had spoken since they had left the church. "Yes, Lydia, that's a good idea. Let's get home as quickly as we can! I am hungry, and Mother did make a pot of chicken and dumplings this morning. There's also an apple pie for dessert." Just the thought of her mother's cooking made Callie's mouth water.

"Yes. Mother and I cooked dinner. I noticed you made yourself scarce." Lydia kicked a stone that lay in the field in front of her. "You always seem to be able to get out of your share of the work."

"That's not fair, Lydia. You know Pa wanted me to help him with the feeding." Since Seth had married and left home, her father rushed to do all the milking and feeding all by himself on Sunday mornings.

"Why does he always pick you and not me?"

"Maybe that is not the way it is. Maybe Mother does the picking, and you know she loves you more than she does me," Callie pleaded her case.

A smile of satisfaction crossed Lydia's face. "Oh, well, let's not argue. We are almost to the creek." Lydia began to walk faster toward the creek. She passed the huge log that was used as a bridge. She went farther down the bank to where large, flat rocks made a path across the creek bed.

"Wait, Lydia," Callie said. "Let's cross here over the log. We will ruin our clothes if we get them wet."
"Oh, you big baby, you won't ruin your clothes. We always cross on these rocks. Do you think that wearing your Sunday clothes will make you fall into the water?" Lydia had a taunting laugh.

Callie had to admit that Lydia made a good point, but her deep, inner feelings told her not to cross the creek over the rocks. She thought, *I will only make Lydia more hostile toward me if I don't cross over where she wants me to.* It was with reluctance that she walked to the edge of the creek bed.

"The water is deeper than usual, Lydia, and these rocks look slick to me." Callie's voice trembled.

"Pull off your shoes, and hold up your dress tail."

Lydia hopped over the larger rocks with remarkable balance. Shoes in one hand and her dress tail held firmly in the other, she crossed the creek without any trouble. However, Callie suddenly felt an overpowering fear. She knew that there was not much water in the creek bed and that even if she did slip into the water, it would be all right. But to the right of the rocks, there was a fast drop-off, and it became mildly deep, at least waist-deep in dry weather. With all the rain they had been having, it would probably be up to her chin. Callie's fear of water caused her to be hesitant.

"Aren't you coming, Miss Beauty Queen? Or are you too good and pretty? Are you afraid you will ruin your dress or maybe catch a cold and ruin your angelic voice?" Lydia loved to taunt Callie.

"I am not a queen." Callie's voice quivered as she responded to Lydia's remarks.

"Mr. Moore thinks you are," Lydia sneered.

"Lydia, for some reason, I am afraid of water. I'm afraid I'll fall in it!" Callie continued to hesitate.

"That's silly. You cross these rocks all the time. Come on. I'll help you."

Lydia beckoned Callie forward. Slowly Callie put her foot on the first rock and then moved to the next. She continued slowly until she was almost in the center of the stream. She glanced at Lydia, who had a strange smile on her face. Then Callie realized what Lydia intended to do. She was going to push her into the water. Callie tried to back up, but Lydia was too fast for her. Lydia gave her a big shove, and she plunged sideways into the deeper part of the creek. Water filled her eyes and nose. When she came up, she could barely catch her breath!

"Help me, please!" Callie gasped.

Lydia stood above, her arms crossed in front of her and a look of satisfaction on her plain face. "Why should I?"

"Lydia, please. Please help me out!" Callie was so frightened that she did not realize that her feet could touch the bottom.

"I won't help you," Lydia smirked. "Walk out by yourself, Your Royal Highness."

Callie regained her footing and stood as if frozen in the creek water. The water wasn't actually that cold, but she was trembling with fear from her head to her toe. One part of her realized that she could just walk out of the water, but another part kept her standing still in her tracks, wondering why she was so afraid of water.

Lydia towered over Callie. Lydia let her dress fall, and the hem touched the water. Lydia was unaware of this because she was so busy enjoying her conquest over Callie. She knew that Callie had an abnormal fear of water, and she could remember why.

Lydia said, "That is exactly where you belong, Miss Callie. You're not one of us. Anyone can tell you do not belong to this family; you don't even look like the rest of us. It's time someone told you the truth. You are nothing but a dirty gypsy!"

With these painful remarks, Lydia left Callie standing in the middle of the creek. She turned and walked up the hill toward the house. Her body shaking, Callie stood alone in the creek and watched Lydia climb up the hill. She took a deep breath as she worked up enough courage to make her way out of the water.

You are not one of our family, and it's time you realized that you're nothing but a dirty gypsy. The words echoed through Callie's mind. She had long ago realized that she looked different than the rest of her family. She was petite with olive skin and blue eyes, but she had never given it any deep thought. Now she was wondering and trying to figure out what Lydia meant.

What did she meant by the remark about me being a gypsy? Callie had seen gypsies camped around and about, but she didn't think she really looked like any of them people. She had always felt as if her mother didn't love her as much as she did Lydia or even Seth. Well, maybe her mother did love her, but it was still a fact that she always made a difference between her and the rest of the family.

As she stepped out of the creek, Callie looked down at her sodden dress. The dress was made from a cheap piece of calico, which had been given to her mother by one of the parishioners. It had a yellow background with small, white and red flowers on it. Her mother had always made most of her and Lydia's clothes.

The dress Lydia was wearing was made from taffeta and had lots of bows and buttons used to decorate the dress to make it fancy. Callie's dress was a simple, high-necked dress with a white collar and a sash made of solid, yellow material. Her mother always said, "You are so pretty, Callie. You don't need fancy dresses."

Now Callie came to realize that she was not like anyone in her family. None of them, except her father, even considered her to be a real part of the family. He never made a difference between her and Lydia. Actually she had always depended on Seth until he married and moved away with his new bride to St. Bernard. Perhaps she didn't belong.

She sat down on the creek bank, and for the moment, Callie forgot all about her fall in the water and her wet dress. She looked into the distance, gazing into the blue afternoon sky. She felt as if she were not a whole person, like something had always been missing in her relationship with her mother and sister. She thought, *I must know the truth about where I belong and where I came from. I'll ask my father, because I know he will tell me the truth. I was so happy this morning, knowing I was getting a chance to sing and develop my voice. But it only took a moment for Lydia to shatter my dreams.*

Two hours later Callie walked into the kitchen. Her father was sitting at the head of the table with his bible open in front of him. As she entered the room, he lifted his head, removed his glasses, and got up from the table. "Callie, where have you been? We've all been worried about you. Lydia said you refused to walk home with her. Why are your clothes so wet? Did you fall into the creek? Are you hurt?"

"No, Daddy, I'm not hurt. Yes, I did fall into the creek." Tears began to form in Callie's eyes and slowly ran down her cheeks.

"Now, Callie." Malcolm's chair made a scraping sound on the floor as he pushed it away to stand up and comfort Callie. "Don't you cry; you're not going to be punished. Your mother and I know that could happen to anyone." He placed a gentle arm around this special child of his.

His gentle gesture caused Callie to burst into tears. She buried her face in her father's broad shoulder as her body convulsed with great sobs.

"Now, now, baby, there's no need for all these tears." He looked down at her dress. "These wet clothes will give you a cold. Go change into something dry, and we'll talk about what happened this afternoon. Sweet child, you know it breaks my heart to see you cry; please dry your eyes. Everything will be all right."

Malcolm lifted her face from his massive chest and kissed her forehead. He loved this child God had given him to raise. He had felt this way about Callie since he had rescued her and held her in his arms for the first time. He knew that God was the giver of the most beautiful gifts. Callie certainly had been that for him. He couldn't ever seem to thank God enough, because she had certainly added many bright moments to their lives. He also knew that Lydia was jealous of her sister and sometimes made life very uncomfortable for Callie.

When Callie returned to the kitchen in her dry clothes, he said, "Let me get you something to eat. You must be hungry, and I know how much you love your mother's chicken and dumplings. While you are eating, you can tell me why you were gone so long."

Callie started to refuse to eat. Her stomach felt like it was tied in a bunch of knots. She knew that the chicken and dumplings would probably make her sick, but she knew that if she didn't eat, her father would be upset. She let him lead her to the table. He pulled out a chair for her, and she sat down. She watched as he filled her plate and placed it on the table in front of her.

Just the sight of all that food made her stomach churn. She played with the food on her plate, moving it around with her fork. She saw her father's eyes become clouded with worry as he watched her trying to force the food down by taking smaller bites. She hurried to finish so that she could get away from the hurt in her father's eyes. When she completed her meal, she asked to be excused and hurried outside to the outhouse, barely making it before heaving the contents of her stomach.

When she went back into the kitchen, her father said, "You're extremely pale. Are you sure you're all right?"

"I'm sorry, pa, but I lost my dinner." She placed her hand on her stomach.

Malcolm rose from his chair and opened his arms to his favorite daughter.

Callie felt safe and secure inside the circle of his arms. She had so many questions to ask, but her mind was in such turmoil that she didn't know what to do. Should she talk to her father now, or should she wait?

"'Baby girl, go wash your face, and then you'll feel better. By the way, what happened between you and Lydia today?" Malcolm had begun to suspect that Lydia was being cruel to Callie when no one was around.

Callie dropped her head. "Oh, I sent her on ahead to help Mother get dinner on the table." She took a deep breath. "Pa, will it be all right if I go lie down for a little while?"

"Yes, sweetheart, why don't you lie down and try to relax? It might keep you from being nauseated."

As Callie entered her and Lydia's bedroom, she looked around the room as if seeing it for the very first time. The faded, green, well-worn satin curtains she had been so proud of just yesterday didn't even look the same today. Her feet made a scraping sound on the puncheon floor as she slowly made her way across the room to the worn chaise lounge. Callie lay down on it. As she stared at the ceiling and thought of her sister's cruel words, weariness overtook her, and Callie drifted off into a deep and troubled sleep. In her dream, she was in a beautiful meadow. The meadow was covered in vividly colored flowers, bright-green grass, and tall trees with sunlight filtering through. Colorful butterflies floated, dipped, and fluttered around her, sometimes landing on her shoulders and in her hair. Everything seemed to be moving in slow motion. She felt utterly at peace, because she felt as if there were a warm presence protecting her. She could feel love all around her. The love seemed to be alive and vibrant. Everything seemed to be touched with this love, even the flowers, trees, and butterflies.

She saw a tall, beautifully dressed woman. This woman appeared to Callie as a kind and gentle person. She had blond hair and wore a pleasant smile. In her dreams, Callie was a small child, perhaps around three years old. The tall lady picked her up and held her close to her heart. She could smell a sweet perfume on the woman who held her. She reached up to touch the lady's face, but there was nothing there. The face was blank; she couldn't feel a nose, mouth, or eyes. However, she did not feel fear. Who was this lady who had no face? Who was this lady whom she had no fear of?

After hearing the truth from Lydia today, instinctively she knew that this being was her mother, because the love that flowed from this lady waltzed through her mind like fluttering butterflies in a quiet meadow. The lady hummed a beautiful song, seemingly unaware of where her footsteps were taking them. They danced to the edge of a swollen bayou, where the gurgling of the waters added music to her singing.

Suddenly a harsh, hateful voice called to the woman. Callie didn't understand the words, but the woman froze. Then she disappeared, allowing Callie to fall into the cold river water. Callie felt herself sinking deeper and deeper into the frigid waters. Her feet kept slipping on the stones on the bottom. Callie was unable to get control of her body so that she could escape from the icy water. She opened her mouth to scream, and water filled her mouth, causing her to choke and gasp to catch her breath.

Callie awoke with Malcolm gently shaking her and talking to her in a soothing voice. "It's going to be OK. It was only a dream. Now wake up, Callie; wake up," he said.

Callie's fear-filled eyes opened, and she looked at her father.

"Callie, are you sick?" Malcolm asked.

"No, Pa, I'm not. At least I don't think I am." Her eyes softened, and her tense body relaxed when she realized that Malcolm was close to her.

"You were having another one of those dreams, weren't you?" Malcolm asked.

"Yes Pa," she said with a shaky voice, "but this one was worse than the others. I dreamed again about the sweet lady with no face, but this time she let me fall into the water." Tears began to flow freely down Callie's cheeks, and her body shook with silent sobs that came from deep inside her soul. "I was drowning, pa; I was drowning!"

"Aw, baby, how awful that must have been!" Malcolm shook his head slowly.

"I was in the water over my head and couldn't get out! What does all this mean, and who is the woman in my dreams? Pa, if you know, you surely must tell me," she pleaded.

"What makes you think I would know, Callie?"

Malcolm dropped his eyes; he couldn't bear to see the haunted look in his daughter's eyes. *Could it be that she actually remembers being left in the cold, raging waters of the bayou? That impossible, because she was only a baby when I found her. There was no way of actually knowing exactly how old she was back then. We randomly selected a birth date for her. How much do I owe this girl? How much should I tell her?*

Would the truth ease her troubled mind, or is it possible she could live a lifetime without learning the truth about the night we first saw her? It's been a long time since we moved from where I lifted her from danger, and I'm fairly sure no one knew about the incident, except my own immediate family.

Malcolm shifted his weight on the bed and cleared his throat. "Callie, I think you dreamed about the water because you fell in the creek this morning. Don't you think that might have something to do with it?"

Callie sat up on the side of the bed. "I guess so, Pa. It's just that I've dreamed all this before I fell into the creek!" She looked down into her lap as if studying her hand. After a pause, she said, "Pa, Lydia said that I wasn't one of you all and that I should have drowned when I was a baby. What did she mean, Pa?"

This statement was very hard for Callie to make. She didn't want to hurt her Pa, and she was also afraid of Lydia's wrath if she somehow found out that Callie had told on her. But Callie knew that she would never be at peace without these answers.

Malcolm took a sharp breath and then let the air out of his lungs slowly, trying to control his emotions and cover the anger he was feeling toward his older daughter. For some time, he had suspected Lydia's cruelty to Callie, but rather than face up to it, he had chosen to ignore it. He knew that Callie hadn't been happy living with Lydia's jealousy and, yes, his wife's indifference to her and favoritism to the other children.

What should I do? Should I tell her the truth? What would the truth do to her? Should I let her go with Mr. Moore and let her become the singer I feel in my heart she is destined to become? This might be her only chance to have a good life. I don't have lot of money, but Mr. Moore said I wouldn't need much, if any, for her education in music. He said that he felt she would make him money once he had trained her. But money is not the issue here. My issue is giving up Callie, the light of my life. But I will not have Callie mistreated by my family, and I can't watch over her every minute of the day.

Thinking these thoughts about what had happened to Callie this morning, he knew that Lydia had pushed Callie into the creek and then had run off and left her. It was time that Malcolm faced this issue and did something about it. "Callie, did Lydia push you into the water?" he asked point-blank, looking her in the eyes.

Callie turned her eyes from her father and began to look out the window. "No, Pa," she said softly. She wasn't a good liar and could never lie successfully to her father.

"Callie." Malcolm cupped her chin in the palm of his hands and forced her to look him in the eyes. "You know I've taught you never to lie. Now I'll ask you one more time. Did Lydia push you into the creek?"

Tears streamed down Callie's face. There was anguish in her eyes. "Yes, Pa, but please don't tell her I told you. Promise." She wiped her eyes with the back of her hand.

Malcolm's body became rigid. This was worse than he had anticipated. Callie was scared to death of Lydia! At that point Malcolm's mind was made up. He would send his daughter to the university.

"OK, Callie, you have my word. I won't tell Lydia that you told me." He pulled her close to his big chest and ran his hand down her long mane of hair. A few moments later, he asked gently, "Callie, would you like to go with Mr. Moore and learn about singing and music?"

Callie pushed her body away from her father and looked him in the eyes. Her eyes lit up. With all that had happened with Lydia, she had forgotten all about the wonderful opportunity Mr. Moore had offered her, and if her pa wanted her to go, then she would gladly go. At least this would get her away from Lydia and her mother. "That would be wonderful, Pa, just wonderful!"

"All right, Princess, just dry your eyes, and I'll get to work on it."

"Yes, Pa. Oh, yes.

Malcolm left her room with a heavy heart. The decision had been made. Callie was leaving him. This decision was the best one for Callie, and it got him temporarily off the hook. *But what should I tell her? Doesn't she have the right to know?* With a troubled mind, he walked into the parlor, where Lydia and Sarah were practicing their singing.

"Is Callie all right, Pa?" Lydia asked, faking concern.

"Yes, she's fine."

"I'm so sorry she fell into the creek, Pa."

"Yes, Daughter, we're all sorry that she fell into the creek."

With these words, Malcolm left the house and went to the barn. He felt that he needed some time alone to pray.

CHAPTER FOURTEEN

The church had a farewell lunch for Callie the Sunday before she left with Mr. Moore. Callie was dressed in one of the new dresses her mother had made for her. The blouse on the orchid dress was made in tiny tucks with buttons down the front. The skirt had six gores. She wore a wide grosgrain ribbon that tied in the back for a sash; the streamer from the bow fell almost to her knees. The width of the ribbon accented her small waist. She wore a matching narrow ribbon in her hair. The dress had puffed sleeves, narrowing at the elbows. Tiny buttons went down the long cuffs of the sleeve Sarah had really tried to make this a happy occasion for Callie. She had put a lot of loving care into the dress.

There was a happy, vibrant look on Callie's face as all the congregation milled around her, wishing her the best and telling her how pretty she looked and how much they would miss her. Lydia watched from a distance, hate and jealousy churning within her. She waited until she saw Callie, her lovely sister, excuse herself and head for the outdoor toilet. She followed a small distance behind her and patiently waited for Callie to come out.

When Callie stepped out, she was startled for a moment at her sister's presence.

"Lydia!" Callie's hand flew to her throat. "You scared me!"

"Really! You mean the queen can be scared? I thought nothing could go wrong in the Royal Highness's world!" Lydia was very sarcastic.

"Please don't talk to me like that. We're sisters, and I love you," Callie pleaded.

"No. I am not your cursed sister! How many times do I have to tell you we're not sisters before you'll believe me?" Lydia spat these words at Callie.

"I don't believe you, Lydia, because you're just trying to hurt me. You've always tried to hurt me. I'm sorry that you're not getting to go with me, but Lydia, I promise you, when I become established, I'll come and get you. Then we'll sing together again and always." Callie extended her hand to Lydia.

"I don't want to sing with you. I'm so glad you're leaving. Furthermore you are not my sister. I hate you, Callie!" Lydia balled her hand into a fist. She would love to smash Callie's pretty face, beat it to a bloody pulp, but she knew she couldn't do that. Not here anyway.

"I can't help it if you don't like me, Lydia, but for heaven's sake, we are flesh and blood." Callie's voice quivered. "I love you, Lydia, even if you don't love me."

"Callie, listen, I'm only going to tell you this one more time. We are not sisters. You're nothing but a filthy gypsy. Pa dragged you out of the river, you simple-minded girl." With these words, Lydia opened the door and went into the toilet, leaving Callie standing like a statue outside.

Callie stood, shocked to the core. She knew that Lydia was telling her the truth. It was all falling into place; the dreams, the difference her mother made between her and the others. But she realized that this was not the time or the place to fall apart. That would have to come later. She squared her shoulders, held her head high, and went back to those who were honoring her.

Suppose these church people are glad to get see me go as well. Have they been nice to me because of Pa, It was obvious to her that her mother was glad to see her go. Her mother had been in the best mood Callie could ever remember since finding out that Callie was leaving.

The late-afternoon sun was weakly filtering into Callie's room. The family had come home from the church dinner. After changing out of their church clothes and neatly hanging them on the nails that were driven around the walls, for that purpose. Callie mother had volunteered to help Callie pack her trunk and prepare for her journey. Callie felt the need to stay busy and get ready to leave this place that she knew didn't want her. She wanted to leave as soon as possible.

Callie slowly folded her shawl and was about to place it in the black, roll-up trunk. As she held her shawl, she looked off into the distance.

"Callie, what are you thinking about?" her mother asked. "Don't you want to leave? You seem so unhappy since we came home from church."

"Oh, Mom, yes, I want to leave, but I will miss you all." She dropped the shawl into the trunk. "Mom?" She had decided to ask her mother about what Lydia told her earlier that day.

"Yes, Callie."

"Mom, I need to know something, and please tell me the truth."

"Of course I'll tell you the truth. That is, if I know the truth. What's bothering you?" Sarah walked to the dresser and removed more of Callie's underwear.

Callie dropped to her knees on the floor. "Mom, Lydia told me I'm not one of you all. She says that I'm just a dirty gypsy and that Pa pulled me out of a river. Is that true?"

Sarah turned toward Callie. When Sarah saw her hunched on the floor, she thought, *Callie looks like a small child, and my heart goes out to her. I do love this child I've raised. Of course I don't love her like I love Lydia, my own flesh and blood. No mother could do that. At least no mother worth her salt could do that, now could she?*

Sarah walked to Callie and said, "Callie, I'm sorry you had to find out this way. Lydia has a cruel streak in her; she shouldn't have hurt you so."

"Then it's true. I'm not one of you." Callie burst into tears. Her shoulders shook, and she put her face in the palms of her hands. Through muffled sobs, she asked, "Then who am I?"

"Child, I don't know." Sarah sat down on the floor beside Callie and gently patted her back. "You know you can always come back to us if the school doesn't work out for you; after all, we're your family, the only family you know."

"Believe me, I'm not ungrateful. I'm thankful to have all of you," Callie said and cried harder.

"Calm down, my child." Sarah placed her arms around Callie.

"Mother, I must find out who I am. Were there any clues, anything at all that might lead me to my family?" she asked through muffled sobs.

"Yes, Callie, there were a few things with you that might possibly help you find your heritage." Sarah got up and walked into her and Malcolm's bedroom. A few minutes later, she returned and gave Callie the ring and locket.

CHAPTER FIFTEEN

Callie was hot and exhausted but very happy. She was now eighteen years old, and after twelve months of training, Callie had just performed her first concert. The concert had been an outside, open-air concert performed on the rolling, green lawn at the school. She and several other girls had entertained a lot of people. Days of practice and anticipation had her nerves on edge. Now that it was over and she had been a success, she was exhausted, but it was happy and satisfied way.

Seth had been the only family member who had come to hear her perform. Malcolm was holding a revival at a church miles away. He had sent word by Seth that he and Sarah deeply regretted that they couldn't come but were very proud of her. She was in their prayers; they were sure she would steal the show! Their praises deeply touched her heart. After the show, Seth and his wife came backstage to congratulate her. She could tell he was beaming with pride because of her performance.

He hugged her close to his body and said, "Way to go, Baby Sister! I'm so proud of you!"

"Thank you, Seth. I really appreciate you coming today. You don't know how much it means to me." Callie pulled away and held both hands toward Mary Beth and said, "I know the trip has been hard on you with the baby coming. I hope we haven't tired you out."

"Oh, no, I'm just fine." Mary Elizabeth squeezed Callie's hands. "Seth and I wouldn't have missed this for the world. We love you so much."

Callie's heart warmed with her sister-in-law's words; even though Callie hadn't spent much time with her, she felt as if she had always known her. She was so happy for Seth, happy that he had found such a sweet and wonderful wife to walk through life with.

"Callie, you sang so beautifully tonight. When Dad told me you were going to a school of music, my first thought was, how can she sing any better than she already does? But I can see that you have trained your voice and you also have gained more self-confidence. Are you all right? Are you happy?" Seth's voice took on concern.

"Seth worries about his little sister all the time," Mary Beth said.

"That's sweet of you, Seth. I'm fine, but of course I miss my family. How are Mother and Pa doing?" Callie didn't ask about Lydia, because the pain was still too great.

"They are fine; they miss you, too. Pa said he misses his little songbird. I asked Lydia to come, but she said she should go with Pa to the revival," Seth said.

Callie could tell by the way Seth talked that he didn't know about the trouble between her and Lydia, the trouble that had caused her to leave home.

"Well, you girls look exhausted! I think it's time we traveled to the inn. Mary Beth needs to lie down and rest. Callie, I think you could also use a rest." As Seth talked, he took a pencil and note-pad out of his suit-coat pocket. He wrote his mailing address on the pad. "Now, Callie, here is our new address. If you need us for anything, please let us know. I don't like the idea of you being so far away from us."

"Oh, Seth!" Callie laughed. "I already have your address, re-member? I sent you an invitation to our concert today. Please don't worry about me so much."

"Well, now that you have my address twice, perhaps you will feel twice as safe."

Callie took the piece of paper. "Thank you so much, Seth."

Callie went to her room. The room was on the third floor, and it was stifling hot. Soon she was wet with sweat. She opened the window and pulled back the heavy drapes to let in the breeze. She removed her makeup, took the combs out of her hair, and let it hang loose and free. She then removed her skirt and blouse. She lay across the bed in her chemise. The breeze that came through the window brought the sweet smell of lilac and honeysuckle. The coolness and aroma were such a comfort to her body. She closed her eyes and drifted into a light sleep.

Boards cracking outside her door roused her. When the creak-ing noise stopped, she knew someone was standing outside her door. She waited for a knock, but when there wasn't one, fear be-gan to take hold. A key was being put into the keyhole, and when she heard a click, the lock opened. She watched as the doorknob turned. Callie sat up in her bed. When Mr. Moore walked into the room, her mouth flew open in surprise. In her fear, she had forgot-ten that she was partially dressed.

"What are you doing in here?" Callie frantically asked when he began walking toward her, his eyes resting on her breasts. She crossed her arms in front of her to cover herself.

"I simply came to congratulate you, Callie. I can see that you were expecting me." He walked closer to her.

"No! I am not waiting for you! And you know I'm not. Now get away from me!"

He placed his hand on her breast. "We have some things to discuss tonight." She tried to pull away, but he held her tight and began rubbing her breast. She trembled with fear. He mistook her fear as a trembling with passion for him. "It's all right to want me so badly, because I'm the one who put you where you are today, and of course you're grateful." His hand slowly moved down her body.

The closer he got to her, the more revolting he became. His breath was sour and smelled of tobacco. His body had a foul odor, and she felt like throwing up.

"Leave me alone! I'd rather not be where I am today if this is the price I must pay. Get out of my room. Now!"

Callie's face was red from anger, fear, and embarrassment. She waited, expecting him to turn around and walk out of the room. Instead he sat down on the edge of her bed. The bed creaked and swayed from his weight.

"Mr. Moore, get off my bed!" Callie tried to pull the bedspread over her body.

"Oh, don't be so childlike. There's no need to hide such a beautiful body." He pulled the spread off her and began stroking her shoulders.

"Keep your hands off me! I'm warning you! If you don't get out, I'll scream at the top of my lungs!"

"Don't be so upset, Callie. You don't understand. I love you, and I only want to make you mine. Then I can protect and take care of you," he said.

"I don't need you to take care of me! Get your filthy hands off me! You are disgusting. Totally disgusting!"

He had made passes at her before, but for the most part, she had managed to avoid him. But she had known she would have to put him in his place. *Why did this have to happen today? My beautiful day is ruined.*

He dropped his hands from her body and said, "How dare you talk to me like this? I'm offering you the world. How do you think all the other successful girls who came from this school got to where they are today? They realized that wonderful things can happen to a beautiful young woman whose body is ripe for the picking. You need a man to take care of you."

He stood up. "Looks like old Malcolm has taught you well. You seem to be all about morals. You'll learn very quickly that you only get what you pay for. If I'm as disgusting as you say, then you must earn your keep in another way. Before I'm through with you, you'll be begging to be mine, and you'll do anything I ask of you."

⋙✦⋘

Callie was hiding in the shadows of the spring house. The sun was dipping low in the sky, gracefully bowing out for the day, and leaving a sunset of red, pinks, and blues. She was nervously smoothing her dress and hair as she shifted her weight from one foot to the other. She whispered to herself, "Why doesn't he hurry? Why isn't he here?"

She was anxiously waiting for Seth to arrive. She had sent him word that he must rescue her soon from the school. She told him she felt as if she were in danger. It had been a month since Mr. Moore had made his threat. She knew that she had hurt his pride. She felt he was going to make another attempt to have his way with her, and this next the he would force himself on her.

Seth sent word to her that she should be ready to travel shortly after lunch on Friday. That morning she and her friend had brought her clothes and belongings to the spring house. She peeked around the side of the spring house, when she heard a horse and buggy enter the long driveway leading to the school.

"It's Seth! Thank God, he's here," she said with relief. When he came nearer, she stepped out of the shadow and waved at him. He slapped the horse with a whip, and the horse sped up. The buggy stopped quickly when he pulled on the reins and said, "Whoa!" He jumped down from the buggy.

"What's wrong, Sis?" Seth had a worried look on his face.

"Oh, Seth! Thank God for you. You're running late, though," Callie said. "There's no time to tell you what's happening right now. I'll tell you later. Let's get my things loaded and get out of this horrible place. We'll talk while we travel."

She handed him the wine-colored tapestry bag she was carrying and said, "Seth, there are more of my things in the spring house. They're hidden behind the milk cans in the corner. I hope there's enough light left to see in there."

After Seth heard the urgency in Callie's voice, he asked no more questions. He went into the dark spring house, lit a match, found her possessions, and quickly threw them on the buggy and helped her up. They were soon on their way. As they were going down the winding driveway, Seth slapped the reins, causing the horse to speed up and leaving a trail of dust rising behind them. She looked back at the beautiful campus where she had spent many happy hours, all ruined because of one dirty, old man.

Once they were on the main road, Seth settled back into his seat and said, "Now tell me what this is all about."

"It's about Mr. Moore. He's such a filthy man. I've had to fight off his advances for weeks. I finally realized just what he's all about last month when he informed me that if I didn't let him have his way with me..."

Her face turned red, and she dropped her head in shame. Her voice choked with sobs. It was a few moments before she could continue her story. "He said if I refused to be the 'love of his life'..." She glanced shyly at Seth and said, "That's just the way he put it, Brother."

She could see the veins in Seth's neck begin to throb with anger. "He said I didn't realize how lucky I was to have the opportunity he was offering me. When I flatly refused him, he asked me how I thought all the other girls who studied under him had become so successful. Naturally, he said, it was because of his help. Seth, that's when I realized I had to run." She removed a silk handkerchief from her purse and dried her eyes.

Seth didn't say a word. He pulled on the reins to slow the horse down and began to turn the buggy around. "Seth! What are you doing?" she asked.

"I'm going back! I intend to defend your honor. I'll kill that pig! I knew the first time I laid eyes on him that he was slime! Pa is just too trusting of people!"

"No, Seth! Please don't go back! Just take me away! I can't take anymore." She began to panic. "I don't want to go back there for any reason."

"Do not even try to talk me out of this. I will always take care of my baby sister!"

Callie saw the anger and determination in Seth's eyes. She realized just how much she loved her brother and how much he'd done for her all the years they had been together. She didn't want him to get into trouble over her. He'd got himself in all kinds of trouble over her and their mother through the years. He defended her when Lydia's jealousy had flamed into a vindictive hate. She knew she must talk Seth into turning the buggy back around.

"Seth," she said in a low voice as she placed her hand on his knee, "please listen to me. I know you're right. I realize Mr. Moore has it coming to him. I fear if you accuse him, then he might say I was also a part if his evil scheme. I swear, Seth, I was never part of any of his evil!" Her voice rose.

"I know you weren't part of it, Callie," Seth said quietly.

"Don't you see, Seth? If you cause a scene, he will tell all kinds of stories about me. There are always some people who will believe him. I simply couldn't live through that kind of shame! Seth, I just couldn't! I'm afraid no one would come to hear me sing." She began to twist the handkerchief in her hand.

Seth's shoulders slumped, and he sat very still for a moment. With a deep sigh, he said, "I can see your point. I don't want your reputation ruined, either. But someday that buzzard will pay for all of this. I can promise you that!" He turned the buggy around and then said, "You can move in with me, or else you're going back to Pa's home."

"No, I'm not, Seth. I'm going to New Orleans!"

"Why?" Seth asked. "How will you live and take care of yourself?"

"The answer to why is because I want to sing and I hear that New Orleans is full of opportunities and my singing has greatly improved. Even though Mr. Moore is evil, he did teach me a lot about voice training. Seth, I'm also still looking for my parents. I must find out where I came from." Her voice was filled with pain.

Seth's heart went out to her. "I know, Callie; I know."

"Now I have some money saved. I still have the money Father gave me, and I've earned a tidy sum from singing," she said with pride. "I can take care of myself. Please don't worry about me. After all, if I run into trouble, I'll just send for my big brother."

"Oh, Callie, you're such a strong-willed person," Seth said.

CHAPTER SIXTEEN

"Hurry, Seth! I can't wait to get on board the boat!" Callie's eyes danced with excitement. She had finally escaped Mr. Moore, and she also had Seth's approval to go to New Orleans. Well, maybe not approval, but at least acceptance. *What a wonderful day*, she thought to herself.

Soon they were at the dock. Seth had hired a robust, black dockworker to look after his horse and her things. As the two walked the dock, she watched the men as they carried baggage from the wagons and carts that were parked along the loading zone and got ready to load them on the boats. People were talking in several different languages. Some were singing old spiritual, slave songs. Callie loved all of the chaos she was seeing and became more excited when she saw the boats waiting at the dock.

She held her breath when she saw the *Natchez Queen* with its twin smokestacks topped with golden crowns. She heard a Dixieland band playing; as she watched, the band came into view, marching to the front of the boat. The band members were dressed in white pants with red- and white-striped shirts. They wore white straw hats with a red band around them. She tapped her feet to the beat of the lively music.

"Callie, may I have your attention?" Seth cleared his throat. "I would like to remind you that you will have to buy a ticket if you want to ride," he said.

"I'm sorry, Seth. I just got just carried away with the beauty and the grandeur of the *Queen*," she replied, pointing at the ship.

"Yes, she's a beauty. This is the first time I've seen her," said Seth. "I would love to sail on that boat."

"Maybe someday, Seth, maybe someday!" A faraway look danced in her eyes as Callie imagined herself on the boat.

"Do you have any idea where to locate the ticket office?" Seth asked.

Callie shook her head as she began to look around. "There, it's over there." She pointed to a small building marked "Tickets." There was a long line. "Do you think we should walk around awhile and then come back later?"

Seth studied the line for a moment. Then he said, "No, the line seems to be moving rather quickly. Let's go on and get in line."

As they drew nearer to the front of the line, Callie opened her purse and handed Seth some money. "Here, Seth, this should pay for my fare. Remember to get me on a boat that has reasonable rates."

When they reached the ticket master, she asked, "Sir, what is your cheapest transportation to New Orleans?"

"Are you two traveling together?" the ticket master asked.

"No. Actually I'm traveling alone," Callie responded proudly.

The ticket master removed his cap, revealing a partially balding head. He scratched his head and placed the cap back on and then said, "The packet canal boat is the lowest priced way to sail, if you don't mind traveling with the mail and some freight. It's a good ride but nothing fancy."

"That will be fine. I want to buy one ticket to the packet canal. When does it sail?" Callie asked.

"In two hours, ma'am."

"Now wait a minute, Callie. You might not be safe on that boat," Seth protested.

"Oh, she'll be safe. I know the captain of this ship personally. He will take good care of her," the balding man interrupted.

"Sir, I do not doubt your word. I'm sure your friend would take good care of my sister, but I prefer that she sails on the *Natchez Queen*." Seth reached for his wallet and removed a large bill.

"No, Seth, please!" Callie pleaded.

"Now, Callie, I will have my way on this. You've had your turn today, so it is my turn now." Seth said in a matter-of-fact voice.

Callie hugged Seth and placed an affectionate kiss on his cheek. When she turned to board the ship, he took her by the hand and said to her, "I'm going to board the ship with you, and I'm going to talk to the captain. I want him to know that you're traveling alone and I expect him to see to your safety."

"Oh, Seth, that isn't necessary," she said, although she knew it was useless to argue with him once he had made up his mind.

When they went aboard the ship, a man dressed in a white sailor's uniform said, "Ticket, please." Callie handed the young man her ticket and then walked past him. Seth followed. "Ticket, sir; you must have a ticket to pass this point," the man said politely.

Seth turned around and said, "I'm not sailing. I simply need to speak to the captain for a moment."

"She sails in ten minutes." The young man's voice sounded agitated.

"Jonathan, let them pass." The ship's captain stepped forward. He had been standing a few feet away from them, welcoming all the passengers aboard the ship. "I'm Captain Deveraux." He held out a gloved hand.

Seth shook the captain's hand. "I'm Seth Hatfield, and this is my sister Callie Hatfield. I just wanted you to know that she will be traveling alone. Please see to her comfort and welfare while she is on board your ship."

"Let your mind be at rest, Mr. Hatfield. She will be well taken care of." The captain tipped his hat toward Callie. "As a matter of fact, there's a lady on board who often sails with us, and she likes nothing better than to take young people under her wing."

"Thank you, Captain." Seth tipped his hat, hugged Callie, and then left the ship.

The captain led Callie to the bar. He looked around and then pointed to a table that was shaded by a large umbrella. "Over there is Mrs. McClain. She's the lady I spoke about to your brother. Let's go over, and I'll introduce you to her."

Mrs. McClain smiled as the two neared her table. The captain said, "Mrs. McClain, this is Callie Hatfield. She's traveling alone. It would greatly please your captain of you would kindly look after her."

"I would be delighted!" Mrs. McClain said. She was a plump lady. Her hair was a dark auburn streaked with gray. She wore it in a French twist. Her fingers were plump and loaded with rings. Her face was lined with wrinkles and lots of laugh lines.

The captain pulled a chair out from the table. After Callie was seated, he motioned for the waiter. "What would you like to drink, Miss Hatfield" he asked.

"Lemonade, please," Callie answered.

"The lady will have a glass of lemonade," the captain said to the waiter. Then he said to Callie, "Callie, now that I know you're in good hands, I'll be on my way. But remember, you will be dining at the captain's table tonight.

After the captain left, Callie's shoulders slumped; exhaustion was overtaking her. All the fear and anticipation was over now that she had finally escaped Mr. Moore and was finally on board a luxury ship sailing for an unknown future.

"Are you all right?" Mrs. McClain reached across the table and put her hand over Callie's. Her bracelets made a jingling noise as she moved her hand.

"Yes, I'm just tired, that's all," Callie said.

"Where are you traveling from?" Mrs. McClain asked.

"I'm from Parades."

"Oh, that's a beautiful place. Does your family live there?"

"Yes." Callie hesitated a moment then said, "Actually I haven't lived there very long. I've been at the school of music for a while."

"Oh! So you're a singer? That's wonderful!" She clapped her hands with glee. "Maybe you could sing for us tonight!"

"Perhaps." Callie took a sip of lemonade from her glass. When she felt someone looking at her, she looked toward the bar. There was a man sitting there, and he smiled at her when their eyes met.

"Who's that man at the bar?" Callie asked.

"That's Stephen Reeves. He's a close friend of the captain's. His father owns a shipping line. He's very rich, and isn't he handsome?"

"Yes," Callie whispered as she looked at Stephen. His eyes were dark and joyful. His shoulders were broad and muscular. A lock of curly hair fell across his forehead.

"I see that he's giving you the eye. I feel I must warn you he's a heart breaker, Callie. He's been known to love them and leave them. So watch your heart when you're around him."

"Oh, I fully intend to watch my heart," Callie replied as she flirted with her eyes.

"Not a bad idea. It isn't wise for a girl as young and beautiful as you are to be naive, especially if you intend to pursue a career in music. Many men will promise you great things if you will give them what they want."

"Oh my!" Callie's eyes were wide with innocence. *How well I know this*, she thought.

Mrs. McClain continued, "I've never had that problem. When I was younger, I wanted to be beautiful with a small waistline and long, straight hair. Instead I was always thick in the middle with kinky, red hair." Mrs. McClain laughed, and then a distanced look came into her eyes. "But you know," she said, "I wouldn't trade my life for anyone's. I met my husband when I was thirty years old. He wasn't what one would call handsome, but we loved each other from the minute our eyes met."

"What a beautiful story! Is Mr. McClain with you on this cruise?" Callie asked.

"He's always with me, my child. I can feel his presence all the time. You see, he passed away three years ago."

"I'm so sorry," Callie's said with sympathy.

"Thank you, Callie. You see, I have nothing better to do than to travel and help damsels in distress."

Callie smiled but said nothing.

"I'm just teasing you, Callie, but if I can be of any help, then I'm here for you," Mrs. McClain said.

Later that evening Callie sat at the captain's table. The captain was seated at the head, and Stephen sat in the chair to the captain's right. Callie was seated on the captain's left side, directly in front of Stephen. Mrs. McClain sat next to Callie.

Callie looked around the long dining room. The carved mahogany table was covered with a white, linen tablecloth. The table was set with fragile bone china, and the silverware was polished to a high shine. The room was decorated with exotic plants and colorful flowers.

Soon the waiters began to serve food: Tender, moist roast beef served with gravy, creamed potatoes; tiny pearl onions cooked in a white sauce; green beans; and French bread. The desert was next, delicate pastry served with vanilla ice cream.

As they ate their dinner, the captain said, "I think we should all get to know each other. Let's introduce ourselves. I'll begin. I'm Captain Deveraux, and I've been the captain on this vessel for ten years. Callie, now it's your turn. Tell us your name and a little about yourself."

"My name is Callie Hatfield, and I'm sailing to New Orleans."

"She's also a singer, and she's going to New Orleans to find work," Mrs. McClain informed the rest of the table.

"A singer! How interesting. Perhaps you'll sing for us tonight. The show starts at seven. I'll have them work you in—that is, if you will do us the honor," the captain said.

"I would be delighted to sing," Callie said with confidence.

Mrs. McClain then took up the introductions. "Hello! My name is Hilda McClain. I'm a widow, and I travel love to travel."

Finally, it was Stephen's turn to introduce himself. "I'm Stephen Reeves, and I am also headed for New Orleans, which happens to be my home. I'm looking forward to hearing you sing, Callie."

CHAPTER SEVENTEEN

Callie's voice floated through the theater like a palpable thing, floating and swaying on the waves of the air as surely as the ship floated on the water. When Callie began to sing, it was as if she became transformed, as if she actually became part of the elements, and as if her heart was reaching out to the audience. She could feel their vibrations as she mesmerized them. After her first song, the applause sent shivers down her spine. The applause didn't stop until she began another song.

Stephen sat as still as a statue as he listened to her captivating voice. Her eyes were closed, and her voice was wistful and lovely. He felt that the words were coming straight from her heart. Somehow he knew that she had suffered much pain. He longed to take her in his arms and comfort her, and the thought about her living alone in a city like New Orleans sent cold shivers down his spine. These emotions were new to him, because usually with a woman this beautiful, he could only think of kissing her soft lips, but Callie stirred feelings much deeper than physical attraction. These feelings were different, almost frightening to him.

After Callie sang her final song, she took a bow and left the stage. She felt all warm and happy inside as she proceeded to her dressing room. The singer who followed her was staring holes through her. The look took Callie off guard. She stood with her mouth open for a few moments. It was as if she were once again looking into Lydia's jealous eyes. She quickly turned and left the theater through the back door. She was determined to not let anyone spoil this special night. She would suggest to the captain that the jealous singer perform before she did; she felt this would take some pressure off the young singer.

Callie wanted to go to her cabin and relive this night over and over in her mind. To reach her cabin, she had to walk all around the ship's deck. As she neared the huge paddle wheel at the rear of the boat, fine sprays of water began to splash against her. She looked up at the clear, moonlit sky filled with twinkling stars, and she realized it wasn't raining.

Callie was overcome with fear once she became aware of the paddle wheel. In her urgency to escape Mr. Moore, she had forgotten her fear of water, and the fear returned in full force. She moved to the side of the boat and clutched the rail. Closing her eyes tightly, Callie could feel the knot in her stomach once again. When she opened her eyes, she saw the black waters churning, moving like something alive and dangerous behind the paddle wheel, as the boat moved down the river.

She took a deep breath, trying to get up the courage to go around the paddle wheel and to the safety of her cabin. Tears trickled down her cheeks. When her feet refused to move, she opened her purse and removed a small, hand-crocheted, silk-lined bag. She opened the bag and removed her baby ring and locket and held them tightly in her hand. This had become a habit with her, especially when she was afraid. She somehow felt close to the mother she had never known when she held the jewelry close to her heart.

After Callie's performance, Stephen went backstage to congratulate her on her performance only to be told that she had gone to her cabin. *She is probably tired from all the traveling she did today as well as her performance*, he thought. He decided to go out on the deck and smoke a cigar.

Once on the deck, he lit a cigar and threw the lighted match into the river. He stood there for a few minutes and then decided to stroll down the deck. After a few moments, he saw Callie. She was close to the paddle wheel, standing near the rail. He walked toward her. The sound of the churning muffled his footsteps, so she didn't hear him approach her. And when he touched her shoulder, she screamed, dropping jewelry from her hand.

Her mouth was wide open, and fear filled her eyes as she looked at Stephen.

"I'm so sorry! I didn't mean to frighten you," Stephen said. He could see she was distraught and reached out to put his arm around her shoulder, but Callie pulled away and looked at down at the deck floor.

"Oh, no! Oh, no!" She cried as she searched for her jewelry.

"What is it, Callie? What are you looking for?" Stephen asked.

"It's my jewelry, Stephen. I dropped my jewelry when you scared me."

"A thousand pardons, Callie. I really didn't mean to scare you. Please calm down. I'll help you find your jewelry." His eyes began to scan the dark deck.

"What am I looking for?" he asked.

"A ring and a locket," Callie replied with a quivering voice.

"That shouldn't be hard to find." Stephen was down on his hands and knees, crawling about and trying to find the jewelry.

Callie knelt down beside him and began to look. Moonlight pierced the shadows on deck, and Callie saw her ring. It had bounced about three feet from where she stood and was lying under a chair.

"I've found my ring!" she said as she went to pick it up. She grabbed it and held it close to her heart, which moved her to tears.

She held the ring out for Stephen to see.

"This is a baby ring," he said as he took the ring from her hand. Turning the ring around in his hand, he remarked, "It's a finely crafted ring; I can see that even in this light."

He struck a match and looked inside the ring's band and saw a small Lilly engraved inside the band. Throwing the match over the side, he commented, "No wonder you treasure this ring. A master craftsman made it. I can't recall his name, but what I do know is that only the rich could afford anything crafted by him." He carefully handed the ring back to her.

"How do you know he made this ring?"

"Have you not ever noticed the tiny Lilly inside the ring's band?" Stephen asked.

"Yes. I've often wondered why it was in there."

"Is this a ring that's been passed down from one generation to another?"

"I don't know. Why?" All of his questions were making Callie uncomfortable.

"Well, the ring is obviously very old. I'm surprised your mother or father didn't tell you the story behind it."

"What story?" Callie asked.

"You know, the usual kind of story parents tell their children when they pass down an old heirloom. Such as who crafted it or who owned it first. Just general things like that, no big issue," Stephen added. He wanted to drop the subject because he could see it was upsetting her. *Why?* He wondered.

Callie shuddered and bit her lower lip to stop its trembling. She stared down at the deck. She thought about telling him a lie, telling him that someone had given the ring and locket to her father as a way of paying him for traveling several miles to hold a revival, but Callie couldn't bring herself to tell a lie. She somehow felt that if she told the lie, it would bring her bad luck in her search for her family.

"Callie!" Stephen called her name and began to follow her. "Callie, please stop!"

Callie stopped and stood still, her back to him. He came up behind her and put his hands on her shoulders.

"Callie, I'm sorry if I upset you," Stephen said.

When he gently turned her toward him, he saw tears trickling down her face. He leaned over and kissed them away tenderly and slowly. For just a moment, all the hurt went away. The hurt was replaced by a strong desire to be held tighter and longer in these arms where she felt safety and warmth.

"I'm so sorry," Stephen whispered. His mouth was just inches away from hers. "I've seen the hurt in your eyes. I wish I could take it all away, but I can't help you unless you tell me what's wrong. In due time, I'm sure you will."

He pulled her closer, and their lips met in a long, lingering kiss. Finally when she began to pull away, he whispered, "You're so beautiful. Your skin is so soft. Your lips taste like honey, and the perfume you're wearing reminds me of my mother's. It brings back memories of long ago when she was still alive." There was pain in Stephen's voice.

"You lost your mother, too?"

"Yes, she died when I was a small boy. There are only a few things I can remember about her. After she died, I was raised by my grandparents." Stephen's hands circled her waist as he gazed down into her eyes.

"At least you know who your parents are," Callie said without thinking.

"Is that what's bringing you so much pain, Callie?"

She nodded.

He lifted her chin, forcing her to look into his eyes. "I'm so sorry, Callie. I wish I could ease your pain."

"No one can ease my pain, Stephen. The only way I'll ever feel like a whole person is when I meet one or both of my parents face-to-face. On that day, I will ask them why they gave me up after creating me. Did they love me? Do they have that same empty hole in their hearts like I have?"

"What about your father, the minister? How did he play a part in all of this?" Stephen asked.

"He raised me. He found me where my parents had abandoned me. He took me in and raised me as his own. He loves me, and he's done the best he could do for me. I was wearing the ring and necklace that I dropped when he found me. This jewelry is the only clue I have to my identity."

Callie didn't know why she was telling Stephen all of this. Somehow it seemed like the right thing to do. The burden was so hard to carry alone.

"Oh, Callie! What a sad story," Stephen said. "You know, you do have the jewelry as a clue. I think I can find out something from them. Will you trust me?" he asked.

"Yes," she said softly. "Will you help me find my locket?"

CHAPTER EIGHTEEN

The days Callie spent on the *Natchez Queen* were unlike anything in her wildest dreams. She and Stephen spent hours standing or sitting together, holding hands, and watching the changes in scenery as the boat moved along the river. She saw towns and islands, flowers, trees laden with Spanish moss, alligators, and snakes. They passed other pleasure boats, rafts, and canoes, all headed somewhere down the river.

Late one afternoon they sat on deck watching a beautiful sunset. Stephen was holding her hand. He said, "Callie, we'll be docking in New Orleans tomorrow. I dread seeing this voyage come to an end. I've been happier these last few days than I can ever remember."

"Oh, I know, Stephen. I feel the same way. Once we disembark, I will have to face reality. I must find a job and a place to live," Callie said.

"Callie, you mean you don't even have a place to stay?"

"No, Stephen, I don't, but don't worry about me. I'll find something. I have some money saved. I'm sure I have enough to last until I start getting paid." She sounded confident. And she was very confident that this was the opportunity she'd been waiting for—a chance to sing!

"No, Callie," Stephen shook his head. "I simply refuse to let you go out alone in a city the size of New Orleans."

"Why?" Callie was shocked by his outburst.

"It's just too dangerous. Now let's settle this. You are to come home with me," Stephen said in a matter-of-fact way.

Callie's mouth flew open in surprise. "Stephen, how dare you ask me to live with you? I'm sorry if my kisses have given you the wrong impression of me. I'll have you know that as badly as I want to sing, my body is one price I refuse to pay!" She stood up and began to walk away.

"Stop this instant, Callie!" Stephen's voice was angry.

Callie turned and looked at him.

"I'm sorry, Callie. I didn't intend to insult you. I mean no harm. I'll swear that I have nothing devious on my mind. It's just that my father's house is huge. It's empty and just waiting for you. We're never at home. In fact I'll only be home for two weeks, and then I'll be sailing to faraway ports. I'll be gone for three months. During the two weeks that I am home, if you will allow me, I'll talk to my father and have him help you find employment. He happens to be a close friend of Mr. James Caldwell, who owns the St. Charles Theater. You might very well get a chance to sing at the St. Charles. If Mr. Caldwell doesn't need any singers at this point, then I'm sure that once he hears you sing, he will find you a position somewhere on a stage in New Orleans."

"Oh, Stephen, this is unbelievable!" She clapped her hands. "I've heard that Jenny Lind sang at the St. Charles Theater," Callie said with dancing eyes.

"Yes, she did. I understand that it was standing room only," said Stephen.

CHAPTER NINETEEN

allie's heart seemed to be beating to the rhythmic sound of the horse's hooves as they made their way through the streets of New Orleans. The horses were pulling a luxurious carriage. The carriage belonged to Stephen's father. When Stephen wanted the carriage, it was always made available to him. Today Stephen's personal driver had met them at the ship's dock.

As Stephen and Callie rode through the town, they held hands. Stephen told Berry, the driver. "Slow this carriage down a little. I want this lady to see the city. As a matter of fact, let's take the scenic route."

"Yes, sir! I'd be happy to show yer pretty lady our grand city," Berry answered.

"Drive us to the St. Charles Hotel first," Stephen said. He squeezed Callie's hand. "Do you remember the large, white dome that we saw miles downriver?"

"Yes!" Callie smiled. "I'm so excited just to think that I'm in New Orleans, and I'm going to see the St. Charles Hotel close up!" Her eyes opened wide when they approached the hotel. It was a six-story building surrounded by a gleaming, white dome. "The dome is so huge! It looked small when I saw it from the river."

"Yes. The dome is very large, so is the hotel."

"Yes, it is! Can we go inside?" Callie asked.

"We certainly may," he said to Callie. He leaned toward the driver and said, "Berry, take us to the entrance door and stay with the horse and carriage, because we won't be long."

Once inside the grand hotel, they saw the elaborate restaurant and the beautiful paintings hanging on the marble walls. Callie stood in awe when they came to the theater. *Just think that Jenny Lind once performed here*, she thought. *How I would love to see and hear her sing just once.*

"Callie, how would you like to perform on that stage?" Stephen asked.

Callie nodded her head. "Do you think that's possible?"

"Yes, darling. I can make that very possible."

After they left the hotel, Stephen instructed the driver to go to the farmer's market. As they rode along, Stephen was enjoying watching her reactions to all the attractions the city held; it was the first time he had seen her with a smile of satisfaction. The sad look in her eyes was replaced with merriment and anticipation. Callie's eyes darted from one thing to another as the two walked through the farmer's market. When she saw a booth with yards and yards of colorful material, she thought of the beautiful dresses that could be made from them.

When they came to a booth selling lace, buttons, thread, and other notions, she reached out to feel the beautiful, white lace with gold threads running through it.

"Callie, would you like to have enough material and lace to make yourself a dress?" Stephen asked.

"My lady, how many yards would you like for me to cut off for you?" the dark-skinned sales lady asked with a French accent.

"Oh, no. I'm just admiring your wares," Callie said to the salesperson. Then she turned and walked away.

Stephen got her by the arm and stopped her. "Callie, don't be so hasty! I would love to buy you some material for a new dress."

"Stephen, I appreciate that, but I already feel so beholden to you. It's enough that you've put a roof over my head. Believe me, I'm grateful for that." She looked into his eyes. "But I won't take advantage of your kindness."

"All right, Callie. I don't understand, but I will respect your wishes." He put his arm around her waist and said, "Let's continue on and see more of the sights this city has to offer."

Callie was amazed at the sights, sounds, and the pungent smell that surrounded them, the smell of fresh fish and freshly slaughtered meats hanging in the air. When she saw the small animals in cages, her heart went out to them. The rabbits, squirrels, and possums were squealing to be released from their cages, not knowing they would be in someone's cooking pot soon. The odor of freshly baked bread drew her to the next booth, where the merchant was calling out, beckoning someone to buy his wares. Stephen smiled and bought a king cake from him.

There was a babel of languages as people spoke to each other in their native tongues. Callie could hear English, Spanish, French, Creole, and Greek spoken throughout the market.

"What a wonderful place to be!" Callie clapped her hands together. "I hope I can shop here someday."

Stephen laughed. "You will certainly have many opportunities to shop here, my little songbird. My housekeeper shops here, and she loves company. She comes here once a month, possibly more often. I'll instruct her to bring you along anytime you wish to accompany her."

"You don't think she'll mind me coming along, do you?" Callie questioned.

"Oh, no, she won't mind; you will love my housekeeper, because she has a heart of gold. And she's also the best cook you'll ever meet. She'll probably be angry with me for buying this cake. I can hear her now. "Mr. Stephen, if you wanted a king cake, you should have told me instead of going out and wasting your money on that one."

"I hope I won't be too much trouble to her," Callie said.

"She'll be glad to have you there with her. Well, I think it's time to call it a day. Let's get to the carriage and go home. I want you to taste her cooking for yourself," Stephen said.

Callie's hand went to her throat, and she held her breath when the driver turned into St. Charles Street. She had never seen houses or grounds this beautiful. Large mansions stood proudly on acres of rich, lush, green lawns, and large trees were laden with green foliage. There were also bushes and trees with all colors of blossoms. Most of the flower gardens she saw had water fountains and were framed by black, wrought-iron railings. When the carriage turned into a long driveway, Stephen said, "We're at home at last, Callie."

Callie couldn't believe her eyes. Going down the long driveway reminded her of a tunnel, because both sides of the driveway were lined with live oaks. Their branches, laden with Spanish moss, seemed be reaching out to her, swaying in a friendly welcome. Next she saw the gardens that were a sea of camellias, azaleas, and wisterias blooming in several colors, all giving off a sweet fragrance. There were magnolia trees along the numerous paths winding through the garden. There were several benches for resting and enjoying the garden's beauty and the peaceful surroundings.

Callie's surprise and curiosity were intensified when they approached the house. She saw the long porches that wrapped around the huge, redbrick house. Massive columns supported the roof. When the butler brought the carriage to a halt, a black butler, formally from Willow Grove. He was dressed in a black coat and a stiff, white, collared shirt descended the porch steps. He opened the carriage door and helped Callie out of the buggy. Stephen had hired several black men from Willow Grove, because when he was a young boy he had spent many happy times at Willow Grown and had grown fond of many of their servants.

Callie's body trembled with anticipation as he opened the massive, carved mahogany door that led to a huge entrance hall. The hall had ceilings that arched above towering columns. Twin staircases rose on both sides of the hall. Callie's eye stopped traveling around the room when Stephen introduced her to the black lady who had just walked into the room.

"Callie, I would like you to meet Sue Ellen, the lady I was telling you about. She will be looking after your needs."

CHAPTER TWENTY

I t was late in the afternoon. The sun had begun to set, changing the sky to hues of beautiful red, pink, blue, and purple and casting a warm, rosy glow over the land and into the windows. After hearing that Stephen was due to arrive home that day Callie was so excited about his arrival that she'd got up early that morning and had Sue Ellen fill her tub with water and had taken a bubble bath. Sue Ellen had followed her instructions but warned her not to expect Stephen early_ or maybe not at all because travel was so unpredictable. "He might not be here for a few days or even a week. Sue Ellen warned again. Never the less Callie didn't want to take the chance. She wanted to look her best when he did arrive. She had changed her dress many times that day trying to look her best for her beloved. She had finally settled on a cream-colored, satin dress, trimmed in scarlet with a red sash and cuffs. The skirt was hitched up with a red ribbon in front to show a scarlet petticoat underneath.

With Sue Ellen's help, she was wearing her hair in ringlets that bounced and a coiled chignon on the back of her head. She had left some of her hair down because she knew Stephen liked her hair down and flowing freely. As Sue Ellen brushed her hair, cold shivers went up and down Callie's spine as she remembered Stephen running his fingers through her hair, kissing her on the neck, and whispering how beautiful she was. She could hardly wait to feel his arms around her once again.

Callie was well versed in the dress and hair fashions of the day. She had looked at every fashion magazine and every catalog she could get her hands on. She had carefully watched the ladies she had seen out in public and noted the way they walked, talked, fluttered their eyelashes and hid behind their little fans in a flirtatious way. Callie had become very good at choosing her clothes and fixing her hair. She rarely had to ask Sue Ellen to help with either.

Since she had begun singing at the theater in New Orleans, she had bought yards and yards of beautiful material. She bought linen, taffeta, satin, and silk, and she hired a well-known dressmaker to make all of her clothes. Callie had soon realized that Sue Ellen was just as good at making the dresses as the professionals, and she then had asked Sue Ellen to sew for her. This worked out well for both of them. Sue Ellen could use the extra money, and Callie was nearby for the fittings.

Callie had been dressed for hours and pacing the floor. She played with her hair and readjusted her clothes. She restlessly walked through the gardens and refused to eat the breakfast and lunch that had been prepared for her. She was still in the gardens when she heard a carriage pull into the long, circular driveway. Her eyes danced with excitement as she recognized Stephen's carriage. Callie stood still and held her breath for a moment, and then she turned and went into the house and hurriedly went up the back staircase and into her room.

When she caught her breath, she went to the dresser, stood staring at her refection, and smoothed her hand over her hair. Then she picked up the pearl-handled mirror to look at the back of her hair. As she turned around, she pushed the hairpins holding her chignon tightly in place. When she was finally satisfied with the way she looked, she took a deep breath and willed her rapidly beating heart to slow down. She took another quick look as she left the room and started down the staircase.

As Callie glided down the winding stairs-case. She felt as if she was floating, her feet barley touching the stairs. Her heart was so light and filled with anticipation.

Even though Callie wanted to rush into Stephen's arms, she didn't want to appear overly anxious, so she paused on the staircase and watched Stephen exit the carriage. He looked very tall and handsome as he stood up, stretching his arms high above his head

"I could stretch a mile high; it's so good to be standing up. That carriage ride was a rocky one, if I do say so myself," Stephen said to the driver.

"Sorry, sir. It seems like I did have to start and stop many times." Berry the driver stepped down from his seat and removed his white gloves and handed the reigns to the coachman, who seemed to appear out of nowhere.

Callie began walking down the stairs. She was almost dancing with joy. Her mood quickly changed when a young woman appeared at the carriage door.

"Stephen," the mystery lady said as she offered him her gloved hand.

Stephen bowed and took the lady's hand. She was dressed as colorfully as a hummingbird. She was wearing a bright-yellow dress with a flowing skirt. An orange sash accented her small waistline, and her hair was jet black, reminding Callie of a raven's wings.

There was an orange silk cord around her head, with jewels suspended from its center over her forehead.

Callie watched as Stephen put his arm around this stranger's waist. Her heart was breaking as she heard him talking to the lady. "Welcome to my humble abode," Stephen said. "Come in, and make yourself at home. You must refresh yourself before you continue on your journey. Perhaps you will consider staying the night or even a week."

"I must leave soon, although you do know that I would prefer to stay. But I will accept your hospitality and refresh myself. Stephen, I've certainly enjoyed our time together, and I'm sorry it has to end." The lady looked at Stephen through fluttering eyelids.

"Are you sure you can't stay for a few days?"

Callie could hear the pleading in Stephen's voice.

"Oh, no. I'm sorry, but I must be on my way." A breeze picked up and moved a strand of hair across her face. She took her hand and brushed it aside.

"Well, only if you insist—and if you promise to not allow so much time to pass before we see each other again," Stephen smiled.

"The road runs both ways, you know." She shook her finger at Stephen. Her bracelet jingled.

"Yes, I know. Father keeps me very busy." He nodded his head in agreement. "I'm sure it's for my own good. It seems that I have become very prosperous and well respected in the business world."

"It is as it seems; you have prospered!" she mocked gaily.

"I've been so happy these last few days. I guess I'll always miss the life of freedom that I once lived. Being with you and your family brings it all back,"

"I'm sure you're sleeping on a soft feather bed now, aren't you?" she said in a teasing voice.

"I guess I'll always miss sleeping under the stars, with Mother Nature as my only mattress," Stephen replied in a wistful voice.

"Oh, come on, Stephen! Don't tell me you would trade all of this for a life under the stars." She made a sweeping gesture with her hands.

Stephen answered in a quiet voice. "Sometimes I would, Alicia; sometimes I would trade it all. Well, so much for remembering. Let's go inside, where you can refresh yourself while I order us some tea. We must visit more before you leave!" He took Alicia's hand and began leading her toward the house.

⥳┼┼⥫

Callie quickly turned and went up the stairs. She wouldn't let Stephen see the tears rolling down her cheeks, almost blinding her. Callie stood on the upstairs gallery, bit her lower lip to choke back a sob, and tried to stand still. She watched the sun going down, turning the world into darkness, matching the darkness in her heart.

Callie wondered, *why did I allow myself to be talked into moving into the same house where Stephen lives? Was it because he told me he would help me find my parents? That's the main reason I moved in, or was it?*

She choked on a sob, her anger almost eclipsing her grief. *How could I have been so vulnerable and allowed myself to believe his lies? It appears as if he's quite the ladies' man, and he knows just the right things to say to make a woman's heart flutter.*

"Alicia, Alicia," Callie said in a mimicking voice. "Come inside, Alicia!" She almost gag on her on words. "I want no part of a man who can't be faithful!"

Callie began to pace back and forth in the hall in front of her room. Then talking to herself, she opened the door and went into her room. "But then again he isn't mine. He never told me he loved me! We've only kissed on occasion. Perhaps my kisses didn't send chills up and down his spine, the way his kisses did to me. Perhaps I've read too much into his actions and the few letters he has written me. I love him so much that I

146

thought he loved me as well. I felt he wanted to be in my arms just as much as I wanted to be in his. Oh, Stephen," she whispered, "you have always been so good to me, making me feel so loved and wanted."

Then she thought, *Maybe you just felt sorry for me, but I don't want or need your pity. I don't want anyone's pity.* The thought of Stephen feeling sorry for her brought a new wave of tears to Callie's eyes.

"Missus Callie, Missus Callie, Mr. Stephen is waiting for yo in de parlor," Sue Ellen said as she tried to open the bedroom door, but Callie had the door locked.

"Thank you, Sue Ellen." Callie tried to control the trembling in her voice.

"I'll tell him yo will be down soon," Sue Ellen replied. Callie soon heard her footsteps on the stairwell.

She removed a lace handkerchief tucked between her breasts and buried her face inside it and cried. Later she wiped her eyes and blew her nose. *I'm alone again, and I can no longer accept charity from the man I love. Perhaps I can stay at the theater. There are a few private rooms there, and I know some of them are empty.* She lay across the bed, exhausted.

Two hours later Sue Ellen unlocked Callie's bedroom door, entered the room, and walked to the bed. Callie lay on her stomach, her hair and clothes in disarray.

"What's de matter, chile?" Sue Ellen asked.

"I have a headache." Callie placed her hand on her forehead.

"I guess yo ain't coming down to dinner."

"Please tell Mr. Stephen that I'm happy he is home but I have a headache and I won't be down for dinner."

Stephen sat alone at the long dining-room table and looked at the romantic table setting that was before him. The red wine

sparkled in a cut-glass wine bottle. He stared at the highly polished silverware that lay on the linen napkin; the beautiful china,
hand painted in tiny, rose pattern and rimmed in gold; and the
crystal chandelier casting dancing shadows over the table and its
settings. He wanted so badly for Callie to join him for dinner. He
had given the cook orders for this special dinner. He had ordered
beef Wellington, buttered potatoes, fresh asparagus, hot rolls, and
lemon pie for dessert. He could hardly wait for his beloved; it had
been so long since he had seen her.

Sue Ellen entered the dining room. "Missus Callie has a headache, she sorry she can't come down. Mr. Stephen."

Disappointment and concern came across Stephen's face. He
pushed back his chair and quickly stood up. "Has she not been well
since I've been away?"

"Yes, she's been well, and she's been so happy singing in de theaters," Sue Ellen said proudly. "Berry says she has a big audience
almost every time she sings. He says de tickets are always sold out!"

"So when did she take this headache?" Stephen asked.

"Tonight, I guess. She's been fluttering around all—" Sue Ellen
quickly placed her hand over her mouth before she said any more.
After an uneasy pause, she said, "Mr. Stephen, I'll bring yo some
food."

"Never mind." He sighed and dropped his napkin on the table.
"I've lost my appetite."

Around noon the following day, Stephen decided to check on
Callie. He concluded that if she still had the headache, then he
would call the doctor. He wanted to see her so badly. Thinking
that she was in pain or in any kind of distress brought him pain as
well.

He walked out on to the long, eight-columned porch that was filled with wicker furniture. A round, wicker table held a tray with two frosted glasses and a pitcher of lemonade. Large baskets of ferns hung all around the porch. Huge pots of flowering, red geraniums lined the inside of the porch. Sue Ellen was bent over the pots, cutting the red blossoms off the geranium plants. She was placing the blooms in a bucket, but she stood up when she heard the screen door close.

"Mr. Stephen, yer lemonade is ready, jus' de way yo like it." She smiled. "Would yo like some fig cookies? Callie baked dem last week."

"Where is Callie?" Stephen looked around.

"I don' think she's coming down dis morning." Sue Ellen straightened the straw hat she was wearing.

"Well, don't you think we should look in on her?" Stephen's voice was sharp, sharper than he meant for it to be. He was just so concerned that Callie hadn't come down last night, and apparently she wasn't coming down today, either.

"Yes, sir," Sue Ellen said as she walked toward the front door. Stephen followed her up the stairs and knocked on Callie's door. When no one answered, the two looked at each other. Stephen opened the door, but Callie wasn't in the room!

"What the..." Stephen stopped in his tracks.

"Where is she?" he asked, and then he noticed that her wardrobe was open and empty. "She's gone; I think she left!"

He began to panic. He opened the drawers to the dresser and chest. "Sue Ellen! She's gone and has taken everything she owns!" Disbelief was in his voice. "Why would she do such a thing?"

CHAPTER TWENTY-ONE

Isabelle stood and gazed out a long window that framed the
flower gardens at Willow Grove. It was a late August afternoon.
She noticed that the gardens were in need of rain. A hot, playful breeze began blowing, making things even drier. Through the
open window, she could hear the rattling of dry leaves and the dying flowers, as the wind made small whirlwinds out of them.

She sighed a deep sigh, because this was the first time in a long
time that she had noticed the yard and gardens. Everything had
become so grown-up and in need of weeding and pruning. She
simply didn't have enough help at Willow Grove to keep the plantation in proper order. Without John's stern leadership, the help
had slacked off.

She decided to go outside and walk around the yard. After a
very hot day, the house was almost unbearable. She decided she
would stay outside until the house cooled down.

As she walked down the long entrance hall toward the front
door, she caught a glimpse of herself in the mirror. When she saw
her reflection, she stopped suddenly, and her mouth dropped. *Who*

is this person in the mirror? This tired, old woman with worry lines etched deeply into her face. New strands of gray showed around her temples. She turned her head from side to side, as she absorbed the fact that indeed she was aging rapidly. In two weeks, Isabelle would turn forty-one years of age, although she looked more like fifty. With another sigh and one more shake of her head, she turned from the mirror and walked outside.

As she walked, she looked down at her worn hands, turning them repeatedly over, studying them, the actions similar to young babies when they first discover they have hands. However, unlike a baby's soft, delicate hands, Isabelle's were wrinkled and dry from hard work and lack of personal care. Taking care of John had consumed most of her time, and she had let herself go.

A soothing, cooler breeze felt incredible to her senses as it blew her hair and the skirt of her black mourning dress. Standing there, memories from her past flooded her mind. Memories of a time long gone by. As she pondered the concept of time, Isabelle became lost in a moment of infinity; many years had passed since she had first arrived at Willow Grove as a young bride. Time had changed so many things.

It was perfectly clear to her that time was at the stern of life. She recalled having heard it said time was a great healer, but the so-called healing hands of time must have skipped over the horrid pain in her heart over losing Jane, because Isabelle was nowhere near being healed. Yes, there had been brief moments when time seemed to stand still, yet those brief moments turned into years that had slipped away from her, flown by actually.

She began to walk slowly through the gardens. She noticed how the once-vibrant summer flowers had begun to wilt and fade. Tall sunflowers bowed their proud heads; the morning glories closed their delicate blooms to the evening sun. The wind picked up, blowing the trees and making a rustling sound, and leaves fell to the ground, to be gone forever more.

Yes, she thought. *It seems as though everything and everybody have their allotted time. A time to live, a time to die, every living thing has internal instructions, a biological time clock.* So it seemed to Isabelle.

"Times running out on all of us," she said to the dying garden. "How much longer do I have before I'm lying in the cemetery beside John?"

Then she looked up into the sky. "I pray to you, God. Just let me live long enough to find Jane and hold her one more time and know that she's all right." She said the prayer aloud, as she had prayed hundreds of times before.

She walked a weedy path that led to an ornate, black, wrought-iron bench. In spite of the heat, a chill went up her spine when she looked up the hill toward the family burial plot. Then she looked at John's grave and wondered, *why can't I feel any grief? Is my heart that cold? After all, he was my husband, and I was anxious for him to die and get out of my way so that I could began my search for Jane.*

Now the time has come to move on and begin searching for Jane, and I intend to use every means it might take to finance the search. I'm going to take all the art, china, crystal, and silver to the antique stores in New Orleans and sell them. I will sell everything I can carry off. And if necessary, I will sell the plantation and use the money to find her.

This had been a long time coming, but Isabelle realized that now was the time for her to take control of her life and her situation. No, she hadn't felt any sorrow over John's death, even though death was a time for sorrow. However, she had felt some guilt because she hadn't grieved over him. When the years of John's oppression had finally ended, she had felt as if a heavy weight had been lifted off her shoulders; the burden she had been carrying for years was now gone. She wanted to get his personal belongings out of the house as soon as possible. She wanted to rid herself of anything that might remind her of him and his evil heart.

Yet, she realized, for the sake of society, she had to go through the proper mourning period. Isabelle knew that she had to wear black clothing for a year, even though she would prefer to wear yellow, red, purple, or any color other than black. This made her feel like a hypocrite. She had felt so hypocritical during the funeral when friends and family had spoken words of condolences in hushed voices. She had graciously accepted their words, pats, and hugs and had fulfilled that social part of this situation.

Isabelle knew Jane was live, in spite of John and the fact that the Pinkington Detective Agency doubted it. The Pilkington agency had been searching off and on for Jane since her disappearance and hadn't found the first clue as to what had become of her. They said that they had questioned several bands of gypsies to no avail. Earlier John had insisted that it was highly possible that the gypsies had sold her and that she could be on the other side of the world by now. Isabelle had felt all along that John was responsible for Jane's disappearance. She had felt that he was the key to the mystery of her daughter's disappearance.

The day John died, she and Ripley were sitting in his room beside the bed. His skin and eyes were yellow. He lay very still, all except his chest, which rose and fell with great effort as he struggled to breathe. The room smelled of death and decay. She knew that John's liver had been affected by all the years of heavy drinking. She knew by his raspy breath that he wasn't long for this world; she felt she had to ask him one more time about Jane.

She laid her hand on Ripley shoulder. Ripley eyes seemed to be glued on John's shuddering body, and she took breaths when he did. Isabelle said, "Ripley, I need a few moments alone with John."

It took a moment for Ripley to realize that Isabelle had even spoken to her. She was so engrossed in the sad scene before her. "Yes, ma'am," Ripley answered as she turned to Isabelle.

After she left, Isabelle took John's wasted hand into hers and softly asked, "John, can you hear me?"

"I'm afraid to die. I'm afraid of what's on the other side," John said in a whisper. She had to lean over him to hear him say, "We need to talk. I must tell you what happened to Jane, but you must tell me about you and Berry." John began a fit of coughing.

Isabelle said as she lifted John into a sitting position, "I will not apologize or try to explain to you anything about me and Berry. You have lived your life being a mean and cruel person, and I owe you nothing!"

As she spoke, he began to choke, and she began to work quickly, putting her fingers down his throat and removing the phlegm that was choking him. John lay back, exhausted. Isabelle got a wet washcloth and began to wipe the perspiration from his brow. Wanting sympathy, he looked at her, yet she felt none for this man she had shared her life with. His body began to shake violently, and she realized that she had to make him talk before it was too late.

"John, what did you do with her? Did you give her to the gypsies? If you don't tell me, I'll never forgive you for this evil thing you have done, and I'll only hope God has no mercy on your soul."

John began to lift his hand toward Isabelle. He lifted it slowly, almost reaching her face, when his strength gave out and his hand dropped to the bed. "Forgive me." His eyes were now pleading.

"I will forgive you, John, if you tell me where my baby is."

"I...left...her on the...banks...of the river." He struggled for air before he continued, "I couldn't kill her myself. I don't know... what...happened to...her." He turned his eyes away from Isabelle. "I went...back...the next day to find...her, but she...was...gone. That's where I was coming from the morning you saw me. I...hope the gypsies took her."

The words came slowly. They were hardly audible because of his weakness and his swollen tongue. Once again John went into another coughing spasm, strangling on the phlegm. Isabelle tried to remove the mass, but suddenly he stopped breathing and began to turn blue. Isabelle called out for Ripley.

Ripley rushed into the room, and as she looked over John, she said, "It's over, Missus Isabelle."

CHAPTER TWENTY-TWO

Sue Ellen and Berry sat quietly on the latter back chairs on the porch of their cabin. Berry's chair was leaning against the house on two back legs. He was busy whittling a whistle out of a stick of pine wood. Sue Ellen was shelling peas. Her apron was full of peas. She threw the empty shells out into the yard, where the chickens were waiting to fight over them, and dropped the shelled peas into an empty pan on the porch.

"Mr. Stephen's gone. He said he needed to get away for a while. I'm fixing to go see Callie. I'm gonna to ask her why she done up and lef' Mr. Stephen. It was de strangest thing I ever heard of. She jus' up and lef' him. Po Mr. Stephen, he's taking this mighty hard; dat man shore is in bad shape. Yep, I never seen nobody just wilt inside like Mr. Stephen did when he realized Callie was gone." Sue Ellen said.

Berry stopped whittling and looked at Sue Ellen. "Yeah, Sugarins, it sho was strange, but us black folks don' need to stick our noses into white folk business. Yo know dat, don' yo, Sugar-ins?" Berry said

"I know, Berry. But I sho do miss dat child. She's the sweetest white child I ever saw." A handful of peas hit the bottom of the pan, making a pinging sound.

"Yeah, well, don' yo worry; she's doing jus' fine singing her heart out," Berry said as he spat a long stream of tobacco juice on the ground.

"All's I know is dat Mr. Stephen sho was down and out when she lef.' He told me fore he go dat if I could talk Missus Callie into coming back to da house, den he would be much obliged. He would welcome her and take her back in, and dat's jus' what I's gonna to do. Shoo! Shoo!"

Sue Ellen grabbed her apron to keep the peas that were in it from falling out. She stood up, and with one hand, she broke off a limb from a nearby bush. She began to shoo away the chickens that were venturing too close to the porch and the pan of peas.

When she almost tripped and fell into the pan, Berry had to laugh at her. He grabbed her hand to steady her. Then he said, "Well, do as you please. Go nose round a little. Get your belly full of white folks' troubles."

"Oh, shut your mouth," Sue Ellen replied and hit him on his knee.

"Where did Master Stephen go anyway?" Berry asked. "When will he be back, Sugar-ins?"

"I don' know. He didn't sail off dis time. He said he needed to sleep on Mother Earth and look at de stars, or something like dat." Sue Ellen sat down and continued to shell peas.

"He's gone to visit Mama Dora and Tomsk." A satisfied smile crossed Berry's face.

CHAPTER TWENTY-THREE

When Callie opened the door to her dressing room, Sue Ellen could hear the loud applause that followed her and people yelling, "Bravo! Bravo!" Once inside the room, Callie closed the door and leaned her body against it.

Sue Ellen could see the tiny beads of sweat on her forehead and above her upper lip. There was a look of triumph in her eyes that replaced the sorrow that was usually there. Callie let out a long breath as she leaned against the door.

"Bravo! Bravo!" Sue Ellen said as she held her hands up in the air and clapped.

Callie's body stiffened as she gasped in fear. Both of her hands went to her heart, and she looked around the room. She saw Sue Ellen sitting in a chair, almost hidden by the colorful dresses and wraps surrounding her. "Sue Ellen, you scared me half to death!"

"Well, I sho didn't mean to scare yo," Sue Ellen apologized.

"I know you didn't." Callie's voice softened. "It's so good to see you." They walked toward each other and embraced. "I've missed you so much." Sue Ellen watched as tears of joy filled Callie's eyes.

"Chile, I missed yo. It jus' ain't feeling right around de big, ole house. De house jus' seems cold and empty wid out yo. I miss yer sweet voice singing and humming. No, it jus' ain't right," Sue Ellen said, reaching to hold Callie in her arms. "Chile, yo have lost some weight. Yer shoulder bone is like a sharp blade. And I bet I could count yer ribs, honey."

"Yes. I have lost a little weight." Callie sighed when she noticed the look of concern in Sue Ellen's face and continued in a teasing voice, "I'm not getting any of your fine cooking." She smiled and patted Sue Ellen on the cheek.

"Well, let's jus' take care of dat right now." Sue Ellen turned around, bent down, reached under the chair she had been sitting in, and picked up a woven basket that was covered with a faded, pink-plaid dishcloth. After she removed the cover, she said, "Take a whiff of dis, child. I brought de orange and coconut muffins you love so much. I couldn't come and see my chile without bringing her some muffins."

"Oh! I'm ravished!" Callie's eyes lit up as her stomach growled. She grabbed a muffin from the basket and took a huge bite. "These muffins are still warm, Sue Ellen, but not as warm as your heart," she said through a mouthful.

After quickly finishing the muffin, she licked her fingers and brushed the crumbs from her mouth and blouse, and then Callie said, "That was the most wonderful muffin I've ever eaten. I sure do miss you and your cooking, Sue Ellen."

"Ain't no use in yo missing me," Sue Ellen quickly teased.

"I can miss you if I want to, can't I?" Callie reached for another muffin.

"Yes. Yo can if yo want to, but yo don' have to. Yo can come back home." Sue Ellen Replied.

Callie put the muffin back inside the basket. In a sad voice, she said, "I don't think I belong there, Sue Ellen. I wish I did, but I simply do not. I really do appreciate all the help and opportunities

Stephen has given me. If I did come back, then I would feel like I was in the way."

"No! No!" Sue Ellen shook her head. "Master Stephen has sent me to bring yo back home. He's been one sad man since yo lef.'

"What do you mean?" Callie asked.

"I mean dat man loves yo! Can't you see? It's written all over his face. Are yo jus' so young yo don' see dat?"

"Oh, how I wish," Callie said under her breath.

"How do yo feel bout Mr. Stephen?" Sue Ellen questioned.

Callie turned and walked to the window. She looked out on the cloudy moonlight. After a few moments, she said, "I have a deep respect for Stephen." She turned to Sue Ellen and continued, "But I feel that our destinies are taking separate paths." Callie didn't want to mention how he had broken her heart when she had seen him with that beautiful girl, Alicia.

"Chile we want yo to come home. Mr. Stephen sent me to fetch yo."

"That's not my home, Sue Ellen. I don't feel like I belong there anymore."

"Why?" Sue Ellen questioned.

"I don't know. I guess I feel like I'm a burden to Stephen. What if he was to meet someone he deeply cares for?" This was all Callie could think to say. She still just couldn't bring herself to talk about Alicia. No, that pain had to forever remain a secret.

"Chile, if yo care for Mr. Stephen as much as he cares for yo, den you don' have to worry bout another woman taking yer man if yo let him know yo love him. Dat is if, and only if, yo do love him." Sue Ellen crossed her arms in front of her body as if to stand her ground.

"Yes, of course I care for him. He's been very good to me." Callie fought to keep from crying.

"Den come back home! Mr. Stephen's so worried 'bout yo! He's afraid some dirty, old man will hurt yo!" Sue Ellen stated bluntly.

"I don't know. I just don't know."

The offer was very tempting to Callie. She supposed that Stephen had a right to be concerned for her safety, because she certainly didn't feel safe living in this hotel. There hadn't been a night gone by that some gentleman hadn't made advances toward her. A few drunken ones had actually had the nerve to put their hands on her. This had been revolting to her. It brought back bad memories of Mr. Moore and his filthy attempts toward her. Now Stephen apparently wanted her to come back to his house, to love and care for her as if she were his sister.

Well, she would have to think about that.

CHAPTER TWENTY-FOUR

Four months later, on Saturday morning as Sue Ellen and Berry sat at their kitchen table enjoying their second cup of coffee, there was a knock on the front door. Their cabin was on Stephen's estate. They were the ones Stephen always left in charge of the place. Since he was away from home so often, it made sense to him for the two to live nearby. Besides that, he felt as if he always had someone to come home to. Stephen had known and loved Sue Ellen and Berry for as long as he could remember.

"Sugar-ins, can yo get dat door while I finish dis biscuit and jelly?" Berry dipped a spoon into a jelly jar and proceeded to spread the clear, red, raspberry jelly over his buttered, hot biscuit.

Sue Ellen pushed her chair back. As she stood up, she wiped her face with the tail of her apron. She smoothed her hair back with her hands as she walked to the door. When she opened the door, warm sunlight flooded the room.

A young man wearing a courier's uniform stood at the door. "Hello, ma'am. I have a message for Mr. Berry Bradford." He spoke with a kind, businesslike voice as he handed her the envelope that contained the message.

"Thank yo," Sue Ellen said with hesitation in her voice. She paused and became very uncomfortable and began to shift her weight from one foot to the other. She said in an unsteady voice, "Can yo read dis to us?"

Sympathy came into the courier's eyes. This was not uncommon in New Orleans. In fact he had deliberately hesitated just in case the lady couldn't read the message. "Yes, ma'am. I will be happy to read this to you."

He reached for the letter, carefully opened it, and began to read. "'To Sue Ellen and Berry: I'm beginning my journey home. I hope all is well. Love, Stephen. PS. I hope to find Miss Callie back home with us when I arrive.'"

The courier smiled and handed the letter back to Sue Ellen. He tipped his hat, turned, and walked away.

Sue Ellen put the letter into her apron pocket as she turned toward Berry. She had a happy smile on her face. "Mr. Stephen's coming home!" She clapped her hands with glee.

"I sho' am glad. It's high time he got back home," Berry said as he chewed on his biscuit. "Sugar-ins, I think Mr. Stephen is still smitten with Misses Callie. Why don' we go see her and make her come back to de house," Berry suggested.

"I believes I will. Now will you wipe dat jelly off yer chin," she said as she playfully rubbed the top of his curly head.

Sue Ellen and Berry arrived at the theater in the late afternoon. Berry went to the kitchen to catch up on all the latest news, and Sue Ellen helped some of her friends with the cleaning while she waited until it was time for Callie's performance to end. She was so anxious and excited to see Callie again. She could hardly wait to tell her about Stephen's message and to ask her to come back home before Stephen's arrival.

After climbing all the stairs to Callie's room, Sue Ellen was out of breath. She was carrying a large, woven basket filled with food for Callie. She sat down in a chair to catch her breath and put the basket down by her side as she waited for Callie to come in.

When Callie came through the door, she was humming a happy song. It was a happy surprise when she saw Sue Ellen. Sue Ellen stood up and walked toward Callie with outstretched arms.

"Oh, Sue Ellen!" Callie cried. "It's so great to see you again!" She laid her head on Sue Ellen's shoulder. Sue Ellen was the closest thing to family she had. She needed to feel the warmth of her body and the touch of someone she knew loved her.

When Callie raised her head, Sue Ellen smiled at her. Her eyes were filled with love. She missed this unhappy child and was happy to hold her in her arms once again.

"Oh, Sue Ellen, are you going to be here for a while?" Callie asked.

"Well, I don' know. Why?" Sue Ellen asked.

"I'm singing for a private party, and I have to sing again in thirty minutes. It seems that there's some people high up in government here tonight. I feel honored to be invited to sing for them. But I want to visit with you as well," Callie said.

"I don' know how long I'll be here. I'll ask Berry."

"Is Berry here?" Callie asked.

"Yes. He's talking to a man dat works here."

"Oh, I miss you both so badly I can hardly stand it," Callie said in a wistful voice. "I've been gone from home—I mean, Stephen's home—for six months now."

"Den why don' yo come home? We sho miss yo, too." Sue Ellen nodded her head as she talked.

Callie looked off into the distance. "Is Mr. Stephen there?"

"No. He's still gone. I guess he's helping his father in dat shipping business."

Sue Ellen sensed the anger in Callie's voice when she spoke Stephen's name, and she wondered, *what happened between Mr. Stephen and Misses Callie?* She quickly decided to keep the news she had come to share with Callie to herself, the message they had received a few days earlier telling them of Stephen's forthcoming arrival. She didn't want to spook Misses Callie.

⥺⇥⇤⥸

Two days later Berry, Sue Ellen, and Callie packed up Callie's few belongings. She had decided to move back into Stephen's house.

Callie's heart was filled with joy and happiness as the buggy once again took her up the long, familiar driveway. When the huge house came into view, Callie caught her breath, just as she had the first time she had seen the place. She moved over in the buggy seat closer to Sue Ellen. Sue Ellen was wearing a red scarf on her head, a wisp of gray hair showing underneath.

Callie reached over and squeezed her hand and thought about how dear this woman had become in her life. She realized that she loved Sue Ellen more than she had ever loved another female figure. She squeezed her hand a little bit tighter, while Sue Ellen patted the top of Callie's hand.

"After we unpack yo stuff, little misses, I'm gonna cook yo a meal fit for a king! I'm tired looking at yer bony body. Den I want to hear yo sing. Ole Sue Ellen wants to hear songs round da house. Berry's always a sucking' on dat Jew's harp, but I wants to hear yer beautiful voice again in Mr. Stephen's house."

"Yes, ma'am." Callie laughed.

Two weeks later they received another message from Stephen. The message read that he should arrive home on the following Monday. When Sue Ellen told Callie the news, a hurt look came into her eyes, and she dropped her head. Her shoulders slumped as she turned around and left the room.

Sue Ellen was greatly puzzled at the sadness that had come over Misses Callie. *What on earth happened?* She wondered. *Callie was doing so well, eating good and putting on weight. She also goes around singing as she helps in the house. She has been spending a lot of time in the kitchen learning how to cook from me.* Sue Ellen was delighted to teach her the tricks of country cooking.

CHAPTER TWENTY-FIVE

Stephen began to make his long journey home. He would've taken a stagecoach and arrived earlier if he had been certain that Callie was waiting for him. Since he was unsure of what awaited him, the gypsy blood that flowed in his veins, or perhaps the sorrow in his heart, made him take the slow way home. He was riding a horse and taking in all the beauty of nature that surrounded him.

What has happened? Why did she change? Has she met someone else? That is surely the problem. I could have sworn she cared for me, and then all of a sudden, she became cold and distant. Perhaps she met a talent scout who promised more and more opportunities to advance her career. Maybe it wasn't such a good idea to get her a singing job. What man wouldn't want to pursue her? Just seeing her would take any man's breath away. When she sings, her voice would touch any man's heart. Yes, I have lost her. I've lost the only one I'll ever love, and don't even know why.

Tears flowed down Stephen's cheeks as he rode on a trail along a riverbank. The trail was shaded by trees hanging full of moss. Wild flowers were scattered everywhere along the trail. He was enraptured by it all. When he saw a large patch of moss-grown land, he pulled back on the reins and said, "Whoa," and the horse came to a stop. He got down and tied the horse to a nearby tree. Then he took a blanket from the saddlebag and laid it down on the mossy ground. Using the blanket as a pillow, he looked up at the clear, blue sky, and a friendly breeze began to blow, cooling his hot and tired body.

"Why hurry home? There's nothing to go home for," he said aloud, closed his eyes, and fell asleep.

CHAPTER TWENTY-SIX

"Sue Ellen, would you please come in here for a minute!" Callie stood in her bedroom door. Sue Ellen was in the bedroom across the hall, dusting and cleaning the upstairs room, preparing for Stephen's arrival. They were expecting Stephen to be home any day now. He should have been home two weeks earlier. Callie feared that something bad had delayed his arrival. Sue Ellen reassured her that he was fine and this wasn't unusual behavior for Stephen.

"What do yo want, child?" Sue Ellen came into Callie's room carrying a feather duster in her hand and a tired look on her face.

"I need you to button my dress. The buttons are in the back, and I can't reach all of them."

Sue Ellen smiled. "Be mighty happy to button yo up, child."

Callie turned her back to Sue Ellen. Sue Ellen laid her duster on the floor and began to button the dress. She started with the top button and made her way down the dress, buttoning the satin-covered buttons. When she came to Callie's small waistline, she couldn't pull the dress material close enough to button.

"Chile, yer getting a little thick through yo belly. I can' button yer dress! Yo needs to put on an nuder one."

"I know. My clothes are getting tighter. It's all of your good cooking, but I'm going to wear this dress today because it's my favorite dress and I absolutely refuse to be outdone!" Callie said firmly.

"I don' know how you plan on doing dat." Sue Ellen's voice was firm. As she spoke, she placed both of her hands on her wide hips.

"That's simple! I'm going to wear a tighter corset under my dress. Now will you please unbutton me so that I can put another one on?"

"All right, chile," Sue Ellen said as she began to unbutton the dress she had just buttoned. "You might as well go to de dresser and get yer other corset so I can put it on and button yo up again. I sho wish yo would jus' buy some new clothes. You look better wit' yer cheeks full anyhow."

After the dress was unbuttoned, Callie slipped out of it and dropped it to the floor. She was now dressed only in the bodice top and bloomer. She went to her dresser and began rummaging through the drawers, hunting for her most comfortable corset.

"If yo are gonna put on dat corset, den jus' take off yer bloomer. I'll put some powder on yer fanny. As hot as it is, yo will sweat and break out wit' heat," Sue Ellen said as she picked Callie's dress up off the floor.

Callie reached for a box of powder from the top of the dresser and then let her bloomers drop to the floor, and Sue Ellen saw the dark spot on Callie's hip. "What's dat on yer fanny, girl? Is it a scab?" Sue Ellen squinted her eyes as she looked at the mark on Callie's hip.

"Where?" Callie asked as she looked over her shoulder.

"Right here!" Sue Ellen walked over to where Callie stood and touched the birthmark.

"That's just my birthmark," Callie answered, unconcerned.

"Turn around toward dat window, and let me look at dat again." Sue Ellen's voice began to quiver.

Callie did as she was told. She looked over her shoulder as Sue Ellen examined her.

It took a moment for the truth to sink in. This was the same birthmark all her children wore. The shock was great. Sue Ellen froze, dropping both hands down to her sides as her shoulders slumped in defeat. Her breath became heavy and irregular.

"Are you all right, Sue Ellen?" Callie asked with concern in her voice while putting the powder box down on top of the dresser. Sue Ellen nodded her head yes.

"Well, you don't look all right," Callie said just realizing that she was naked. She picked up a shawl that lay at the foot of her bed and wrapped it around her body. "Perhaps you need to sit down."

When Sue Ellen opened her mouth to speak, nothing came out. She tried, but her voice squeaked and croaked, sounding like a young man's when it began to change. "Nothing wrong, child, nothing. Let's put dese bloomers on yo befo' yo catch yer death of cold."

"You got awful quiet all of a sudden. You also stopped fussing over me," Callie said lightly, wondering, *what happened, and why has Sue Ellen become so upset over my birthmark? Or is she upset because she thinks I'm going to lose more weight?* Callie was puzzled.

Sue Ellen didn't trust herself to speak again. There were too many questions crowding her mind. What if she were staring at her husband's child, the girl who had changed their lives forever? The child they had been told was stolen or disappeared many, many years ago.

Sue Ellen realized that she had to leave the room, because the air had suddenly become oppressive. She picked up the feather duster from the floor. The light feather duster felt like so much weight to her. "I must go down to de kitchen and check da pot of stew I lef' on the stove." Sue Ellen seemed to be speaking and walking in slow motion. This day had suddenly turned into a day of trouble for her.

Later in the afternoon when Sue Ellen went home, Berry was sitting in a rocking chair on the porch. An old, gray cat lay near the rockers of the chair and seemed to be swinging his long, bushy tail to the lively tune Berry was playing on his harmonica. When Sue Ellen stepped up onto the porch, she gave Berry a long, hard look. He had lived with her long enough to know just what that look meant. Sue Ellen was angry!

When Berry winked at her, she didn't so much as crack a smile. He laid down his harmonica and said, "Sugar-ins, do yo want me to build a fire in de cooking' stove?"

She looked at him for a long moment before answering. Then in a gruff voice she said, "No! I brought home some cold cornbread from de big house. Your black hide can eat milk and bread for yer supper!" She held her head up high and walked into the house. She had very little to say to him the rest of the evening.

After the two went to bed, Sue Ellen turned her back to him. He put his arms around her and tried to draw her near. She pushed him away when he tried to nibble on her ear, and then she sat straight up and beat her pillow with both of her fists. Berry jumped up out of bed.

"What's going on, Sugar-ins? You're gonna beat de feathers clean out of dat pillow!"

Sue Ellen's body became limp, as she placed her face on the pillow and began to cry. Berry reached for his wife, but she pulled away. She was crying deep, soul-wrenching sobs, and her shoulders heaved.

"May de Lord help us Sue Ellen. What kind of woe has we got now? What's come upon us now? Has you got an ailment?"

"No I ain't got no ailment. You de one dats got de woe."

"What yo talking bout?" There was surprise in Berry's voice.

"I'm talking bout finding de chile dat belongs to yo and Missus Isabelle! Dat's what I'm talking bout, Berry!"

"What? When and where?" That was all Berry could say.

"You ain't gonna believe dis, but Misses Callie is yer child," Sue Ellen cried.

"What on earth is yo talking bout, Sugar-ins?" Berry stood up and rubbed the top of his head.

Sue Ellen sat up in bed. "I saw de birthmark! I saw it today! Dat same birthmark dat all my chillun's wear!"

Berry said nothing. He simply looked off into the distance for a long moment. Then he said, "I'm not de only man in our family wit' dat birthmark, so don' go getting your horse befo' yer cart, Sue Ellen."

CHAPTER TWENTY-SEVEN

Sue Ellen thought things over for a few days and began to settle down some. She decided that it would be best to ask Callie some questions. Callie had talked about her parents. She had said she was the daughter of a traveling preacher. Well, maybe she truly was, but where had she got the birthmark? Had the preacher's wife jumped the fence? Well, it was time she figured things out. The suspense was taking a toll on her. She had been staying away from Callie as much as possible and could tell that Callie was puzzled and hurt by her behavior.

The following morning when Callie walked into the kitchen, she asked Sue Ellen what her plans were for the day.

"I'm bout to go to de garden and cut a fresh bouquet. I never know when Mr. Stephen is coming home. Would yo like to help me, Callie?"

"Oh, yes, Sue Ellen." Callie quickly walked across the room and got her straw hat and garden gloves, which hung on a hook beside the door. The two went outside.

The sun was warm and bright. Butterflies were all over the colorful zinnias. The two ladies began clipping off the flowers and putting them in the handwoven basket Sue Ellen had brought outside with her.

The two worked in silence. Callie couldn't stand the suspense any longer and asked, "Sue Ellen, have you been angry with me?"

"No, chile. I jus' been feeling poorly dese last few days, dat's all."

"What's wrong?" Callie was concerned. *If something happens to her, what will happen to me?* She wondered.

"Jus' de change, I guess, jus' de change." Sue Ellen straightened her hat and continued cutting off the flowers to put in the basket.

"I hope you feel better soon. You look very tired," Callie said.

"I am tired, Callie. dat porch swing sho does look good to me." As Sue Ellen started toward the porch, she staggered.

"Oh my, Sue Ellen, I'm so sorry you're not feeling well." Callie took her by the arm to steady her. "You must sit down and rest. I'll finish picking the flowers; don't you worry." Callie fussed over Sue Ellen.

"Why don' we both set a spell?" Sue Ellen wiped the sweat off her brow with the sleeve of her dress.

"All right, we will." Callie asked, "Would you like something to drink?"

"If yo don' care, I sho would like a glass of water."

Soon the two were seated on the porch. Callie was in the swing, and Sue Ellen sat in a wicker rocker. Sue Ellen took off her bonnet and began fanning herself with it. "I'll bet it's good to be back home, ain't it?"

"Yes, this is the most beautiful place I've ever seen! And I actually feel as if I belong here," Callie said in a wistful voice.

"I know yo love dis place, but how could it feel more like home to yo dan your other home? How can dat be? Sue Ellen asked.

"I feel at peace here with you and Berry. I feel safe," Callie said in a soft voice.

"Don' sounds much like yer home was too happy, Callie. Was yer preacher daddy rough on yo? Sometime preachers are like dat wit' their chillun's."

"No, my father was the kindest man I've ever known."

Sue Ellen couldn't help but breathe a sigh of relief when Callie referred to the preacher as her father.

"Den why don' yo ever go for a visit?" Sue Ellen asked.

"My father is kind, but my mother and sister were mean to me." Callie dropped her head. She really didn't want to talk about her past, and thinking back brought her too much pain.

"Why?" Sue Ellen kept pushing.

Callie continued to stare at the porch floor, and then she began to speak. "Because I'm a gypsy! Malcolm is not my real father. But he's the only father I know. He raised me. I'm a gypsy."

"How do yo know dat?" Sue Ellen was now sitting on the edge of her seat.

"My sister told me." Callie nervously began running splayed fingers through her hair.

"Yo ain't never seen yer real daddy?" Sue Ellen ask.

"Not to my knowledge. I'm still searching for my mother and father. Stephen said he would help me."

"Well, if anybody can find dem, Mr. Stephen can, specially if dey are gypsies!"

"Stephen doesn't know I'm a gypsy. I was afraid he wouldn't want me if he knew who I really am."

"Den how's he gonna find them?" Where is he gonna to start?"

Sue Ellen could have told Callie about Stephen's gypsy heritage, but she had learned long ago to keep her mouth out of white folks' business. Besides that, she had all she could handle on her plate today.

"I have a clue. It's the only link I have to my real mother. I have two pieces of jewelry that belonged to her," Callie said. No sooner were these words were out of her mouth than she wondered why she had told Sue Ellen all of this. She had kept it a secret for so long.

"Can I see dat jewelry, chile?" Sue Ellen asked.

Reluctantly Callie left the porch, went to her room, and got the small, drawstring bag that held her jewelry. When she was back outside, she sat down on the swing beside Sue Ellen. She took the jewelry out of the bag and placed it in Sue Ellen's hand.

Sue Ellen quickly recognized the necklace and the ring. Yes, she had seen this jewelry many, many times. This was the final proof that Callie was her husband's child.

CHAPTER TWENTY-EIGHT

Early the following morning, Sue Ellen and Berry nervously stood outside Callie's bedroom door. The door was slightly ajar. Berry began to slowly open the door wider, holding his breath all the while, hoping the hinges wouldn't creak and wake her up. He breathed a sigh of relief when the door was finally open. He stood quietly as he looked down at Callie as she slept. Callie was sleeping on her side, one hand under the side of her face. Her long, black hair was spread wildly over her pillow. A lock of her hair fell across her face.

The longer Berry stood and looked at Callie, the more emotion he felt. Soon tear drops began to form in his eyes and run down his cheeks. *What if this young girl is Missus Isabelle's child? Not just Isabelle's child, but mine and Missus Isabelle's child*, he thought.

Everyone had known about Missus Isabelle's pain and sorrow as she searched for her missing child. Since everyone thought that John Bradford had fathered this child, no one knew of the pain and constant sorrow that was in Berry's heart over the child he had fathered and lost. Many times he had looked at his and Sue Ellen's children and wondered if his other child was dead or alive. He wondered if she was hungry or being mistreated.

In his own way, he had also searched for her by listening to lots of conversations, looking into stranger's faces, looking for a half-breed who might look like him or Missus Isabelle. He did this many times, looking for a clue, any clue, that would lead him to his missing child, a child he realized he could never claim even if he saw her being mistreated. He could at least see that she was somehow reunited with her mother. Sue Ellen said that she had seen the identifying birthmark. If it was true that Callie was his missing child, then he had been with her all this time. God had answered his prayers. Praise the Lord!

When Sue Ellen saw Berry's shoulders shaking with sobs, she whispered, Get on out of dare, Berry." She pulled at his arm. When Callie began to stir in her sleep, Berry quickly closed the door, and the two scurried down the hallway.

When they stopped at the end of the hall, Berry said with pride in his voice, "She's a pretty little thang, ain't she? But I still don' know if she's mine; I ain't seen de birthmark yet."

"She ain't going to show yo her fanny!" Sue Ellen said with jealousy in her voice. "Jus' cause her mama showed yo her fanny, don' mean she will!"

When Berry realized that Sue Ellen was jealous, he said, "This sho is hard on yo, ain't it, Sugar-ins?" He put his arm around her shoulder. "She ain't nowhere near as pretty as our chillun. She's got too much white blood in her. Her lips are too thin, and her nose is too skinny

Sue Ellen smiled. "It's all right, Berry. I don' hold nothing against yo no more. It's too late for dat."

This was the second time Sue Ellen had told her husband about Callie's birthmark. Only the first time, her name had been Jane. Both times had been very painful for her. She was trying very hard to overcome the anger and the jealousy she felt. She still couldn't bear to even think about Berry lying with another woman! It simply tore her heart out.

After she had talked to Callie and seen the jewelry, it had taken Sue Ellen a few days to calm down. One part of her wanted Callie to leave and get out of their lives, but the other part wanted to take her in her arms and comfort her. She now understood all those looks of pain and loneliness she'd seen in Callie's eyes. She also loved Callie almost as much as she loved her own children. Over the years she had heard of Missus Isabelle's quest for her missing child, and that her health had gone down, and that she was grieving herself to death. She had also heard about John's death. Well, that wasn't such a bad thing!

Sue Ellen's thoughts went back to the sorrows she remembered seeing. She had seen slaves grieving when their babies were taken from their arms and sold to another master. She did have some sympathy for Callie. No, she couldn't be cruel and vengeful. She must forgive Berry and move on. After all, someday when she died, she wanted to go to heaven. She wanted to hear the rustle of the angel's wings. The good book plainly said, and she had read it many times, if you are holding any hate in your heart against anyone, then you can't get through the pearly gates. Oh, how she wanted to go through those gates someday!

The next day in the kitchen, Sue Ellen gave Berry a small, woven basket covered with a red- and white-checkered piece of oilcloth. "Here's yer lunch, Berry. It's yer lucky day. There's a piece of steak, de size of a plate in dare and a piece of praline pie. I bought de steak thinking Mr. Stephen would be home. When he didn't make it home, I decided we sho better eat it befo' it ruins. I'll have to make myself eat dat for my midday meal, too." She smiled.

When Berry opened the door to leave for work, Sue Ellen said, "Tell you what. I'll walk wit' you part of de way to yer work."

As the two walked along Berry said, "Sho' is a beautiful morning. Listen to de birds singing. Yo know, Callie can sing as beautiful as any bird I've ever heard!"

There was pride in his voice. Callie had performed in the club where he worked. In fact he had played the harmonica a few times as she sang. People were talking about her singing; she was becoming very popular in the short time she had been in New Orleans. Then he saw the hurt look in Sue Ellen's face.

"Sue Ellen," he said, taking her by the hand and squeezing it. "I'm sorry. I sho is sorry dat I did yo wrong!" Berry was apologizing for the hundredth time.

"Berry, I loves yer old black hide, and de good Lord made us black. I feel we've done de best we can wit' our lives. It ain't been easy, but we can' take what happened out on dat child. I'm proud of her, too. She may or may not be yers but I believe she's yers."

"Lawdy Lawd! Sue Ellen, yo sho is a fine woman, and dis old black man loves you." He gave her a playful pat on her bottom.

She looked at him with a twinkle in her eye. "Don' yo go starting something' yo can' finish."

CHAPTER TWENTY-NINE

After singing her heart out for the audience, Callie was coming off stage. As she walked toward her dressing room, Berry hurriedly came up behind her. He tapped her on the shoulder, and when she turned around to see who was trying to get her attention, Berry said excitedly, "Missus Callie, there's a lady in de audience who would like to meet yo! Do you have time to talk wit' her?"

"Berry, who is she?" Callie asked.

"Her name is Missus Isabelle Bradford," Berry replied.

"Why does she want to meet me?" Callie questioned.

"She said dat she is a fan of yers and dat she could help yo further yer career."

"Well, can she?" Callie asked sharply.

She was tired and hot, and her nerves had been on edge since Stephen had arrived home, because he had been so withdrawn from her. The few times their eyes had met and held for a few seconds, she could see the lonesome, longing and pain that she, too, felt. After those special moments passed, they would ignore each other again.

When they talked to each other, it was if they were two strangers talking, polite but showing their deep feelings for each other.

"I don' know. Do yo want me to send her away?"

Berry dropped his head as he talked to Callie. Her sharp words were breaking his heart. *Reckon what she would say if she knew that I'm her pa*, Berry wondered. He would never dare tell his beautiful and talented daughter that she was the pride of his life. No, for her sake, he had to hide in the shadows, but hopefully he could live out the rest of his days close enough to her that he could watch her live her life. Yes, as beautiful as she was, she would marry and have children. Berry shook his head slightly and smiled at the thought of his and Isabelle's grandchildren.

Callie saw the look of pain that crossed Berry's face when she spoke to him so roughly. She felt ashamed of herself. Berry had always been so kind and good to her and everyone else. "No Berry, please don't send her away" she pleaded.

Then in a softer voice, she said, "I'm sorry I was rude to you. I wouldn't hurt you for the world. I couldn't have made it all these months without you and Sue Ellen. I love you both." Tears were running down their cheeks as the father and daughter embraced each other.

Berry pulled away from her first and breathed a deep sigh of relief. What would he have done if she had refused to meet Missus Isabelle? Sue Ellen and Berry had met with Isabelle a few days earlier and talked things over. Isabelle just couldn't wait any longer to meet Callie, the child she had brought into this world many years ago, also known as her daughter Jane. She had been going to every one of Callie's shows since she had found out who she was.

"Berry, you look as if you're in a trance. I didn't mean to be hateful!" Callie took a glove off her left hand and wiped the tears from her face. "Berry, please go and tell her that I will meet her at a table on the balcony." She glanced at a clock on the wall. "I'll be there in thirty minutes."

She smiled and began to walk away, but pausing, she turned around and said, "Tell the waiter I would like a tall, frosted glass of lemonade when I get there."

CHAPTER THIRTY

Callie walked onto the balcony. She paused and looked to her right and then to her left, looking for a signal from a lady named Isabelle. Soon a waiter motioned her to a table, where a middle-aged lady was sitting alone. She smiled and motioned for Callie to come to the table. Isabelle had taken a long look at Callie when she stood and looked around on the balcony. She saw a resemblance to Berry's side of the family. Something about the way she carried herself or the way she lifted her head to the side reminded her of Berry's mother. In spite of the fact that she was a slave, she had carried herself with dignity and poise.

Callie walked toward Isabelle, and Isabelle was overcome with emotion as she recognized this beautiful young lady who was once her small, baby girl. She was feeling a strong urge to run to her and tell her who she was and smother her with kisses. Perhaps even dance with joy!

I mustn't do anything embarrassing or foolish, she thought. She had promised Berry and Sue Ellen that she would say nothing until she was sure, beyond a shadow of a doubt, that this girl was her lost child. Isabelle actually had to bite her tongue to keep from shouting for the joy at the moment. *Oh, how long my arms have been empty! Empty and aching to hold my only child!*

The waiter who had seated Callie had a white towel draped across his left arm and a frosty, tall glass of lemonade sitting on a round tray in his right hand. He asked, "Would either of you ladies care to try one of our delicate pastries?"

"As a matter of fact, I believe I'll have one. I'm hungry." Thoughtfully Callie placed her index finger on her chin. "I think I'll have a bowl of shrimp gumbo, but later I will surely try your pastries."

"Yes, ma'am! I'll bet singing as beautiful as you do works up an appetite," the waiter said.

"I'll have the same," Isabelle said.

The waiter looked at her and smiled as he backed away from the table. *Yes, I'm hungry. Since I talked to Berry three days ago, I haven't been able to eat much*, Isabelle thought.

Berry and Sue Ellen had come to her hotel room. She had been reading and had fallen asleep in her chair when she'd heard the knock at the door. *Who on earth is knocking on my door at this hour?* She had wondered. She had dropped the book on the floor and stood up to answer the door. To her surprise, there were Berry and Sue Ellen. She was very happy to see them again. She opened her arms, and she and Sue Ellen had hugged. After the embrace, Isabelle had said, "It's just wonderful to see you two again. But why are you here this late in the evening?"

"Missus Isabelle, we are here on some unfinished business. Could we jus' come in yer room?" Berry had said in a gentlemanly fashion as he stood holding his hat in his hands.

"Well, yes, yes, of course." Isabelle had stepped back to let the two enter. *What could be wrong?* Isabelle had wondered. She followed and sat down on the edge of the bed.

Sue Ellen could see that Isabelle was disturbed by their visit. The two hadn't seen each other but a few times since Sue Ellen had seen the birthmark years ago. The few times they had seen each other had been awkward moments for the each of them.

"Missus Isabelle," Sue Ellen had said as she went to the edge of the bed and placed her hand on Isabelle's shoulder. "Don' be skerd or get yo'self in a tizzy, but we have come wid' some good news." She had paused and looked at Berry and said, "Yo tell her, Berry."

Berry had cleared his throat, shuffled his feet on the floor, and begun, while turning his hat around and around in his hands. "Missus Isabelle, my sweet Sue Ellen has found yo chile. De one yo have been looking for all dese years."

"What!" That was all Isabelle could say as she had looked back and forth from one to the other. She couldn't believe what she had heard.

"Dat's right, Misses Isabelle. Yo chile is de singer da sings at da palace."

"How do you know?"

"I jus' know. I saw de birthmark again," Sue Ellen replied. Sue Ellen's eyes narrowed as jealousy began to overcome her. She fought down these feelings as she watched the color drain from Isabelle's face.

"Well, for heaven's sake! How did you see the birthmark? It was on her fanny!" Isabelle was anxious and scared as she stood up and began pacing the floor, wringing her hands.

"Sue Ellen works for Mr. Stephen, and Callie, yo daughter, lives wit' Mr. Stephen," Berry continued as if Isabelle hadn't said a thing. "Sue Ellen was helping her get dressed, and she saw de birthmark." Berry still couldn't say aloud "our daughter" when referring to Callie.

"Callie? Is that the name she goes by now?" Isabelle began to feel faint and sat back down on the edge of the bed. *This is all so confusing. How could this be? My child has been with familiar people all this time! Is this girl really my daughter?* She'd had so many disappointments in the past, so it was hard for her to believe this news.

Callie—or Jane, if you will—was now sitting across a wrought-iron table facing Isabelle. Her search had finally ended; she knew that she had truly found her baby! Her spirit was singing songs of thanksgiving and joy. Here was her baby all grown up. With the little, turned-up nose, the full mouth, and the olive skin. Her talent as a singer was inherited from her father.

The waiter arrived at their table with a round tray held high in one hand. After he served the food, he took a slight bow before leaving the table. Callie stirred her lemonade before removing the long teaspoon from the glass. She looked across the table at Isabelle and then asked, "Have we met before?"

"Perhaps we have. Isabelle said, and thought. *Yes we first met on the day you were born.*

"What brings you to New Orleans?

I'm searching for my daughter," Isabelle said as she picked up a spoon. The spoon made a clicking sound against the soup bowl as she stirred with a slight tremble in her hand.

"Searching for someone you love must be the loneliest feeling in the world." There was a wistful sound in Callie's voice.

"What do you mean, Callie? Have you ever lost anyone?" Isabelle leaned forward in her chair.

"I just said it must be awful for you."

Callie looked around the balcony at the wrought-iron rails that edged the two-story building. Looking down on the street, she saw men lighting the gas streetlamps, trying to shake the lonely feeling that overcame her.

Isabelle saw the sadness in Callie's face. Changing the subject, and pausing to take in a spoonful of her soup, Isabelle then continued, "I admire your talent so much. I'm just curious as to where you were trained."

"Well, actually I suppose most of my training was from my father, Malcolm Hatfield. He's a preacher. My sister and I sang in church as far back as I can remember." Callie didn't want to go into the time she had spent in the New Orleans School of Music. Even though Mr. Moore had taught her a lot, it still made her stomach churn thinking about him. She certainly did not want to talk about him.

"How interesting. Being the daughter of an evangelist must have been an interesting life. Did he pastor a large congregation?" Isabelle asked, wanting to learn all she possibly could about the beautiful, young girl sitting before her.

Callie dabbed her lips with a napkin. "No. My father preached anywhere he felt the Lord led him. We didn't have very much money, but he always kept food on the table and a roof over our heads."

"I can see that you are very fond of your father. I'm sure he is very proud of you. You are a beautiful and talented person."

Isabelle's voice broke she wiped her eyes with her napkin. *So many horrible things could have happened. Things I once imagined might be happening to you. I haven't had a moment of peace since you disappeared from my life. Thank God, Malcolm found you. He was a guardian angel send from God. I truly believe that.*

CHAPTER THIRTY-ONE

Stephen was sitting on a stool in the bar of the restaurant. He had chosen a seat at the darkest end of the bar. He intended to watch Callie from where he sat. He'd been there for several hours, slowly sipping glasses of bourbon on the rocks. He realized that he'd been drinking heavily, but the bourbon spread warmth throughout his body and helped him cope with Callie's coldness toward him.

No, I'm not spying on her. Yes, I am, he thought. He was confused as to what had happened to her. *Why had she changed?* He was trying desperately to uncover this mystery. He'd been watching her closely; sometimes he even felt guilty for his actions, but he strongly felt that if there was another man in her life, he would bow out gracefully. From the first time he had laid eyes on her, Stephen had known that he would love her forever. He knew that she was his soul mate, the one God had made especially for him.

"She sho' can sing, can' she?" Berry complimented Callie as he wiped off the bar in front of Stephen.

"Yes, yes, she can," Stephen said, startled. He sat straight up as if Berry had startled him although he had known that Berry was cleaning tables tonight. Stephen had been watching him earlier and had noticed that he had lingered and watched Callie singing every time he passed theater door.

"Why don' you go inside de theater and get yo'self a seat, Mr. Stephen? Yo can' see Missus Callie from here. Yo been sitting here a long time." Berry picked up an ashtray and emptied it into the trash can underneath the counter.

"I'm fine sitting here, Berry, just fine." Stephen took another sip of bourbon. True, he wasn't close enough to the stage to see Callie, but her sweet voice carried very well, inside the theater and out to the street. He watched the people stop on the street just to hear her sing. Oh, how he loved to hear her sing! He could hear a longing in her voice as she belted out her songs. *I wonder what she's longing and searching for; I wish it was me*, he thought.

When the show ended, Callie left the stage, and Stephen left the bar. He was hoping to get a glance of her before she went to her dressing room. He began to walk toward the theater door. When he saw her coming in his direction, he quickly stepped back into the shadows. He watched as she walked through the restaurant and onto the balcony and was detained by some fans. This distraction allowed him to get back to the bar without her seeing him.

"What's going on, Berry? Is she singing again?" Stephen asked Berry. Stephen knew that Berry watched Callie closely and assumed that he was only concerned with her safety.

"Nothing, Mr. Stephen. She's jus' going to meet Missus Isabelle Bradford on de veranda," Berry said as he looked in Callie's direction and continued to shine the shot glass he held in his hand.

Soon curiosity got the best of Stephen. He felt that he had given her enough time to be seated and dropped a gold coin on the bar to cover the price of his drinks. With a glass of bourbon in his hand, Stephen eased his way toward the veranda and paused to watch as her fans were stopping her and asking her to sign autographs. They were handing her pieces of paper, envelopes, and their cooling fans as well. She was talking, laughing, and being very kind to everyone.

Oh, how he missed the old Callie and that bubbly personality. What had gone wrong? Living in the same house with her had been difficult. She went out of her way to avoid him, but he could still smell her sweet perfume and hear her softly singing as she went around the house helping Sue Ellen. Most of the time when they ate their meals together, her coldness was like a wall of ice between them. Stephen had begun to deliberately stay away at mealtimes. He just couldn't take much more of her coldness. When he was home, she stayed out of sight. It made him sad as he tried to figure out what had gone wrong.

She must have found someone else. He took another swallow of his drink and walked around the restaurant. He talked to old friends and a business acquaintance while he tried to regain his composure. When he felt that Callie had had time to be seated, he walked to the veranda, and there she was, sitting at the table with Isabelle Bradford.

Mrs. Isabelle must be a fan of hers, Stephen thought.

CHAPTER THIRTY-TWO

Isabelle and Callie looked up in surprise when Stephen came over to their table.

"What a wonderful surprise! Two of my favorite ladies together," he said, and they offered him their hands. He kissed Isabelle's first and then Callie's. His lips lingered longer on Callie's hand, and the touch of his lips sent shivers up her spine. She could smell the aroma of his cologne, as well as the smell of bourbon and expensive cigars. She was so overwhelmed by his presence and his manly smell that she was almost speechless.

"Stephen, what a nice surprise! It's so good to see you again!" Isabelle said.

"It's wonderful to see you as well, Mrs. Isabelle," Stephen said. Turning to Callie, he said, "Callie, I enjoyed your performance tonight."

"Thank you, Stephen. I didn't realize that you were in the audience."

"I was sitting at the bar. I wouldn't miss any opportunity to hear you sing. You sang beautifully."

"She certainly did sing well tonight, Stephen. Why don't you sit with us for a while and reminisce about old times?" Isabelle asked.

"How long have you two known each other?" Callie asked. It was obvious to her that they had been friends for a long time because of the way they seemed to be overjoyed to see one another.

"I've known Stephen since he was a small boy. I knew his family very well. Do you remember when I came to your campground early one morning and Mama Dora took me into her wagon? You were asleep; she woke you up and told you to go outside," Isabelle said, tears rolling down her cheeks because she had gone there hoping Mama Dora would give her something to abort this beautiful, talented lady who was sitting in front of her.

"No, Mrs. Isabelle. I don't remember you coming into our camp, but I remember seeing you and your husband when we were camping on your land. You two were very gracious to allow our tribe to camp on your land; not everyone was that gracious. I believe I will sit down with you two ladies. It's good to see you once again, Mrs. Isabelle. I like to reminisce about old times and traveling with my family. You and your husband always welcomed our gypsy tribe," Stephen said as he pulled a chair out to sit down.

Gypsy! Callie's eyes opened wide. *Is he kidding?* She wondered. *If he's telling the truth? We might actually be related.* Callie remembered Lydia's words when she had said, "You're nothing but a dirty gypsy."

Stephen said, "This may come as a shock to you, Callie, but I'm part-gypsy. My mother was a full-blooded gypsy, and I spent most of my childhood traveling with my mother's people. We roamed from place to place and often spent months on Mrs. Isabelle's land." Stephen nervously tapped his fingers on the table.

"My, my! How exciting!" Callie was very interested in what Stephen had to say. "What happened to your mother?"

"Sadly she passed away years ago." Sadness came into his voice.

"She was a beautiful woman," Isabelle said.

"I can barely remember her, but the gypsies say that my cousin Alicia looks a lot like her. I suppose that's why I'm so fond of her," Stephen said. Alicia was the girl Callie had seen Stephen hugging, which had greatly upset her.

"I haven't seen Alicia since she was a small child. She was very pretty and full of life back then," Isabelle said.

"She still is. In fact she came by just a few months ago. I found her at the farmer's market. She was buying taffeta and lace for the women in the tribe. She wanted to see our home. We drove out there, but she only stayed long enough to refresh herself and then said she must be on her way. I tried to talk her into staying a few days, but she wouldn't hear of it. Callie, I wish you could have met her. You would have enjoyed her company," Stephen said.

It took a few moments for Callie to sort out all of this information. *Alicia is his cousin! I've been so wrong!* Callie began to laugh with a hint of hysteria. The relief was so great. "Oh, Stephen, I would love to meet your cousin!" She reached over the table and placed her hand over his. She squeezed his hand tightly, like she never wanted to let go.

Stephen didn't know what to think about Callie's sudden change of behavior. As he sat there with Callie holding hands, he saw that she had suddenly turned back into the sweet, loving person he had once known. *What was said that changed her?* Stephen thought it through, and he realized it must have had something to do with Alicia. He remembered that Callie had changed the day he had brought Alicia to his home. That was the night she wouldn't come downstairs and eat dinner with him. She moved out soon afterward.

She must have seen me with Alicia, Stephen thought.

Callie was greatly relieved to hear about Alicia, but then a thought entered her head. *What if I am a gypsy? What if I am somehow Stephen's cousin as well?* All these thoughts and all the good news were confusing her.

"Well, Stephen, it's possible that I'm a gypsy as well. You two might as well know that my stepfather rescued me from the bayou when I was just a baby. There was a gypsy campground nearby, and the family thought I could possibly be a gypsy. But since I was wearing expensive jewelry, they had their doubts about where I came from. I've spent a long time looking for my family, but I really don't expect to find out who I really am," Callie said.

Stephen and Callie looked at Isabelle when they heard her quick intake of breath. Callie saw her sway forward in her chair and the color drain from her face. Stephen quickly wet his napkin with cold lemonade and held it to her brow.

Isabelle was overwhelmed with emotion because she had promised Berry that she wouldn't tell Callie she was her daughter until she was sure beyond a shadow of a doubt. Well, there was certainly no doubt anymore. She had truly found her daughter. The words Mama Dora had spoken years ago came to her mind: "This unborn child you are carrying and my Stephen's lives will be intertwined in the future." It was very obvious to Isabelle that the two loved each other. She couldn't let Callie go on any longer thinking that the man she loved was her cousin.

"Are you all right, Mrs. Isabelle?" Callie asked.

"I've never been better, Callie. I have something to tell you. I hope you will be as happy about this as I am. You see, Callie, I'm your mother!"

CHAPTER THIRTY-THREE

Callie was sleeping peacefully. The early morning sunshine flooded her room through the tall, double windows, and a soft breeze crept through the thin, airy curtains across her bed. She was resting well, having peaceful dreams, as a slight smile played on her lips.

She awoke to the sound of a rooster crowing. Her heart beat rapidly, she quickly sat upright in bed and clutched the covers tightly to her chest. *What on earth is that noise?* She wondered as she listened intently. After a few fear-filled moments, she realized that it was only a rooster. Apparently he had decided to claim the awakening of a new day underneath her bedroom window.

After breathing a deep sigh of relief, she began to look around the unfamiliar room. She looked at the faded wallpaper covered with yellow roses and pale-green leaves; she had been told this was her home, but she didn't feel at home in this large, ornate, iron bed with feather mattress. *Why does this room look so strange to me?*

She realized that it seemed strange because it had been late when she and Stephen had arrived at the plantation. The room

197

hadn't looked the same in the lamp- and candlelight. She was at her real mother's home, the house where she was born. She smiled when the thought crossed her mind. *Why, I could very well have been conceived on this very bed I'm lying in!* She let out a deep, peaceful sigh. There was joy and contentment in her heart for the first time in her life. She couldn't remember ever having these types of feelings. She couldn't remember ever having feelings of belonging. She had felt some security with Malcolm and Sarah, but somehow she had never felt as if she belonged with them. Lydia had always made sure of that. Hopefully all of those hard times were behind her now.

With joy and a song in her heart, Callie stood up on the floor. The carpet felt cool and soft as it tickled the bottoms of her feet. She slipped into her robe and then went to her trunk to choose a dress to wear today and decided on a cream, light-weight dress trimmed in green ribbons. After putting it on, she walked over to the dresser and looked into the mirror. Enjoying how she looked, she sang a happy tune.

She lifted her hair off her shoulders and playfully turned around and around in front of the mirror. When she began to brush her hair, she realized that even the reflection of her own image had changed. The person she saw had found her identity. The old Callie was gone, as were the sorrow always in her eyes and the downcast look on her face.

They had all been replaced by the twinkle in her eyes. Her face now showed the confidence of a woman who knew where she belonged and how much she was loved. Callie became very anxious to see the house and grounds that her mother had told her would someday belong to her. She hurriedly dabbed on some face powder and allowed her hair to hang loose and free.

As Callie descended the winding stairway, she could smell the aroma of a country breakfast being prepared. The smell of rich, roasted coffee greeted her once she stepped off the stair landing. She followed the smell to the kitchen and heard Stephen's laughter as she entered. His hair was tussled, his shirt wrinkled, and he was in his socks. When he saw her entering the room, he stood up and walked over to her. He put his arms around her waist.

"Well, sleepyhead! Did you finally decide to get up?" he teased her as he gently placed a kiss on the tip of her nose.

"Yes, Stephen. I slept very well."

She pulled away from him, raised her arms above her head, stretched her body, and yawned. Stephen took her hand and led her to the small table in the center of the room. When seated, she noticed a black lady standing at the stove with her back to them. The woman was putting fresh slices of country ham into a skillet. The meat sizzled and popped when it hit the hot skillet, sending off an appetizing aroma throughout the room, causing her mouth to water and her stomach to growl. From the things her mother told her, Callie assumed this was Ripley, the black lady who had been with the Bradford family for a long time.

"Mr. Stephen, don' yo need more coffee?" Ripley asked as she picked up the coffee pot. When she turned around from the stove, Callie saw sweat glistening on her face. When she saw Callie, Ripley eyes lit up with love. A huge, toothless smile spread across her face.

"Lowdy, Lowd! Miss Jane!"

Ripley hand began to tremble so much that Callie was afraid she might spill the hot coffee on her hand. Callie walked quickly across the room and gently took the pot from her hand. She sat the coffeepot back on the stove and then turned to Ripley. Tears streamed from Ripley eyes and down her dear, wrinkled face, a face that had been wrinkled by worry as well as years gone by.

"De Lord Jesus has been mighty kind to us, specially me. I thank yo, Lord, for letting me see dat baby I rocked in my arms so long ago all grown-up and so beautiful." Ripley looked up at the ceiling as if she were seeing straight into the heavens, picked up the tail of her apron, and wiped her eyes and nose.

"I take it that you must have been my nurse when I was a baby," Callie said.

Ripley turned her back to Callie and hung her head. "Yes, 'um, I was, and I'll always blame myself for yo disappearance, Miss Jane."

"Why? Why would you blame yourself?" Callie placed her hand on Ripley shoulder and gently turned her around to face her. Even though this was the first time Callie had met her, she had a deep respect for Ripley, because her mother had told her what a wonderful person she was and how faithful and loyal she had been throughout the years.

"'Cause I left you alone wit' Master John. I've had to watch your mother suffer all dese years as she searched for yo." Her voice was filled with guilt and shame as if she had committed a crime, blaming herself for Callie's disappearance. Now that Callie had returned, Ripley was at last laying down a heavy burden.

"But John was my father. What was so wrong with him taking care of me?" Callie was becoming extremely confused and wondered what was going on.

Stephen pushed his chair away from the table. He went to the two ladies and placed an arm around each of their shoulders. "Now, ladies, this should be a joyous morning; let's allow this day to be a day of new beginnings. As we gypsies would say, 'It's time to travel on.' Move on to another summit in our lives. Let's leave our yesterday far behind and rejoice in today."

Ripley smiled a sad smile as she straightened her back and wiped the remaining tears from her face with the back of her hand. Stephen led Callie back to the kitchen table, pulled out a chair with a bow and the sweep of his arms, and said, "Please be seated, my love."

Then he planted a kiss on her forehead. "You two ladies be seated. I'll finish up breakfast and then serve you all."

Stephen was very tenderhearted. He couldn't bear to see all the pain and guilt that was written all over this dear black woman's face. Maybe this small act of kindness could somehow ease some of the pain. At least it could let it be known that no one blamed her for that fearful night when Callie had disappeared into the unknown.

"But I'm gonna make red eye gravy and eggs to go wit' de ham and biscuits," Ripley protested. Everything was becoming very strange to her; most of all was this handsome, young man treating her as an equal, which had never happened to her before. It was all so baffling.

"I can make red eye gravy," Stephen protested.

"Don't make any for me. I'm not very hungry this morning. If I could just have a cup of coffee, that will be good enough for me," Callie said as she began to wring her hands under the table. She had suddenly lost her appetite. Too many mysteries and too much confusion had caused her stomach to feel tied up in knots.

Stephen pulled a chair out for Ripley. After she was seated, he brought two steaming cups of coffee on a wooden tray and sat it before them. Knowing what she liked, he fixed Callie's coffee with just the right amount of cream and sugar. He said, "I love this place! I've been here many times before.

"I doubt dat, Mr. Stephen." Ripley shook her head and began to stir cream into her cup. "Yo being from Orleans and a seafaring man. Maybe yo dreamed of dis place sometime or nother."

Stephen laughed. "I've not always been a sea captain or in New Orleans. I have mixed blood. My mother was a full-blooded gypsy; I'm proud to say I am half-gypsy. I was raised by my maternal gypsy grandparents. We were drifters, movers, and I learned at an early age to value my freedom. Thankfully I learned to have a business head on my shoulders from my father.

"As a child," Stephen continued, and he looked off into the distance, as if recalling a beautiful memory, "my tribe would load down the caravan, hitch up the horses, and round up the cattle, sheep, and chickens, and then off we would go to seek a new adventure and see what was on the other side of the mountain, living one day at a time. What a life." He let out a sigh.

"You's a gypsy?" Ripley was shocked, even though he had mentioned it previously. She had been so overwhelmed with happiness when she had seen Callie that she hadn't even paid much attention to what he was saying.

"Yes, I am." Stephen, taking it as a compliment, was proud of his heritage.

"What tribe?" Ripley rolled her wide-open eyes and thought, *was he one of the gypsies who took our sweet Jane away? It shore is strange; she left with gypsies, and now she's been brought back by one.* Her back stiffened as she wondered about the strange coincidence.

"Tomsk and Mama Dora were our leaders and my grandparents."

Ripley was so shocked at Stephen's revelation that she sat her coffee cup down so abruptly that hot coffee splashed on the table. She said, "Den yo have been here befo', dat tribe came, 'bout every summer. We looked forward to dem coming; even ole, hateful John liked to see dem. Cause they was good and honest people. They do anything they could do to help out."

Then Ripley looked at Callie. "It was one of dem mean gypsy tribes who took yo away!"

CHAPTER THIRTY-FOUR

The screen door squeaked when Callie opened it. She paused a moment before going out onto the porch. She wanted a few minutes to familiarize herself with the house and grounds. As she looked around with curiosity, nothing seemed familiar. She must have been terribly young when someone took her away from her home and family, because nothing struck her as memorable.

She went to the edge of the porch; everything looked freshly groomed. This pleased her because her mother had told her that the yards and gardens were grown-up and not in as good of shape as they once were. Just the thought of her mother going through all the trouble of having it cleaned up just for her and Stephen put a smile on her face.

A warm feeling came over Callie. She thought about the bond and warmth she had seen between Lydia and the other woman she had called her mother. She shook her head, as if trying to clear the negative thoughts that seemed to be taking over. She smiled and walked to the back porch. She stepped off the porch and saw her mother sitting several feet away. She was in the flower garden, sitting on an ornate iron chair. Her hands were resting on the ornate table in front of her. The table was set with a coffeepot, cups, napkins, cream pitcher, and a sugar bowl, which sat on a silver tray.

Isabelle was wearing a long blue dress and blue, quilted satin slippers. Her hair was brushed and pulled to the back, tied with a white ribbon. This must be the faceless woman Callie had seen so often in her dreams. The one her very soul ached to be close to. Oh, how they both had suffered, but by the grace of God, perhaps the suffering was over. Hopefully she would be with her mother for a long time.

Isabelle seemed to be in deep thought, with a distant look in her eyes. The deep lines in her face looked relaxed, making her appear a bit younger than she was. For a few moments, Callie hesitated about whether or not to disturb her mother's apparently peaceful and serene moment.

There are so many unanswered questions I need answered to know who I really am. I've heard so many stories, and Ripley has only added to my confusion, telling me I was kidnapped by the gypsies. Perhaps I'm like Stephen and have mixed blood; perhaps that's why we have understood, respected, and loved one another as much as we do. Unknown to us, has this been the force or power that has contributed to our love for each other at first sight?

It suddenly came to Callie's mind that when she had been reunited with Isabelle, Isabelle had referred to John as her husband but never as her father. *I simply must know the truth.* She began to walk toward her mother.

Isabelle caught Callie's movement out of the corner of her eye; she turned her head and saw Callie coming toward her. She smiled when she stood up and began walking toward her daughter with her arms outstretched; they embraced when they met. Then holding hands, they turned and headed toward the iron table where Isabelle had been sitting. Each time Isabelle took a step, she stepped with caution, because the soles of her shoes were wearing down.

"My, my! Aren't you quite the early riser! I thought you would sleep a little later since you were so late getting here last night. I hope you and Stephen slept well," Isabelle said after the two were seated and she had poured Callie a cup of coffee.

"Actually, Mother, I'm not an early riser. Being a singer and singing in the theaters I'm often up late hours. I suppose I've adopted the habits of most other stage performers. I indulge myself by sleeping late. Stephen is the early riser." Callie took a sip of coffee. "Actually I planned on sleeping in this morning, but it seems as if your faithful rooster had other plans in mind." Callie laughed.

Isabelle laughed and slapped the table with the palm of her hand. "Well, if that old rooster thinks he's going to disturb my baby, then he's totally wrong! I'll have Ripley wring his neck. He's likely to find himself in a pot of dumplings if he doesn't watch his step!" Isabelle was rolling with laughter.

"Oh, Mother, there's no need to go that far!" Callie shook her head and laughed. *Mother. How strange that word sounds coming off my tongue. How strange and wonderful it is to actually know and be near my real mother. It's still like a dream, but if this is a dream, then I hope I never wake up.* "Mother, this is such a beautiful place. I can't wait to see more of it. I know Stephen will love it also."

"Oh, he's already been out and about," Isabelle said. "But I think he came back and went inside."

"Told you he's an early riser."

"Where is he now? Do you think he would want to join us?"

Callie replied, "I don't think so. The last I saw him he was in the kitchen entertaining Ripley."

"Oh, what a beautiful and glorious day, Callie. I am so happy." Isabelle's voice choked with emotion.

"Yes, it is wonderful, but it seems so unreal. I thank God for this day. I always knew as a child that I wasn't at home, but I never dreamed that my actual home would be so miraculous." Callie looked at all the beauty that surrounded her. She could see several small cabins in the distance and assumed them to have been slave cabins.

"I am sure you must have been like me. I had different pictures in my mind on your birthdays. I always tried to imagine what you looked like However, there was no way I could have ever envisioned such beauty as yours! One must simply see how beautiful you are to appreciate you. Even your pictures on all those billboards don't do you justice."

"Thank you, Mother, but perhaps you're seeing me through a mother's eyes. You know the old saying "we all think our crows are the blackest.'" Callie laughed. "Was the way I looked your biggest surprise?" Callie laughed a bubbly, happy laugh.

"Perhaps. But I suppose your beautiful voice and great talent was definitely a huge surprise," Isabelle said as she looked off into the distance and thought, *I shouldn't have been so surprised. She is Berry's child as well. Berry and his family have always had musical talent. They could dance, sing, and play many musical instruments.*

At an early age, I can remember visiting Willow Grove with my parents. We children would sneak out of the yard and go to the slave quarters to hear the sweet music the Negroes made with their homemade instruments, like the drums, jigs, combs with thin cloth wrapped over them, and of course harmonicas. I loved to hear the sweet, sad songs coming from the tired, weary Negroes. I could hear so much emotion when they sang and played.

Isabelle reached for another sugar cube for her coffee. "Now it's your turn to tell me what surprised you the most."

"Well, I guess having a different name came as a shock and surprise. I'm so accustomed to answering to Callie. It's going to be difficult to answer to Jane, but," Callie said, holding up her index finger, "I'm adapting to my new name. It never occurred to me when I found you that the name I was wearing wouldn't be my real name. I've longed to know who I really am. Now that I actually know, I must get used to this new person, family, and name."

"Oh, darling, let's not worry ourselves about a name; that's the least of our worries. If you wish to be called Callie, then Callie it will be. A name doesn't change you. Whatever name you decide to be called can't change the sweet, wonderful person you are. The only important thing is that we are together again."

Tears of happiness flowed freely down Isabelle's cheeks as she reached across the table and squeezed Callie's hand.

"You're right. Why can't I use both names? I'll keep Callie as my stage name because my fans know me by that name."

"That's fine with me, Jane," Isabelle smiled. "You know, I'm getting hungry. I'm going to ring the bell and have Ripley bring our breakfast."

"No, Mother. I'll go inside and bring it out. Ripley looks tired this morning. Of course this is the first time I can recall seeing her. I don't mind bringing our breakfast out."

Truly Callie didn't want her mother seeing how emotional Ripley was this morning.

"What a kind heart you have," Isabelle said with pride.

CHAPTER THIRTY-FIVE

As Callie walked across the garden toward the house, Isabelle's eyes followed her daughter. She thought, *she's such a kind-hearted young lady, but of course she had no choice; she's mine and Berry's child. I realize I've always been too tenderhearted for my own good.*

Is she a love child? No? Yes, perhaps one might say she is, because Berry and I have always had a deep respect for each other. Our bond is a love for humanity and hatred for that cruelty both of us had fallen victim to from John's evil heart. Jane is the result of human kindness running out of control.

As Callie stepped on the porch, Stephen opened the screen door. He was carrying a platter covered with a white towel. "Ripley decided it's about time you ladies had a tad of breakfast; underneath this simple, white cloth lie the grandest biscuits and country ham you've ever tasted. Speaking of taste, may I sample a kiss from your honey-dipped lips, my fair lady?"

Callie laughed as she stood on her tiptoes and placed a long, lingering kiss on Stephen's lips.

"That's my girl," Stephen said as he held her tightly with one arm, trying to hold the platter steady with the other hand. "Are you ready to go back to the garden and eat breakfast with your mother?"

"I certainly am." Callie's eyes danced with happiness.

As the two walked the garden path side by side, Stephen asked, "Well, did you ask about your father, like you said you were going to?"

"No." Callie hesitated a moment before going on, "No, Stephen, it has been such a beautiful morning for the two of us. I was afraid to spoil it."

"That's a wise decision, my love. I can't remember even seeing you this happy and content. May you always have this much happiness in your heart."

When the two reached the iron table, Stephen placed the covered tray down on the table and then pulled out a chair for Callie. Once she sat down, he took the towel off the platter, exposing the ham and biscuits. On the platter were bowls of homemade peach preserves and a dish of creamy, yellow butter molded into the shape of a rosebud. Stephen filled their coffee cups and placed the napkins on the table.

"All right ladies, you must eat, drink, and get strong." He bowed low, laughing as he straightened up. Callie and Isabelle couldn't keep from laughing as they watched him.

"You seem very happy this morning. Are you this cheery every morning?" Isabelle asked as she picked up a napkin and dabbed the tears of laughter from the corner of her eye.

"Actually I'm just being kind," said Stephen. "I want you both to be comfortable."

"What are your plans? Am I included?" Callie ask and smiled

"Well, if you must know, it is my intention to explore this beautiful plantation."

Callie's heart leaped with joy when she heard the man she loved speak so highly of her mother's lovely estate. She absolutely adored his enthusiasm!

Isabelle was overwhelmed with happiness as she watched the couple sitting in front of her. She could clearly see the love they had for each other, a lasting love that was hard for her to comprehend. This love Callie and Stephen had was the kind of love she had always yearned for yet never received. Isabelle reached for a biscuit and cut it in half, and then she spread creamy butter over it. The butter melted quickly and sank into the hot biscuit. She took a smell bite, then dabbed her mouth with her napkin and then said to Stephen, "I hope you will enjoy yourself. Go to the stables, and saddle up the horse of your choice."

"Thank you so much. I believe I'll take you up on that," Stephen stated as he stood up and looked at the green pasture on the other side of the road. A peaceful feeling came over him as he gazed at the fields. Remembering the days of his youth. When he had roamed these fields with his grandfather and grandmother, Mama Dora and Tomsk.

"It's a small world. I feel a deep connection with this land."

"I'm sure you do Stephen. Your tribe camped here for months at a time. I simply adored your grandmother," Isabelle said.

"Do you remember me, Callie?" Stephen said. As quickly as he asked the question, he was sorry, because he realized that she had probably been taken away too young to remember him.

"No, Stephen. The last time you were here was before Callie was born. But your tribe came back, but you were always with your father when they camped here," Isabelle smiled. Then she looked off in the distance and reminisced about the last time she had seen Stephen. The memory was still so vivid. Jane had leaped in her womb the first time they had met. She recalled Mama Dora's prediction that they would be a part of each others lives somewhere down the road.

"Mrs. Bradford, are you all right?" Stephen asked with concern. She seemed to be in deep thought, almost as if in a trance.

"What?" Isabelle asked. "Oh! Yes, I'm sorry. I was just thinking about Mama Dora and about how much I loved her. Stephen, you must invite her to the plantation when they come by again."

CHAPTER THIRTY-SIX

After Callie and Isabelle finished their breakfast and Stephen left for his adventures, they sat for a while longer engaging in small talk. Even though Callie was anxious to ask her mother about her father, she hadn't found the proper opening in their conversation to bring it up. She was becoming restless.

Finally she pulled back her chair, stood up, and said, "Mother, I'm going to cover these dishes and coffeepot with this towel." She shook out the dish towel and covered them. "Do you think we could go for a short walk? I would love to get a little closer look at your flowers; perhaps you can identify some of them for me."

"Why, yes, of course, I think that's a marvelous idea!" Isabelle rose from her chair and smoothed out the front of her dress with her hand. "Callie, you have no idea how much happiness and joy you have brought me just this morning! Your very presence has once again made me realize the true meaning of joy. All those empty, dark years I've had suffered without you are finally over. Now there's no dark curtain between us; everything is coming to light."

Callie said, "Of course I know what you mean about the joy you're feeling! Even though we've been apart all these years, when we were reunited, it was as though an emptiness inside of me had finally once and for always been filled. There was once an empty void in my soul, and now it has been filled and replaced with the same joy you speak about. Even when I was a small child and thought Sarah was my mother, I always knew there was something missing, something not quite right. I could never put my finger on it. My father, Malcolm, or the man I called father, was a good man. He did all he could do to love and protect me. My mother and sister, however, were anything but kind. There was always an emptiness I couldn't explain." As she said this, Callie choked back tears.

Tears began to run down Isabelle's cheeks. "Both of our hearts have been lonely hunters. Thank God, because he has granted us deliverance. No matter what anyone said or tried to make me believe, I never thought for a second you were dead."

"Did someone lead you to believe I had died?" Callie's voice was startled. *This is the first time I have heard about this. Why would anyone think that?*

"Mother, a few years back, I was told that I was rescued from a raging river. I was also told that I had been kidnapped by a band of renegade gypsies."

Callie didn't mention Ripley name because she didn't wish to cause any friction between the two ladies. Callie dropped her head and turned away from her mother and began walking slowly down a path to the flower garden. Isabelle followed closely behind her.

The mood had been broken; a mood that had been filled with so much joy now turned into a moment of questions. Perhaps this was the time of truth, the time for Callie to ask all the questions she had about her father. Questions that had been going around in her mind for a long time. If only she could muster up the courage to just ask her mother a few questions. *Who is my father? How is this so hard for me to say?* Try as she might, Callie still couldn't ask her mother what she longed to know.

Soon Isabelle was walking beside Callie and took her by the hand. The two walked hand in hand down a wide, stone path. The path was lined with yellow and purple pansies. The grass and flowers were glistening, sparkling with the morning dew.

"Oh, look at those tiny hummingbirds!" Callie pointed toward a honeysuckle bush that grew along the path.

"They are busy sucking the nectar from the honeysuckle flower. Aren't they beautiful with their long beaks?" Isabelle said as they paused for a brief moment to watch the tiny birds humming as they went from one flower to flower, sucking the nectar.

"There are more humming bird bushes up the path. Let's walk on to the bench, where we can sit down and watch these beautiful little creatures for a while," Isabelle suggested.

When the path curved, Callie saw a cemetery surrounded by many live, oak trees with Spanish moss hanging from their branches. Even though the sun was shining brightly, there was very little light coming into the cemetery. A chill went up Callie's spine when she saw the black, wrought-iron fence that was in desperate in need of repair. The heavy iron-gate sagged on its rusty hinges. There was a fountain in the center of the graveyard, a granite statue of an angel covered with mold and mildew. Weeds grew among the tall monuments, which were darkened with slime and mold.

Callie knew that this was her chance to ask her mother about her father.

"Is this where my father is buried? If so, may I please see his tomb?" Callie pleaded.

CHAPTER THIRTY-SEVEN

When Isabelle heard Callie's question, her body became stiff, almost as rigid as the statues of the angels that stood inside the cemetery, and her hands began to tremble. She reached out to steady herself against a nearby tree because she realized the time had come. The question had been asked, and she knew she had to make a decision, the decision that had haunted her since she was reunited with her child.

Over the years since Jane's disappearance, Isabelle hadn't actually thought about what she would tell her daughter when she found her. She had been so preoccupied with her search. *Should I tell her the truth, or will it be easier on my child if I lie to her? If one lie can save my daughter from a lifetime of shame, perhaps that is what I should do.*

Why should this beautiful, young woman who has already been through so much pain and suffering have to pay for the sins of her parents? As far as I know, no one except Berry, Sue Ellen, John, and I know she isn't John's own flesh and blood. I know Berry or Sue Ellen wouldn't tell a soul, because it would bring too much embarrassment upon themselves.

Isabelle was trying to reason with herself. *And she will inherit the entire Bradford plantation when I pass from this world, just as if she were a true Bradford blood heir. Jane deserves all of this. However, John didn't deserve to have the credit of fathering this wonderful daughter. He didn't deserve any respect from her.*

What if Callie someday gave birth to a black baby? Is it possible that the child would pass as a gypsy child? No, I've lived long enough to realize the truth always comes out in the end.

A scripture from the bible came to her mind. Ecclesiastes 10:20: "Even in your thoughts, do not curse the king, nor in your bedroom curse the rich, for a bird in the air will carry your voice or some winged creature will tell the matter." Yes, it was inevitable; the truth will always come out. Whether it be birds or angels, all people will be trapped in their own lies.

Isabelle thought, *many years I've lived in fear. First I feared that John would find out he wasn't Jane's father, and he did. I can't stand any more hiding from the truth.* Once Isabelle decided this, she sighed a deep sigh.

Looking at her mother, Callie asked, "What's wrong, Mother? Are you all right? You looked as pale as a ghost. You surely must have loved him very much if it upsets you so deeply to see his tomb. If it does, then we won't get any closer to his grave." There was concern in Callie's voice.

Isabelle shook her head as she reached out her hand to Callie. "No, my child. I didn't love him that much. Please lead me to that bench over there, and I'll tell you all about your father." Her voice was weak.

She silently prayed as they walked through the cemetery gate and to the bench. *Lord, please guide me through this. I realize the time of lying is over. Please give me the strength to tell her the truth. And please grant her strength to live with the truth. Please don't let her hate me. I couldn't bear to lose her again.*

"Mother, you're so quiet. Have I done something wrong?" There was alarm in Callie's voice.

"No, Callie Jane, it isn't you who has been wrong," Isabelle said as she sat down on the bench. Callie sat down beside her. They looked into each others eyes. Callie's eyes were filled with questions; Isabelle's eyes were filled with pain. And her voice trembled when she spoke. "Callie, that isn't your father who lies in that tomb."

Confusion came into Callie's eyes. "That's not John Bradford buried there?"

"Yes, John Bradford is buried there. John was my husband, but he is not your father. Your father is still very much alive."

Callie began to scoot away from her mother. She was speechless for a moment. Then she said, "Then Lydia was right! I am a gypsy! I'm exactly what she said I was. She was telling me the truth the entire time." Callie was angry. Not because she now thought she was half-gypsy but because Lydia had been right.

"No, you simply don't understand. Please don't be upset," Isabelle pleaded as she reached for Callie's hand.

"I'm not upset because I'm part-gypsy. After all, I am with a wonderful man who is part-gypsy; therefore, I don't know why I am so upset." Callie's voice became softer as she began to calm down. "I think it's because I must know the truth about my past. Please tell me how we became separated. Was I really stolen by a band of gypsies? Or was I actually fished out of a river like Lydia said I was?"

Isabelle felt a chill linger over her body and began to shiver. It was as if a dark cloud had passed over the sky, yet the sun shone brightly as usual. *Fished out of a river? God, help us. The poor child knew the details of John's cruelty.*

Isabelle needed a few more moments to decide just how to tell Callie the truth as kindly as possible. "I feel the need to take a walk; please walk with me and hear me out. I'll tell you everything you need to know."

She and Callie got up from the bench. Isabelle walked a few feet in front of her. In a distraught voice, Isabelle began to speak.

"Callie Jane, I'm going to tell you the truth. When you are finished hearing this, I pray you won't hate me." She paused and then as an afterthought said, "Or your father. You do have a right to know who your father is."

Isabelle turned to face Callie as her hand went to her brow. And her face took a look of anguish.

Isabelle opened her mouth to speak, but no words came out. She felt as if she would surely choke on all the words she had to say. She took a deep breath and swallowed hard, and in a trembling voice, she said, "As painful as this is going to be for the both of us, I will tell you. Callie Jane, your father is a black man. He once lived on this plantation as a free man."

Her voice became strained. While looking down at the ground, she continued, "His name is Berry Bradford, and his wife's name is Sue Ellen. When I finally found you, I was shocked and happy when I realized that you had been with them for a long time. In spite of all of John's efforts to keep you away from me, you were with your real father all this time. When I found you, I thanked God for answering my prayers concerning your safety."

Isabelle raised her eyes and looked at Callie. Then Isabelle said, "Life seems to be one big circle, it seems as if we all go back to where we began."

"Berry is my father?" Callie gasped, interrupting her mother. Her body had become stiff, and her eyes were huge as she looked at her mother with disbelief. "How could that be? What are you saying?" She began to slowly shake her head and said, "No, no," in a quiet voice.

Isabelle didn't know what to say or do. She felt that it was best to be silent for a moment and let the shocking truth sink in to her daughter's mind.

After a few moments, Callie said, "What you're telling me is that Berry was a free man on this plantation and that you two were lovers! I'll bet it was a shock when you realized you were pregnant with me!" Callie ran splayed fingers through her hair. Her voice was filled with anger and shock.

"No, we were not lovers!" Isabelle's heart seemed to jump into her throat when she saw the anger in Callie's eyes.

"Then he raped you?" Callie snapped. Her voice was a mixture of disdain and condescension.

"No, he didn't rape me. Let me try and explain this to you." Isabelle's voice quivered. "John Bradford was a cruel, drinking man. He drank almost daily. When he had too much to drink, he became extremely evil and abusive. He would take his evil out on someone. Berry and I were no strangers to John's brutality. I've seen him beat Berry unmercifully. He still has deep scars on his back from the beatings."

"I've seen those scars. He told me that they came from an evil master." Callie nodded her head.

"Now I must finish my story." Isabelle smiled a sad smile. "On this particular night, John was very drunk, and he was after me. He came into my room, and I was terrified. He slapped me and ripped off my gown. I knew in my heart that if I didn't escape, he would kill me. You see, he was angry and abusive because I hadn't given him a child. That night I fought back.

"When he threw me across the bed, I kicked him in the stomach. He was so drunk that he lost his balance and fell. When he fell, I ran away from him. I stumbled down the steps into the yard. When I got into the yard, I could hear him coming down the steps. He was in a terrible rage, cussing, kicking, and promising me that when he found me, he would surely kill me."

She took a deep breath before continuing, "I crawled underneath the shrubs near the house. My heart was beating so fast. I was certain he could hear it. He hunted for me for a long time. Then the dew began to fall. I began to think about snakes and the way they crawl at night. I decided to go to the barn and hide there. I didn't realize Berry was in the barn delivering a colt."

As Callie listened, she saw her mother's eyes begin to twitch. She had never seen that before. Even though her heart went out to her mother, Callie felt that she shouldn't interrupt her. It was important that the truth come out, important that Isabelle unburden her soul.

"I was terror stricken when I got inside the barn. I don't remember every detail. When Berry heard me crying, he came to see what was wrong although he probably knew. He came to help me. He held me close as he talked to me, trying to calm me down. Soon we heard John cussing. We knew that he was headed toward the barn. I began to cry harder. Then Berry placed his hand over my mouth. He led me to a hiding place in the barn that only he and his family knew about. Berry was also frightened.

"When we got to the hideout, which was simply a tunnel in a huge stack of hay, we were both trembling so badly that it's a wonder John didn't find us. When we heard John leaving the barn, Berry soon calmed down. He began to try to comfort me. I suppose comfort turned into something else, and you were conceived. I pray you won't hate either of us. Because that was the one and only time it happened. You were the only good thing to come out of the horror that night."

As Callie listened to Isabelle's sad story, she saw pain and fear in her mother's eyes. The wrinkles in her face deepened, and her shoulders slumped. In the few moments that she had been talking, she looked years older.

Isabelle held her face in the palms of her hands and began to cry. Through muffled sobs, she said, "You have every right to be ashamed of your mother and father. I wouldn't blame you." She paused and then said, "I'm sure Berry wouldn't blame you, either. We have both hung our heads in shame for years."

"Mother, I'm not ashamed that Berry is my father. I am just surprised, that's all. Just to think that I've been living close to my real father and didn't know it! Berry is the kindest man I've ever known. He's even kinder than Malcolm." Placing her hand on her mother's back, Callie gently patted her.

Isabelle raised her head and looked off into the distance. "Life will always be full of surprises, Callie Jane," she said in almost a whisper.

"Does Sue Ellen know I'm her husband's child?" Callie felt as if she had to know the whole story, no matter how painful it was to her mother.

"Yes, she knows," Isabelle answered.

"She was so kind to me when I lived in Stephen's house! What a wonderful person. Her soul must be completely filled with love." Callie shook her head.

"Yes, she is a very fine woman," said Isabelle. "Berry said that from the start, they didn't realize or have any idea who you were. How could they? Apparently she was helping you dress one day and saw your birthmark. That's when she realized that you might be Berry's child and the child I had been searching for so frantically."

"Oh, I remember that day. I always wondered why she stopped helping me dress. She said she was sick at her stomach, and I'm sure she was," Callie said.

"This has been very difficult for Sue Ellen. That's how she found out the truth in the first place," Isabelle said.

"Really!" Callie responded.

"Yes, when you were a baby, I tried extremely hard to always change and bathe you myself. But one day Sue Ellen bathed you. That's when she discovered the truth. I was so ashamed and so sorry that I had hurt such a wonderful friend."

"What did she say?"

"Not a whole lot to me. It was just the horrible shock on her face and the deep hurt in her eyes." Isabelle breathed another deep sigh.

"It seems as if my life, my birth, has been like a bolt of lightning that has hit everyone's life very hard." Tears flowed down Callie's cheeks. She dropped her head. "Perhaps I should have never been born."

Now it was Isabelle's turn to comfort Callie. She reached for her and held her close. And she spoke in soothing tones to her daughter. "Oh, baby, it's all right. You've been such a great blessing in all our lives. I adore you so much. Sue Ellen cares for you, too. That's how I found you; she and Berry couldn't wait to see us reunited. If she was a spiteful person, then she could have taken her revenge out on you."

Isabelle hugged Callie even closer to her.

"You're right, Mother." Callie raised her tear-streaked face. "Now that I think about it, Sue Ellen and Berry were kinder to me after that."

As Isabelle watched the pain in her daughter's eyes, she said, "Oh, baby, I've been so wrong telling you all of this. I should have kept the truth in my own heart. I should have let you continue to believe John was you father."

"No, Mother, you did the right thing, although I don't understand why John didn't abandon the both of us," Callie said.

"My guess is this John wanted to save his dignity and honor. He also wanted me to suffer for my sins. After your disappearance, he enjoyed watching me suffer. It was so obvious. I suppose he knew it would cause too much suspicion if the two of us disappeared. When I decided to go shopping with my mother, I left Ripley in care of you. I never thought about John taking full care of you. I assumed she would do all of the bathing and changing. I didn't dream he would see the birthmark. John must have somehow known you weren't his child. He seized the moment to get me away from you. Because he wanted to try and destroy you. How I despised that man!" She looked toward his tomb as she talked.

"If he was so terrible, why did you leave me with him?"

"It was like this, Callie. When you were born, John was so happy. He loved you dearly. You were that heir he had been waiting for. His attitude changed toward me and everyone around us; he became kinder and generous. John insisted that I go to New Orleans to shop with my mother. Actually he gave me a tidy sum of money to spend on the trip. He told me to buy myself some new clothes and to dress you like the princess you were. I left you, never dreaming of the horror and pain that I would be face with when I returned."

"He threw me into the water! It was him who threw me into the terrible water!"

"How do you know that?" Isabelle asked.

"My stepsister told me, and my stepfather said it was true. He fished me out of the water. Lydia said my shawl was the only thing that saved my life." Callie's voice trembled.

"Oh, my poor baby. You've had such a hard life! I should have let you believe John was your father. I should have spared you the shame."

"Mother," Callie interrupted, "I've already told you I'm not ashamed that Berry is my father. I've thought all along that I was half-gypsy. It's just that I'm surprised." Callie placed one arm around her mother's shoulder. "At last we've found each other, and that's all that matters."

Callie could hardly bear seeing the pain and shame in her mother's eyes and couldn't hardly bring herself to look into Isabelle's eyes.

"What about Stephen? What will he think? Maybe you shouldn't tell him. Maybe it would be for the best that he goes on believing John is your father," Isabelle said.

"No, Mother. I won't lie to Stephen. He will accept the truth. He has lived in two utterly different worlds. He doesn't judge people by the color of their skin. Neither does he judge people by how much property they own. He looks at people's kind deeds. He likes Berry, and so do I. Do you think Berry and Sue Ellen would ever consider coming back here to live?" Callie asked, trying to change the subject and get her mother's mind off the wretched day when the two had been separated.

"No, I highly doubt it. I don't think either of them would ever be happy tending the earth again. Berry is using his God-given musical talent. He's entertaining people, making others smile and enjoy life," Isabelle explained.

"But I've heard him speak of this plantation. He said that it would always feel like home to him. He said that he wanted to be brought back here for burial when he dies. He also said his parents were buried here. Is that right?" Callie questioned.

"Yes, that's correct. His grandparents are buried here, too."

"Where is the graveyard for the slaves?" Callie began looking around her.

"I'll show you sometime," Isabelle said.

When she saw the confusion in Callie's eyes, because of all the information she has been given. She tried to change the subject. "Callie, you got your talent from Berry. You can sing exquisitely. You know how to bring great joy to others with your voice.

Callie was so filled with confusion that she excused herself from her mother, and made her way back to the house Ripley met her at the door

"How yo doin' Missus Callie I'm glad to see you back where yo belong. I know Missus Isabelle is happy." Ripley smiled a toothless smile.

Yes Ripley I'm happy for everyone. Will you please excuse me, I feel a headache coming on. I think I need to lie down."

"Yes mam.

Callie hurried and climbed the stairs, and breathed a sigh of relief that she was alone and could sort through her thoughts. The words she had just heard from her mother had raddled her world. What if Stephen wouldn't want her now? *Oh God it will break my heart if I lose Stephen, I love him so much. Just when I think I have found my place in this world, my world shatters again.* She said, then cried herself to sleep

═╬╬═

Three hours later she was awakened with a start by Stephen kisses. She sat up in the bed and looked around the room with confusion in her eyes. When she remembered what her mother had told her and tears filled her eyes.

"What's wrong darling?" Stephen ask.

"Oh Stephen I couldn't bear to lose you please don't go! Please let's stay together."

"What are you talking about? What on earth has come over you?" Of course we will stay together. You must have had a bad dream, to wake up with a thought like that one." Her actions were very disturbing to Stephen.

She sat up higher in the bed and hugged a pillow tightly to her chest. "No Stephen it wasn't a nightmare. This is a reality, John Bradford is not my father…

Stephen interrupted her "Why would that make me want to leave you?"

"Because Berry is my father I'm Berry's daughter and I'm not ashamed of it. He is such a kind man. But this has been such a shock. All kinds of thoughts are going through my mind, I'm a person with mixed blood, I'm afraid that you wouldn't me anymore."

"What kind of man do you take me for?" There was anger in Stephen's voice.

"I'm a person with mixed blood, does that make you stop loving me?"

"Of course not I will love you until the day I die."

"Then let's put all of this behind us and move on to our lives together, where is your mother, I'm sure this has been very difficult

225

for her. We should both talk to her and let her know we love her and let's make sure that all of our pasts remain in the past." He took her hand a helped her out of bed then said, dry your eyes and fix your hair and we will talk to her together. Her life has been a lonely one as well."

They found Isabelle in the garden where Callie had left her. She was sitting on a bench starring off in the distance, lost in her thoughts.

They walked quietly up behind her. Stephen gently placed his hand on her arm, "Mrs. Isabelle, he said softly, don't be sad, Callie has told me that Berry is her father. I have no problem with that and neither does she."

Isabelle hung her head, and said, we didn't intend to be together that night in the barn but we were, and that night Callie was conceived. I'm so proud of her. I'm also sorry that her life up to this point has been so painful. I pray that she will forgive me."

"Mother I have forgiven you." Callie reached out and wrapped her arms around Isabelle.

Three weeks later Isabelle and Callie were setting in the beautiful gardens at Willow Grove. Isabelle was encouraging Callie to continue pursuing her career in music

I'm so happy that you are here with me. But please don't ever give up on your singing."

"Give up her singing. Why would she do that?" Stephen asked as he walked toward them.

"How was your ride?" Callie asked.

A look of love radiated from Callie's face as she looked at Stephen. He was dressed gypsy fashion, wearing a shiny red shirt, tight black pants, and a black hat.

"What's this I'm hearing about you not singing anymore?" Stephen asked.

"Oh, I'm not thinking about giving up my singing; we were just talking," Callie said.

"Then you do realize you must never stop singing. It's your gift from God. I feel if we ignore and don't use the talents God has given us, then he just might become angry with us. You bring so much hope and joy to those around you when they hear you sing. You must always sing, and I must sometimes take the time to wear these clothes because they are a part of who I am," Stephen said.

"Yes, that's who you are, and I am proud of you." Callie spoke softly.

"I've been riding over the plantation; it certainly is a beautiful estate." Stephen took his hat off and rubbed the sweat from his brow.

"Yes, I think so, too. I admire it. And I feel as if I am finally home. It's a shame to leave it and go back to New Orleans to sing," Callie said as she looked at the scenery around her.

"Well, perhaps we could make it possible for us to stay here and you sing. We could turn the plantation into a grand hotel and build a theater where you could sing. Mrs. Isabelle would you have any objections?" Stephen asked.

"I certainly do not. I'd be willing to do all I can to help run the business you are talking about. It's high time that laughter and happiness lived here," Isabelle said.

Stephen looked at Callie. He could see that she was indeed happy. The haunting, searching-for-someone look was gone from her face. He placed his arm around her small waist. "I think Callie is more than delighted."

"Well, sir, you seem to be mighty happy yourself!" Callie said in a teasing manner.

"Yes, my love, I am happy! The only thing lacking in my life is making you my wife and living the remainder of our lives at Willow Grove."

Stephen's eyes were filled with true devotion as he knelt on one knee and asked, "Will you do me the honor of becoming my wife?"

"Oh, Stephen! I would be honored to become your wife."

CHAPTER THIRTY-EIGHT

True to his word, Stephen soon had the plans drawn up for the new theater. In a few weeks, the sound of hammers and saws traveled clearly through the morning air. When the theater was dried in, meaning the sides were standing and roof was covering it, Callie was amazed at the size of it. It seemed to be gigantic, standing tall and proud, and then it dawned on her that it was her responsibility to keep the theater filled with her singing. She was still very unsure about herself and her talent. Fear soon overcame her. After all, Stephen had built this building based on his faith in her talent.

Later in a troubled voice, she asked Stephen, "Do you truly think I can draw in a crowd big enough to fill this entire theater? It will take a lot of fine singing to do that."

"Yes, my little songbird, and there will be standing room only. You obviously don't realize just what a fabulous singer you are. The critics are comparing you to the famous singer, Jenny Lind!" Stephen's eyes lit up with excitement.

Stephen's words and his faith in her frightened Callie, even though she knew they were words of praise. She felt a heavy load falling on her shoulders. Yes, she realized she was a good singer, but there were many good singers in New Orleans. It also was overwhelming that the critics were comparing her to Jenny Lind.

Could she live up to Stephen's expectations? Could she fill the theater every weekend? She didn't know if she even wanted to sing that much. She was hoping to start a family sometime soon. Maybe have a child or two. She was so happy having found true love with Stephen; she wouldn't ask any questions about what he expected of her. True, she didn't want or intend to give up her singing, but did she want it to consume her life? Her shoulders slumped as she wrapped her arms around her body.

Stephen saw the frown and look of unhappiness that came over her as her shoulders slump in despair. "What's wrong, darling? Why are you unhappy? Is this theater not to your liking?" Stephen's voice was troubled.

"Indeed, I adore the theater," she said with reluctance as she turned from him and began to walk away.

He reached out and caught her by her shoulders and turned her around to face him and lifted her face to him. "Now, darling, tell me what's wrong; have I done wrong?"

"You haven't done anything wrong, Stephen. It's just that I thought when we married, you might want to start a family. How on earth will I sing if I'm in the family way?" Her voice was grieved because she realized that this was no way for a lady to talk to a man even if she was his bride-to-be.

A broad smile came over Stephen's face as he listened to her confession. "Oh, how happy those words make me," he said, picking her up off the ground. He began swinging her around and around, laughing all the while.

"Stop, Stephen! You're making me dizzy!" Callie complained.

Stephen sat her feet back on the ground. "Callie, I don't care if we even open the theater; you can sing in New Orleans whenever you want to. We will start a family as soon as we are married, if that is what you want. I built the theater just for you. I thought it would bring you happiness, but plans can always change."

"No, you don't understand. I do love the theater, and I do want to sing. I just don't want all the pressure of keeping it open to fall on me. What if I become sick? I guess what I am saying is I want both. I want to sing and have a family."

"Then, my lady, you shall have both. The theater is built to accommodate large symphony orchestras, plays, ballets, dances, and all kinds of things. You can perform once a month if that is what you want. What you don't realize is that your name will bring people in. When this theater is finished, we will soon start the construction on our luxury hotel to accommodate our customers.

"Of course we will have babies. Have you noticed that my dad and your mother spent a lot of time sitting on the porch swing? When I asked them what they were talking about, they smiled and said "Our grandchildren; we are thinking up names for our grandchildren."

Stephen's father had arrived three months earlier. Stephen had sent him a message informing him of his upcoming wedding. He also told him about his plans to start constructing a grand hotel and theater. He had asked his father to come help if it was at all possible. Stephen knew that his father could be of great assistance in purchasing materials for the theater, having made his fortune in the shipping trade. He knew how to buy and sell. His father had come as soon as possible after receiving the message.

The two men were very excited about the project, because they were together and also were the planners, buyers, and financing the project. As if that was not enough, they picked up hammers and saws and labored with the men they had hired to build the theater. Callie liked to watch the two men work as they climbed tall ladders and walked on scaffolds. They loved every moment of the physical labor and being together. She enjoyed watching Stephen work while his muscles rippled underneath his sweat-soaked shirt. The sun darkened his skin, making him even more handsome, if that was even possible.

The theater was nearing completion. The tall mahogany walls were shinning from polish as well as illumination by the lights from the crystal chandelier. The lobby floor of the grand place was marble. The working crew had finished as quickly as possible because there was soon to be a wedding. Stephen announced that he wanted their wedding to be the first major event in the theater.

Now the family—William, Isabelle, Barry, Sue Ellen, Callie, and Stephen—were inside the theater planning the wedding with Mr. Hubbard, a well-known wedding planner. Stephen and Callie stood side by side, holding hands and listening to his advice. Neither one could hardly wait to be united in marriage; they both wanted their day to be perfect. One could feel the love and warmth that came from them when they were together, whether they were standing side by side or just in the same room.

Isabelle and William were leaning against the wall, discussing what their grandchildren would look like. When Callie heard her mother's laughter, she glanced at her. She was thrilled to see the old hurt, strained, sad look gone from her mother's face. She suddenly thought. *Has my soon-to-be father-in-law have anything to do with this .change?*

"Callie, Mr. Hubbard is talking to you," Stephen said.

Stephen's words brought her back to the present. "I'm sorry. What were you saying?"

"I asked where you would prefer to stand." He had his note-pad open and ready.

"I don't know." Callie placed her index finger under her chin. She then looked at Berry and Sue Ellen. "What do you all think?" she asked.

"Lawdy Lawd! I don' know, child." Berry took his hat off and scratched his head. He laughed and said, "Don' matter where yo stand if yo do like me and Sugar-ins did at our wedding; we jus' jumped de broom."

When Mr. Hubbard laughed, Berry said, "It worked. We been together ever since ain't we, Sugar-ins?"

Berry reached for Sue Ellen's hand. Some slave owners wouldn't allow their slaves to marry, so they had developed their own cere-mony. The broom symbolized health and strength. The Bradford's did allow some of their slaves to marry. They would have allowed Berry and Sue Ellen to marry in the traditional way, but they pre-ferred to marry in the fashion that their people had done.

"That is awfully precious," Callie said with excitement. "I didn't know that. Would you like to have a wedding? The two of you could be the first ones to marry in the theater. We would be honored. Wouldn't we, Stephen?"

"No, I sho don' want no showy wedding." When Berry saw disap-pointment in Sue Ellen's face, his dear darling wife he had hurt so badly when he had fathered the lovely young lady standing before him, Berry began to shuffle his feet. "I would marry my Sugar-ins a hundred times and in any way she wanted. If she wants to marry in dis big ole building, den so be it."

"That settles it. We will be having two weddings in the grand theater!" Stephen declared.

Sue Ellen's face lit up with a large grin, and then she said, "Maybe we do dat, but not on yer special day."

CHAPTER THIRTY-NINE

After the decisions were made concerning the weddings and Mr. Hubbard realized just how big Stephen and Callie's wedding was going to be, he suggested that instead of trying to schedule a series of luncheons and particular parties, it would be more sensible to host one big appreciation party. However, since so many of the guests were already arriving, they decided to just have a dinner for the guests already present, as well as one for the wedding party.

When Stephen, Malcolm, and Sarah walked into the entrance of the theater, Sarah stopped in her tracks. A small gasp came from her.

"What an extravagant place," she said as she looked around the hall. Marble statues stood proudly on the marble floor; a large fountain stood in the middle of the hall. Marble tables stood against the walls, which were decorated with bouquets of white carnations and red roses.

When the question arose of who was going to give Callie away, she began to think the matter over. She was very puzzled and didn't know which way to turn since she had learned the truth of Berry being her biological father. Even if she hadn't known that, she would have been honored to have him walk her down the aisle, because she found him to be the most kindhearted, loving person she had ever known.

Of course this would be almost impossible since no one outside the family knew he was her father; it would've brought great hurt and shame to Sue Ellen and her children. This thought took Callie by surprise. She hadn't thought about the fact that she indeed had real brothers and sisters, although they would likely never know they were remotely related to her. Sue Ellen was so kind and good to her even after she'd learned that Berry was her father. Oh, how much pain her birth had been to all those involved, especially Sue Ellen. *I doubt I could live if my beloved Stephen ever fathered a child with someone else while he was married to me!*

Then her mind went back to the question at hand. *Who will give me away? Who has been my father figure?* Malcolm, of course. Yes, Malcolm loved her. He had taught her right from wrong; he had even cried when she left. Malcolm and Sarah and their family had arrived several days earlier with Seth, his wife, and two beautiful daughters. Lydia had also arrived; she was now married and seemed to have matured. She had apologized to Callie earlier for all her dreadful behavior. Callie forgave her. She realized how important family was, even if some members did have their faults.

Callie saw Malcolm enter the room, she walked over to greet him, after she greeted him they stepped into the huge room, they saw the velvet drapes that covered the tall windows. Thick, luxurious carpet covered the floor. One wall of the room was covered with a large black fireplace. A string quartet sat in front of the fireplace and played soft dinner music. The tables were covered with fine linen and beautiful crystal, china, and silver. Fresh crimson-red roses were the centerpiece of each table.

The guests were seated. The waiters were dressed in black pants, white shirts, and red bow ties. First they brought out the cheeses, fruits, and other delicious appetizers. Then the brisket followed, served with sweet potatoes and a salad tossed in an oil and vinegar dressing. Last there came the sweets, delicate pies, and cakes.

Three days later, the wedding was held onstage in the theater. The stage was decorated with red roses and an abundance of candles. The musicians were from the theater where Callie had been per-forming; they had volunteered to play at the wedding and were on-stage behind the draped curtain, where they played a Mozart rondo.

As Stephen stood onstage with the preacher, the best man, and the other attendants, he looked over the crowd and waited for Callie to walk down the aisle. He couldn't help but smile when he saw all the different cultures and races represented.

Berry and Sue Ellen sat on the front row. Sue Ellen looked lovely wearing a red satin dress with a red hat to match. Berry sat proud-ly by her side in his navy-blue suit and a white and blue striped shirt. On the other side of them sat Stephen's father, William, and Isabelle. They were both glowing with happiness. On the other side of Berry sat his grandmother and grandfather, Mama Dora and Tomsk.

Tomsk wore tight black trousers and a white satin shirt with tight cuffs and sleeves that bellowed out over his cuffs. With his broad shoulders and salt-and-pepper hair, he was a dashing man. Mama Dora sat proudly beside him, wearing a long-sleeved, high-necked green silk dress. Her hair was adorned with a gold-colored tiara.

Of course Sarah and her children were in the front row. The thought crossed Stephen's mind that if the angels were looking down, which they must be, they would surely see all of the color and beauty. It must look like an intricate bouquet of people.

The rest of the theater was filled with business associates, politicians, musicians, and numerous friends. In the back of the theater sat Tomsk tribe with Berry and Sue Ellen's children. If any of the well-to-do people didn't approve of the guests, they dared not utter a word, as it was the wedding of a rising young star and the son of a wealthy shipping man. These families had a lot of pull and control.

Stephen stood at attention when he saw the two young flower girls starting down the aisle. Callie had chosen Seth's daughters for the honor. They were dressed in floor-length dresses and had flowers braided into their long, flowing hair. They were each carrying a basket with rose petals.

The orchestra began to play the wedding march, and the entire room stood up. Stephen looked to the door and caught his breath when he saw his elegant bride-to-be and Malcolm standing at the entrance of the church. They began to walk down the aisle. She was wearing a V-waistline dress. Her chapel veil traveled two feet behind her.

An exquisite ceremony began. After everyone was seated, the ushers assisted Isabelle and William onstage, and the service began. The minister read from Ecclesiastes 5:9–12:

"Love is patient and kind; love is not jealous or boastful, it's not arrogant or rude. Love does not insist on its own ways. It is not irritable or resentful. It does not rejoice at wrong, but rejoices at right. Love bears all things, believes in all things, hopes in all things, and endures all things. Love never ends so hope, faith, and love abides these things, but the greatest of these is love."

After the ceremony Callie and Stephen turned toward each other with looks of love in their eyes.

ABOUT THE AUTHOR

Cameron Cole is the pen name of Sara Jo Thurman and Virginia Cantrell.

After the passing of Mrs. Thurman, Virginia continued the writing of *Love Bears All Things*. Sarah was an accomplished educator, devoted wife, loving mother, and dear friend. In addition to teaching and inspiring students, Thurman loved writing.

Virginia Cantrell has written two other books. She owned and operated a skating rink for many years but has since retired. Cantrell now lives on a farm in Middle Tennessee. She enjoys spending time with her children and grandchildren.